PERIL IN PARADISE

An Ivy Snow Mystery

Janet Winters

Janet Winters
Barngoddess Enterprises
P.O. Box 86
Ligonier, PA 15658
ISBN: 9798365126848

Peril In Paradise/Janet Winters

This Book is Dedicated to
Grant Thomas Winters
Beloved Son and Fellow Author
June 14, 1995 - October 28, 2021

CHAPTER ONE

"OFFICIALS SUSPECT DRUG REACTION IN FLORIDA HORSE DEATHS"

My first day in paradise and I'm greeted with these ghastly headlines. I picked up the morning edition of the *Palm Beach Daily News* that sat neatly in front of the door to our suite at The Breakers. Jaycee, Trina and Sloane were still asleep after a dreadful flight from Philadelphia International to West Palm Beach Airport.

I carried the paper, along with a steaming cup of French Roast to the balcony overlooking the Atlantic. The gently rolling aqua waves cresting in foamy white belied the horrors of the tragedy set out in print before me.

"Polo fans say that few things are as exciting as seeing majestic horses maneuver over a 300-yard-long field. But as anyone attending the U.S. Open Tournament last Sunday can attest, few things are so shocking as seeing those same horses stagger and drop dead. Twenty-one polo

ponies belonging to Vincente Villa's team died either before, during, or after the match."

Oh my God! Vincente Villa? Vincente. I hadn't thought about him in years. Or should I say I've pushed him out of my mind every time thoughts of him drifted into the corners of my consciousness. It was just too painful to remember.

"Mom, where are you?"

I heard Jaycee calling from inside the suite.

"I'm here honey. Outside on the balcony."

Jaycee emerged dressed in her khaki riding tights and emerald green "Wellington Equestrian Center" t-shirt. She was ready to head for the show barn where Pirate, and her friend Trina's horse, Dynamo, were stabled for the Winter Equestrian Festival. I took one look at her face, and I knew that she knew.

"They're dead...aren't they mom? It's real."

I shook my head "yes." I knew my daughter and her psychic tendencies, so it didn't surprise me in the least that she would know about the death of those horses before she'd even seen the morning paper. Tears welled up in her azure eyes and rolled down her cheeks as she slumped into the chair next to mine.

"I saw it all in my dream, Mom. All those horses falling to their knees and rolling on the ground in agony."

"Oh honey." I moved beside her and put my arms around her shoulders. I didn't know what to say. It was hard enough seeing the still photos of the horses in the newspaper, but to see it all in motion as Jaycee did in her dream was almost unbearable.

"How did it happen, Mom? Why?"

"I don't know, Jaycee. The authorities are looking into it right now."

"What if it's an airborne disease? What about Pirate and Dynamo?"

"I'm sure they're okay. They're stabled far enough from the polo barn."

I wasn't sure if I was trying to convince her, or myself. Until the cause of death is determined, it could be anything, and it could be highly contagious. Jaycee wiped her tears and headed back inside to cajole the ever-tardy Trina to get a move on. It was important that they got in several hours of practice every day. The competition was extremely tight, and neither girl had ever shown in a venue of this magnitude. The tragedy of the dead horses, and fear for their safety would weigh heavily on their minds, making it difficult to concentrate. Concentration and focus were key if they hoped to place high in the rankings. Fortunately, they had Sloane and me in their corner.

As my mind conjured up memories of Sloane, and her horse Sherlock, gracefully executing every jump in the arena at the Barcelona Olympics, she poked her head through the door inhaling the salty morning air.

"Hey Ivy. Morning."

"Good morning, Sloane, how did you sleep?"

She yawned and stretched as she stepped into the sunshine. "Great! My bed is like sleeping in tiramisu."

Only the best at The Breakers, I thought. She sat down at the table and poured herself a cup of coffee from the room service tray. She already looked like perfection even though she'd just rolled out of bed. Wavy golden hair, crystal blue eyes, creamy complexion. A modern-day Grace Kelly. That was Sloane.

"So, what's up with Jaycee? She looks like she just lost her best friend."

I pushed the front page of the newspaper across the table. As she read, I could see the muscles in her face tighten. Her eyes grew wide as she read the horrific story.

"Vincente Villa's horses. Oh God Ivy, Vincente Villa!"

"I know."

The startling sound of my cell phone blurting out a digitized version of Blondie's *Call Me* broke the ominous mood. I saw that it was John Garrett on the other end, and I hit the answer button with a sense of relief. John always had that effect on me, but never so much as in the past few weeks as I felt our relationship growing into something promising.

"Hello darling. It's good to hear your voice" I said.

"I would have called last night, Ivy, but I was afraid I might wake you. How was your flight?"

I wasn't about to waste precious airtime with the gory details, so I let "fine" suffice. After all, the plane did get us here...eventually. Besides, John had more important things on his mind. As a detective with the Pennsylvania State Police, his plate was perpetually full of everything from misdemeanors to murder. I was amazed that he could swim in those shark infested waters daily, and still display his tender side with me. He did though, and that's why I found myself falling deeply in love with him. Since my failed love affair and disastrous marriage, I vowed to approach any romantic encounters with extreme caution...if at all.

“How’s your hotel?”

“It’s absolutely fabulous! Sloane and I got the girls settled in last night. I’m glad that we decided to stay here instead of with Crystal and Robert. Her invitation was sweet, but I thought it best to let the newlyweds settle into their new home.”

“That kind of surprised me...you two being such close friends.”

“There will be a lot of comings and goings with the show schedule. It’ll be very disruptive. Besides, we'll be seeing them almost every day anyway. Robert rented a box at the showgrounds so they could watch the girls compete, and they’ve invited us to dinner to see their new home. Crystal seems very happy...at last.”

Sloane gave me a look that said, ‘wrap it up.’ The girls were anxious to get in the saddle.

“By the way Ivy…”

Huh oh! I knew that this was John’s way of approaching an unpleasant subject.

“Did you hear about what happened to those polo ponies?”

"Yes John. We're all upset. It's front page news down here."
"Yeah, well the story is getting some pretty intense coverage up north too. News reports are starting to imply that it might not have been an accident."
"Really? I read that the deaths were probably caused by a bad batch of supplements or something."
"All I know is that there's a lot of money involved. Those horses were worth a hundred grand each. Belonged to some rich Argentine banker by the name of Vincente Villa. Know anything about him, Ivy?
"Ah, no. Not really."
As John and I said our "goodbyes" I felt my stomach churn. I had just lied to John about Vincente Villa...why?

The Gulfstream G650ER taxied down the runway just as Vincente checked the time on his Rolex. Twelve p.m., precisely on schedule. It had very well better be for the money he paid that pilot to transport him from one place to the next...with plenty of downtime in between flights for that guy's extra-curricular activities. No-nonsense this time. He had to get from Zurich to West Palm Beach Airport as fast as possible.

Vincente had received word from his polo team captain, Enrico Alverio, that twenty-one of his prized thoroughbreds had dropped like flies during the match. He was shocked and outraged. How could this happen? He babied those horses, hiring only the best trainers, riders and veterinarians to care for his string. Alvero, who oversaw the stable during Vincente's absence, was a world-class horseman, and consultant to The Royal Family. He had coached Prince Charles personally. Things like this just didn't happen to people like them.

Not even his Gulfstream could travel fast enough to get him home. He picked up the dedicated iPhone from the passenger seat pocket and hit the speed dial for Bianca. She didn't pick up, of course. He was only her husband after all. He marveled at the fact that when they were together, she had that phone at the ready, constantly. She was ever available to answer any call she deemed worthy, but when *he* called it invariably went to voicemail. He'd have to text, and she'd better see it. He wanted his car waiting for him on the private landing strip when he arrived.

Bianca, however, had other concerns. She glanced down at her phone to see Vincente's name on the caller ID, and promptly ignored it. If it was important, he could leave her a message. He was probably calling to whine about those horses. That was all he cared about, his banking empire, and his horses. What about her? What about her needs? She told him before he flew to Zurich that she needed the Gulfstream to get to Paris for her fittings. She had gone to all the trouble of replacing her entire wardrobe from the spring collections, just to make *him* look good, and he couldn't care less about getting her to her fittings on time. The couturier fitters would be furious. Well, spring was just around the corner, so he'd better get that plane back here PDQ. Or better yet, why didn't she just order a Gulfstream for herself. She'd get the same model he has...his and hers, how sweet.

Her phone rang again. The one that she had secretly installed in her private bath. This time it was a call she would certainly take...Enrico.

CHAPTER TWO

Crystal Prichard Montrose carefully arranged each place setting on her Edra dining table. Christofle "Malmaison" Platinum china glowed next to sparkling Baccarat wine goblets and Tiffany sterling flatware. The contemporary Versace candelabra worked perfectly with the lush arrangement of Birds of Paradise creating a sophisticated, yet tropical tablescape perfectly at home in her Palm Beach penthouse.

Crystal fussed around the table, adjusting forks and spoons. She was slowly adjusting to the modern aesthetic that she and Robert chose for their new home, although she had to admit that there were times when she missed the coziness of her shabby chic Victorian back in Wellington, PA. No sooner than they exchanged vows, Robert was on the phone with South Florida's hottest interior designer to decorate their recent purchase on Ocean Drive. He was determined to have the whole place, if not completely furnished, at least well on its way when they returned from their honeymoon in Paris.

The apartment itself was in a new building that replaced a recent teardown. It was perfectly suited to their needs. Four bedrooms, all ensuite, gourmet kitchen (although Crystal couldn't boil water), a library for Robert and an open concept living/dining room with an amazing view of the Atlantic from the penthouse balcony. All the furnishings, art and accessories were new, except for Sargent's portrait of Robert's grandmother. It was the only thing he brought with him after selling Heart's Desire, his estate in Pennsylvania, to Sloane Parker. It hung proudly over the mantlepiece in his library. The building was especially equipped with an over-sized private elevator to accommodate Robert's wheelchair.

The penthouse set a perfect stage for their new life in Palm Beach. At first, Crystal toyed with the idea of hanging out her real-estate shingle on Worth Avenue, but Robert wasn't keen on it. He said that he preferred that they work together developing contacts in the area to pursue a new line of investments, in the equestrian community, that fairly ran the business and social scenes on the island and beyond.

Crystal bit her lower lip as she rearranged the place cards for the third time. It was her first dinner party as the new Mrs. Montrose, and she wanted everything to be perfect. She wanted to make Robert proud, and hopefully make a good impression on their guests, several of whom she never met before. One such guest was Ross Spencer, a Texas oil baron who single handedly transformed a plot of swampland slightly north of the island into the Palm Beach Polo Club, a facility of international renown. In just a few short years, the club built a reputation worthy of attracting the world's best teams, such as one owned by Venezuelan banking magnate, Vincente Villa, another guest for this evening. Crystal hoped to avoid discussing his recent tragedy, but that was unlikely since his team captain, Enrico Alvero, 8-goal superstar, would also be here. Thank God Ivy and Sloane were coming. She knew she could count on them to help her make the evening a success. She shivered in the chill air conditioning.

"Darling, everything looks wonderful."

She turned to see her husband coming from the kitchen. "You peeked!"

"Yes, I couldn't help myself. The hors d'oeuvres look delicious."

"What do you think of this seating arrangement?"

Robert perused the table. “Looks fine as it is, but a little unbalanced, don’t you think?”
“What do you mean?”
“Well, you and I at either end, then we’re looking at Ross Spencer and his girlfriend, Lena, Vincente and Bianca, then there’s Enrico, Sloane and Ivy. We seem to be a man short.”
Oh no. Crystal hadn’t thought of that.
“Don’t worry my dear. Set another place. We have a surprise guest coming.”

The girls climbed into the back of the pearlescent white Range Rover that I rented for our stay in Florida. I convinced myself that it was a practical choice since white would reflect the sun’s brutal rays, keeping us cooler in tropical temperatures. The dove gray leather interior would have a calming effect on the girl’s pre-show nerves. The truth is that it’s just a damn beautiful vehicle, and I’d always wanted to drive one ever since I lived in Europe. The GPS with the British accent alone was a vivid reminder. My mind drifted back to those days, and then, of course to Vincente Villa. Seeing his name in this morning's paper sent an electric current through my body. I guess that's the way it is with first loves.

I slammed on the brakes barely missing the bumper of the Mercedes in front of us.

"Ivy, pay attention to the road, or you're going to get us killed!" said Sloane.

"Sorry."

"Where is your head anyway?"

I looked in my rearview mirror, and saw that Jaycee and Trina were absorbed with the music coming through their headphones. It was like being in the cone of silence, so it was safe to talk without being overheard by "inquiring" teenage ears.

"I was going down Memory Lane."

"You mean Vincente?"

"Of course. You know that I wouldn't be able to keep my mind off him after seeing his name in the news."

"I thought you would have gotten over all that by now."

"I am ...I mean I was."

"You know what they say Ivy, "*Memories warm you up from the inside, but they also tear you apart.*"

"I know! I know!"

Jaycee interrupted and broke the spell for the confessional. "Mom, are we almost there?"

"Yes honey, just a few more minutes."

I'd been so distracted that I'd hardly realized that we were traveling through the majestic horse country of Palm Beach County. Fabulous equestrian estates, one after the other, provided eye candy as we approached the showgrounds. Miles of rolling fence line, state- of-the-art stables, and magnificent mansions, surrounded by Royal Palms dotted the landscape. We were in our element! I pulled the Range Rover into the parking lot nearest the stabling area where Pirate and Domino had their stalls. The place was buzzing with riders, trainers, grooms and stable hands getting ready for the first classes of the day.

"You girls get your horses tacked up, and we'll meet you in the practice ring" I said.

As Sloane and I headed across the grounds, I caught sight of a horse trailer lumbering down the road in the distance. The Villa Stables logo was emblazoned across the sides, adorned with a black ribbon.

CHAPTER THREE

"R-O-S-S… I don't have anything to wear!" Lena's high-pitched whine assaulted his ears from deep inside her mirror lined dressing room. He winced. "What do you mean you don't have anything to wear? I would think that thirty square feet of closet space jammed full of designer clothes might provide something!"

"No. I mean I don't have the *right* thing to wear. All those society women, and movers and shakers will be there, and I'll just look stupid."

Ross rolled his eyes. It wasn't enough that he handpicked everything in Lena's wardrobe himself, since all her taste was in her mouth. Now she was complaining about not looking *right* when she had no idea what the *right* look was. He hoisted himself out of the king-sized bed and shuffled across the thick white carpeting into her dressing room. He approached the first dress rack and searched through the collection looking for the magenta silk sheath that looked so great on Lena. With her platinum blond hair and smoky blue bedroom eyes she could easily channel Marilyn in that dress. Who cared what the society bitches thought? It was the other men's envy he craved.

"Really, Ross? This one?"

Her insecurity could be infuriating sometimes. That was one thing his supermodel ex-wife never

knew… insecurity. "Yes Lena...this one. You'll knock 'em dead."

"If you say so, Ross" she cooed.

He returned to the bedroom and removed a gilt framed oil painting of a Texas landscape to reveal a built-in wall safe. He deftly turned the dial left to right, exacting clicks in all the right places, and springing the door open. He removed a large mahogany box with a heavy brass clasp. He opened the box to reveal a red velvet lining laden with resplendent jewels. Diamonds, rubies, emeralds… necklaces, bracelets, rings. A true treasure trove! Ross selected a diamond lariat, set in platinum. Simple, but striking. The perfect accent for magenta silk. He took the necklace to the dressing room and fastened it around Lena's neck.

"Oh Ross, for me?"

"For tonight."

Jewels only belonged to the women he married… and then, only with a prenup.

Vincente gave up trying to reach Bianca. Who knew what she was up to anyway? She'd better not have forgotten about tonight. He placed a call to his secretary, who dispatched a car to meet him at the airport. He'd have just enough time to get to his stables, meet with Enrico, and then head for home to dress for dinner. He arrived at the stables to find Enrico, and his veterinarian, Dr. Julia Forrest, waiting for him. "Welcome back, sir" Enrico held out his hand. "It's a hell of a thing to come home to. Is there any news from the lab?"

Dr. Forrest checked the email on her smartphone. "No, not yet. They're running a lot of tests. I've never seen anything like this before."

"Just my horses. None of the other horses that were on these grounds were affected. Could this have been a deliberate act of sabotage?"

"Maybe" said the vet. "But it could also be something that your horses were exposed to that none of the others were."

Enrico shook his head. "We were winning. We were winning every match. The Gold Cup was as good as ours, and then, on to the Argentine Open."

Vincente thought that Enrico might start to cry. But, no… too macho for that. "Keep me posted doctor. Enrico, I'll see you later at the Montrose dinner."

Vincente climbed back into the black Lincoln and instructed the driver to his home. He hadn't been at Casa Verde for over two weeks, and he wouldn't be back now if not for what happened to his horses. His thoughts drifted back to the last time he'd been in residence, and the terrible fight he'd had with Bianca. She'd never been a very warm person. Her stock in trade was a cold venomous kind of charisma that fascinated men. Like an Acacia, she attracted with her beauty, and repelled with her thorns. Bianca could have had any man she wanted. As heiress to a cereal fortune, she was wealthy in her own right. She achieved fame in the Saddlebred arena, winning World Championships in Louisville for four consecutive years. She had a flair for fashion and was writing a book on Palm Beach lifestyles. She belonged to all the best clubs and chaired all the important committees. A socialite who was the envy of all the other socialites. Yes, Bianca could have married any man she wanted, but for some reason, she wanted him. At least that was once true. The chauffeur deposited his bags in the foyer, as he set off to find his wife wherever she might be in the eight thousand square feet surrounding him.

Bianca was in the tub, up to her neck in bubbles, when she heard Vincent climbing up the winding marble staircase toward the master bedroom. She sighed and rolled her eyes, dreading his anticipated tirade over the unanswered cell phone calls. It was true that she was no longer in love with Vincente Villa, but she was his wife. The wife of a man she created. The moment they met she recognized brilliance in the fledgling banker. She knew that with his brains, and her father's connections she could fashion him into an international financier of great importance. They would be a renowned power couple, with her maintaining control. But controlling Vincente was more challenging than she had anticipated. The macho Argentine blood running through his veins did not easily comply with her domineering nature. She did, however, have one satisfaction that could never be denied. She'd been able to take Vincente away from that bitch, Ivy Snow.

Dr. Julia Forrest checked her iPhone for the fifth time in both anticipation and dread of news from the lab. What she told Vincente Villa was true, a multitude of tests had been ordered to try and determine the cause of death that swept through his string of polo ponies. These tests took time...and time was not up yet. She tugged at a strand of her curly silver ponytail that escaped from beneath the baseball cap that was a de rigueur part of her work ensemble. Wrangler jeans, worn for comfort and durability, a shirt and sweater combination that changed with the temperature, and a white lab coat with her name and practice logo prominently displayed over the left breast pocket, completed the "uniform." Perhaps the lab coat was impractical in the field, but it was a symbol that differentiated her from the trainers, grooms, farriers and other equine professionals that populated the horse world in South Florida.

Julia had not yet adjusted to the Florida climate. Kentucky proved more temperate, even though the summers could be brutal. She missed Kentucky, and it wasn't just about the weather. Her phone rang, and she answered in her heavy drawl. It was Ivy Snow's daughter, Jaycee. Something was wrong with her horse, Pirate. She quickly climbed into her green Ford pickup, which was outfitted with the equipment and supplies necessary to address most equine health issues.

As she pulled into a parking space across from the stable where Pirate was stalled, Jaycee ran out to meet her.

"Dr. Forrest! Thank God you're here! Something's wrong with Pirate. He's sweating and breathing heavily. I'm afraid he'll colic."

"Okay. Let's take a look. Where's your mom?"

"She's on her way. I called her first, and she told me to call you."

Julia approached Pirate's stall and quietly slipped in so as not to startle him. One look and she could see why Jaycee was concerned. Pirate was soaked in sweat, his breathing uneven. Julia checked his vitals. His temperature was elevated. She checked for guttural sounds with her stethoscope, faint, but there… thank heaven! He was still on his feet, which was a good sign. She went out to her truck and returned with a dose of Banamine, which she quickly injected. She brought him out of the stall, and instructed Jaycee to walk him up and down the aisle while the medicine took effect. It was important to keep a horse moving when in danger of colicing.

"He looks like he's doing better, Doctor," said Jaycee.

"We got him in time, Praise the Lord. All the travel and change in temperature must have stressed him out. He'll be alright now."

As the veterinarian loaded her truck, Jaycee had a strange vision. She saw a huge tree spring up out of the ground. It had deeply furrowed black bark, and sturdy branches that canopied out low to the ground. When the vet started the engine, the tree dropped all its leaves, withered, and then disappeared.

With Sloane riding shotgun, I turned into the showgrounds just as Dr. Forrest's truck was leaving. She gave me a thumbs-up and sped onto her next emergency. I breathed a sigh of relief, knowing that Pirate would be alright. I just can't imagine how Jaycee would cope if she lost him.

"See, I told you that everything would be alright," said Sloane.

"Thank God. She's been through so much in the last couple of months. Finding out about Bart, the kidnapping, and almost losing Jayson to drugs."

"I know, Ivy, but she's strong. Stronger than you give her credit for."

"She has to be...*seeing things* the way she does."

Jaycee's psychic abilities were both a blessing and a curse. Oftentimes she knew too much for her own good. It was up to me, her mother, to protect her, but it wasn't always easy. Her visions were most vivid when danger was near, but they were often cryptic and elusive… even to her.

I pulled into the parking space that Dr. Forrest had just vacated. Jaycee and Trina came running up to the Range Rover.

"Mom! Pirate's okay!"

I jumped out and threw my arms around her.
"Thank Heaven!"
Tears welled up in Jaycee's eyes.
"What's wrong?"
"I don't know, Mom. I'm so happy about Pirate, but there's something weird going on."
"What do you mean?"
Jaycee told me about her vision.
"There's something up with Dr. Forrest. She might be in danger" Jaycee said.
I kissed my daughter on the head, and braced myself for...who knows what?

CHAPTER FOUR

I pulled the Range Rover up to the front entrance of The Breakers and handed the keys to the valet. Practice was cut short because of Pirate's ordeal, but at least Trina was able to work Dynamo, so all was not lost. Sloane suggested that we change into our suits and head for the pool. A nice refreshing swim would hit the spot before the evening's festivities. Donning a swimsuit strikes fear into the hearts of most women over forty… and I was no exception. I'd kept in pretty good shape since my days on the U.S. Olympic Equestrian Team, but gravity was no friend to any woman.

Sloane must have felt the same way. She appeared in an ankle length Lilly Pulitzer cover-up, with a wide-brimmed fuchsia hat and oversized shades. She was striking. I did my best to keep up in a gauzy white tunic, with matching turban and strappy gold sandals. The girls looked adorable in their bikinis. Ah… those were the days!

The pool area was populated with chic sun worshippers, slathered with SPF 100, no doubt. Sloane and I were lucky to grab a table with a generous shade umbrella to protect our lily-white skin. The girls opted for lounge chairs to capture maximum rays, then headed straight for the water.

"Let's live dangerously and order a Margarita," I said.

"You're on!" Sloane signaled the waiter. "So, do you have any idea who will be at Crystal's tonight?"

"Not entirely, but I do know that Ross Spencer and his *significant other* of the moment will be there. Crystal said that Robert is interested in finding out more about what his future development plans are. Maybe get in on the ground floor.

"Hmm" ... I suggest that Robert take a good hard look at Mr. Spencer before getting involved," said Sloane.

"What do you mean? What do you know about Ross Spencer?"

"All I know is that his Texas oil money is being spent to make this the equestrian sport capital of the world."

"Well, yeah. That's kind of obvious."

"I'm not sure I'd totally trust that guy if I were in Robert's position."

"Why not?"

"Let's put it this way… Ross Spencer is not only the type that wants to own, he wants to *rule!"*

"I get it. A kind of macho complex. Superiority on steroids."

"Definitely. I don't think that it would be a very good fit. Let's face it Ivy, Robert is used to being in charge. He's a shrewd investor, but not the silent partner type. I see a *Clash of the Titans* with those two."

I thought about that as I ran my tongue over the rough salt crystals remaining on my Margarita glass. "Robert's ideas may have changed now that he and Crystal are married. I mean he still wants to make money, and keep his fingers in the pie, but maybe he wants to pull back a little. You know, travel, spend more time with his bride."

"A leopard never changes his spots," she said. That comment earned Sloane an eyeball-roll behind my shades. "What about her? Spencer's girlfriend, Lena?"

"Anna Nicole Smith all the way."

"My, we're catty today!" We both laughed. We were in dire need of some comic relief.

I reached into my beach bag in search of the sunscreen. I had every intention of getting in the water.

"Not so fast," said Sloane.

I looked up at her, knowing what was coming next.

"If you think I'm letting you off the hook where Vincente Villa is concerned, you're sorely mistaken."

"That's all in the past, Sloane. I don't think it's a good idea to dredge it up."

"Neither is it a good idea to keep it buried. Let's face it Ivy, you have had a lot of difficulty where love is concerned, and I think a great deal of it can be traced back to Vincente."

I leaned back in my chair and closed my eyes. Maybe she was right. My unfinished business with Vincente might have played a part in my disastrous choice of Bart Skeleton as a husband. I must have fallen prey to the ludicrous notion that the way to get over one man was to get under another. The fact that Bart is a narcissistic bigamist nearly destroyed me. Now, here I am embarking on a new relationship with John, and what do I do? Lie. Start a web of deceit… a web with Vincente at the center.

"Mom, are you asleep?"

I sat straight up. Sorry, just deep in thought."
Come on in. The water's great!" Jaycee stood over me, dripping all over my new tunic.

"Okay, okay." I shot Sloane a sheepish grin and headed for the pool.

"Of course, you know I want to be with you, my darling." Enrico cooed smoothly into his cell.

Bianca smiled into the receiver of the Princess phone that she had installed in her bathroom. She insisted on having a landline there to provide anonymity for incoming and outgoing calls. "Well, you know it's impossible now that Vincente is back in the country. It's all because of those dead horses."

"It's a great tragedy, darling."

"Yes, I know, and I feel terrible. But I don't understand why he has to come all the way back here. They're already dead. It's not as though he can bring them back, although he does think he's omnipotent."

"An investigation is being conducted. He wants to be here for that."

"I suppose so, but it's keeping *us* apart."
"I will see you tonight at the Montrose dinner."
"It's not the same, and you know it! We have to be very careful. Wait… I think I hear someone coming. Ciao for now, darling." She hung up the phone and stepped out of her bubble bath into a thick white terry robe.
"Bianca, are you in there?"
It was Vincente. "Yes, I'll be out in a minute."
Bianca took a deep breath. "So, you made it" she said as she opened the door to their bedroom.
"No thanks to you. Why didn't you answer my calls?"
"I misplaced my cell. I didn't hear it ring" she lied.
Vincente glanced over at the phone sitting on top of her dressing table.
She ignored him. "Well, you're home now, and not a moment too soon to dress for dinner."

Vincente didn't like her tone. Tonight was going to be an important night. He didn't want her screwing it up with her vicious comments, as she's been known to do… especially when she drank too much, which was often.
"Bianca let's call a truce. Robert and Crystal Montrose are new to Palm Beach, and they're

willing investors. We want to see that a generous portion of those investments are made with Villa International."

Bianca smiled. That was a worthy mission, so she would do her part to impress them with her striking beauty, innate charm, and Harry Winston jewels.

CHAPTER FIVE

Robert glided his wheelchair through the French doors leading to their master suite. He could hear Crystal humming some unrecognizable tune over the sound of the pelting shower. “Darling, could you please hurry it up in there?”

She stuck her head out of the shower door. “I’ve got plenty of time. The guests aren’t due until eight.”

“I’ve asked Ross Spencer to come at seven thirty for a pre-cocktail cocktail. I want to talk a little business before the others arrive.”

Darn. Why couldn’t he have told me that sooner...MEN! All they need is a few swipes of the comb and a good dinner jacket, and they’re set to go! She dried off, slipped into her lavender silk dressing gown, and headed for her closet. Fortunately, she knew exactly what she’d wear. As a matter of fact, she’d made a beeline for Saks on Worth Avenue as soon as the invitations for the dinner party were sent out. She chose an AKRIS sleeveless dress with fitted bodice and flirty knife pleated skirt. The cool chartreuse hue was the perfect complement to her flaming red hair, which she pulled back into a severe chignon. It was her new Palm Beach look, a far cry from the bohemian curls of her single girl days.

She stepped out into the living room, just as the buzzer rang from the lobby below. She instructed the doorman to send Ross Spencer and his *significant other* up to the penthouse. Robert joined her at the door, as she welcomed Ross and the magenta clad platinum blond on his arm. Introductions were made as they convened to the living room.

Lena looked around in awe of her surroundings. She'd never seen anything like the display of contemporary artwork that graced the walls of the Montrose home. She didn't get it, but she knew it cost big bucks. She joined Ross on the sofa, realizing that they were the first guests to arrive. She poked him in the ribs, whispering "we're the first ones here!" Ross forgot to tell Lena about the pre-cocktail cocktail. He thought it best if she made herself scarce, so he suggested she powder her nose. Crystal obliged to show her the way.

"Nice place you've got here, Montrose," Ross said.

"Thanks. Glad you could make it. I suppose things over at the showgrounds are pretty busy this time of year."

"Peak season now, but we go full throttle all year."

"Yes, I imagine so. You've done quite an impressive job here in Florida. What's next on the agenda?"

Ross smiled to himself. So that's what Montrose is up to. He wants in on the next phase of the equine empire here. "Have you ever been to Paris, Montrose?"

"Yes, a number of years ago, why do you ask?"

"They'll have nothing on us."

What do you mean?"

"The Grand Palais...that's what."

Robert was visibly puzzled. He was familiar with the Grand Palais, but what that had to do with South Florida, he couldn't imagine.

Crystal and Lena returned, followed by a server with ice cold Martinis for all. The buzzer rang again. It was just shy of eight o'clock. She opened the door to greet Vincente and Bianca Villa. Crystal had never seen such an opulent piece of jewelry as the one hanging around Bianca's neck. It was a riot of diamonds in every shape and color, fashioned into an artful piece that grazed her decolletage. She was so mesmerized that she had trouble tearing her gaze away to look at Bianca's face. But it was a gorgeous face, featuring luminous brown eyes and an electrifying smile, all framed by the raven waves of her long lustrous hair. Crystal felt like Little Orphan Annie by comparison. She glanced at Vincente. They made a dashing couple. She quickly collected herself and invited them to join the party in the living room.

Robert came forward to shake hands. Vincente looked up to see Ross Spencer rising from the sofa. Their eyes met. A vibration of animosity passed between the two. The contempt that they had for each other was palpable. Everyone fell silent. Crystal turned to Robert with a *do something* look. He quickly snapped to and made the unnecessary introductions. The buzzer rang again, momentarily saving the situation. Crystal hurried to the house phone, relieved to hear that Sloane and I had arrived. She waited for us at the door to the penthouse, reluctant to return to the living room. As soon as we walked through the door, she hustled us into the powder room. "We've got trouble," she whispered.

"What do you mean?" Sloane asked.

"We've got a room full of people who hate each other. Robert invited these people... he didn't know that they knew each other. And now... it's a disaster!"

I took Crystal by the arm. Don't worry, we're here now. Everything will be alright." We moved to the living room, and I froze. Standing before me was Vincente Villa. My heart skipped a beat.

The arrival of Enrico Alvero provided some relief for the overcharged mise-en-scene, at least temporarily. As drinks were passed around, the conversation was stilted, as no one was sure of the nature of relationships between fellow guests... public or private. Poor Crystal. Her first experience as a hostess in Palm Beach was reminiscent of Agatha Christie's *Ten Little Indians.* I had to hand it to her though, she was doing a splendid job under the circumstances. She managed to steer the conversation to neutral subjects for all concerned. The opening of the Palm Beach Antiques Show, the newest culinary offerings at Ta-boo, and the much-acclaimed spa at Eau Palm Beach. To Ross's horror, Lena mentioned that she had once done nails there. The room remained uncomfortably charged.

I couldn't help feeling the weight of Bianca Villa's stare. The woman was an incorrigible bully. As if her vile behavior of the past wasn't enough, now she had to taint the atmosphere with her icy chill. I couldn't help but notice that her venomous glance was not reserved strictly for me. She kept a close watch on Sloane and Enrico Alvero, enjoying a very friendly discussion on the other side of the room. Between keeping tabs on me, and the Sloane-Enrico tete-a-tete, it was as though her head was on a swivel.

As the hour grew closer to nine, and dinner, we awaited the arrival of Robert's "mystery guest." Crystal called earlier to tell me that someone, a man, would be joining us for dinner. Robert wouldn't even hint as to his identity. Crystal hoped that it wasn't some celebrity. She'd always been the star-struck type and would never be able to make it through the evening if the likes of Johnny Depp, or Leonardo DiCaprio walked through the door. I told her not to worry, that I would take over as hostess with the mostess if that were to occur.

The buzzer did its job once more, and the suspense would soon be relieved. This time Robert answered the door and ushered the final guest to the party. He was a tall, silver-haired man, with eyes the color of Delft Blue. He greeted us with a generous smile. Robert introduced him as BBC sportscaster, Lloyd Snow.

I gasped! It was as though Muhammed Ali's glove landed a blow to my left jaw. I stood stunned, unable to move. Robert turned to me, his face lit up, grinning from ear to ear. He looked like Santa Claus handing out Christmas presents to forlorn orphans. Lloyd came toward me. I recoiled. The room was frozen in stunned silence.

"Ivy, it's been a long time."

I took a deep breath, trying to recover from my shock. I had not seen Lloyd Snow since my mother's funeral twenty-five years ago. There was a good reason for that.

"Hello Lloyd" was all I could muster.

Poor Robert. Stunned and confused, he tried to decipher the situation, and keep the evening from going down in flames. I took pity on him.

"It's been a long time, hasn't it?"

"Yes, Ivy. How have you been all these years?"

"I'm getting along."
Sloane broke away from her conversation with Alvero to intervene. "Lloyd, amazing to see you again."
"Sloane Parker. I don't believe I've laid eyes on you since your Olympic days."
"What brings you to Florida, Lloyd?"
"I'm covering the horse show for the BBC."
"Oh! I thought you'd retired from broadcasting years ago."
"I did. But I've come out of retirement… at least temporarily."

Crystal took the opportunity to break up the awkward situation. "Dinner is served" she announced in a voice that was just a tad too loud.

I had to let Sloane take the wheel of the Range Rover back to the hotel. I was in no condition to drive, and it had nothing to do with the Martinis or the Sauvignon Blanc.

I was stressed out, and emotionally exhausted. Making it through dinner, seated next to Lloyd Snow, and across the table from Vincente Villa, was almost more than I could handle. The proximity of Lloyd's body next to mine made me want to recoil into my shell...like a snail. Afterall, the fact that I had an impervious shell was due, in part, to Lloyd.

I tried my best to avoid Vincente's gaze, but each time I looked across the table, our eyes met. I didn't taste a morsel of my food.

"Wow, Ivy. I didn't think you were going to make it through the evening without going catatonic," said Sloane.

"Can you blame me?"

"No. As a matter of fact, I'm amazed at how well you handled it. What would Robert have been thinking to have invited the three of you on the same night?"

"Robert doesn't know anything about Vincente and me, and as far as Lloyd Snow is concerned, he knew that Lloyd was married to my mother, but he couldn't know about what took place in the past. He thought he was putting together some kind of sentimental family reunion. I never told Robert or Crystal about Mother and Lloyd. It's something that I wanted to keep buried in the past."

“I’ve never heard you talk about it. I wouldn’t know anything myself, if I hadn’t been there to witness the whole sordid thing.”

“Can you believe how Lloyd prattled on about looking forward to meeting his grandchildren? Since Jaycee is down here, I guess they’ll be no avoiding that. Why did he have to come back into our lives?”

Sloane pulled the Range Rover into the hotel driveway. “It had to happen sooner or later, Ivy. Just like meeting up with Vincente is, well, destiny.”

“Destiny playing a dirty trick," I said.

CHAPTER SIX

"Honestly Robert, could it have even been a bigger disaster?" Crystal buried her head in her hands. Robert poured himself a second cup of Breakfast Blend. "It was kind of rough… sorry darling. But how was I to know about all these crazy dynamics? I just wanted to get a feel for what's happening business wise down here, and maybe kick start a bit of a social life. As far as Lloyd Snow is concerned, I never knew there was any bad blood between him and Ivy."

"How do you know Lloyd anyway?"

"Oh, it was just one of those chance meetings years ago at the Union League. He was over here covering the Devon Horse Show, and Monty Wilson brought him to the club for dinner. Had a game of bridge afterward. I heard he was in town covering the horse show, so I asked him to dinner. Thought Ivy would be thrilled to see him… guess not! Do you know what's gone wrong between them?

Crystal buttered a slice of whole wheat toast as she thought back to the few conversations that she'd had with Ivy about her life before she married Bart Skelton. "I haven't the faintest idea. She told me a little about her days training for the Olympics, but that had more to do with Sloane Parker, and their friendship. She said very little about her childhood… only that her father was killed in a racing accident on the Pocono Speedway. She said that her mother married a Brit, Snow, who then adopted her. Her mom died sometime afterward. It was all very vague, but she also told me about an Argentine named Vincente who had been her first lover. I guess the mystery as to *his* identity has been solved."

"That's for sure. I think it was obvious to everyone that an electric current was passing between those two."

Crystal laughed. "You'd have to be blind to miss it. His wife certainly didn't. She was shooting dagger eyes at Ivy all night… and Sloane too, for that matter. Boy, Sloane and Enrico Alvero were really hitting it off. Did you notice?"

Robert looked at Crystal, and they both smiled, thinking the same thing. "Looks like Bianca Villa has a lot on her plate," said Crystal.

The phone rang. It was Ross Spencer inviting Robert to lunch at the Polo Club.

"Mom! We have to be at the grounds by ten or we'll miss our chance for the practice ring" cried Jaycee.

I never would have thought that the festival would be so crowded. Of course, top riders from all over the world came here to compete, but the scheduling was so tight that you had to make every minute count. They'd have to do something about that. All the riders were complaining.

"Okay honey, I'll call down for the car." Sloane and Trina appeared in my doorway ready for action. The time pressure was affecting even Trina, who usually had a *manana* attitude toward everything in life.

As soon as we arrived at the showgrounds, Sloane and the girls headed for the stables to tack up the horses. I wanted to look around the parking lot for a shady spot. We were going to be there for most of the day, and I didn't want to drive home in an oven. The shade of the palms really didn't do much to solve the problem, but it helped. I found a suitable spot at the far end of the lot, and as I maneuvered the Range Rover into the space, a burgundy Rolls Royce Corniche convertible pulled in alongside me. I turned to see Vincente's handsome profile as he put the car into park. I shook my head. Was it a dream? When I awoke this morning, I wasn't even sure that the dinner party at Crystal and Robert's last evening was real. How could it be? It was so bizarre. But this… this was real.

My hand trembled as I opened the door and climbed out of the car. I had no idea what I would say to him. He came around to my side, and we stood under the palm tree. I looked up into his eyes, and at that moment, it was as though a lifetime had not passed. He could feel it too...I knew.

"Ivy, I couldn't believe that it was you last night. I thought I'd never see you again."

"I thought the same, Vincente."

"What happened...all those years ago...I must explain."

I couldn't imagine what sort of explanation would make it right between us.

"We can't talk here; everyone knows me," he said at a whisper.

"Yes, and word would get back to Bianca, I'm sure."

"When can I see you...alone?"

"I don't know, Vincente." I didn't know if I would or *could* see him.

"Please, Ivy. There's so much I must tell you. Not just about us, but about Bianca, and Lloyd Snow. You have a right to know."

"Alright, but I can't get away until tomorrow. Meet me at IL Bellagio in West Palm at six." I broke away and walked...sprinted across the parking lot toward the stables. What did he mean? What could have happened all those years ago, that I knew nothing about? Curiosity drove my need to know...but that wasn't all.

Robert's chauffeur guided the pearlescent Escalade up to the front door of Testa's at precisely eleven forty-five. He had the SUV outfitted with an electronic lift that made getting his wheelchair in and out of the vehicle a breeze. He liked to arrive at his appointments early to give himself ample time to get situated without making anyone else uncomfortable. The maître d showed him to a private table in the corner of the room that had been reserved by Mr. Spencer. Because of the early hour, there were few patrons in the place, which afforded

Robert the luxury of wheeling across the room with a scant audience. He ordered a Vodka Gimlet and awaited the arrival of his host. He didn't have to wait long.

Ross Spencer sauntered through the doorway of Testa's as though he owned the place. Maybe, as a silent partner, he did? He was dressed in his Palm Beach uniform. Navy Polo blazer, fawn chinos, and today, a flamingo pink Izod shirt. Saddle tan Ferragamo's, sans socks, completed the ensemble. Robert thought it was pedestrian.

"Hello, Montrose. Thanks for coming on such short notice."

"No problem, and it's *Robert."*

"Of course," Ross Spencer said, displaying something that was almost a grin. "I wanted to continue the discussion we'd started last evening...the one interrupted by the arrival of Vincente and Bianca Villa. How do you know them, by the way?"

"I don't know them well. We met the other day at the Everglades Club." Robert was reluctant to give out too much information, not knowing where Spencer was going with all this.

"I'd be careful dealing with Villa if I were you."

"Why do you say that?"

"Ah, just a feeling. Forget I said anything." The waiter arrived with Ross Spencer's "usual" ...Stoli on the rocks. Robert could sense the pattern of routine. Ross leaned forward and lowered his voice. "What I really wanted to talk to you about is my plan for expanding the equestrian facilities here. My vision is to make this place the unquestionable capital of the equestrian sport world."

"And how do you plan on doing that?" asked Robert.

"By outdoing every other competitor, that's how. It's just like any other business. Build the best, and they'll come."

Robert didn't know all that much about the horse world, but business, he knew. "That's an ambitious goal, but probably achievable for you. You've got the money...the development know-how. Look what you've done here already." Spencer sat quietly, with a faraway look in his eyes. Robert could almost see the wheels turning.

"Yes. It's come a long way from the swamp it used to be, but there's so much more that can be done," said Ross.

They both ordered the "special" Grouper with a bourbon caper glaze. Ross pontificated on the wisdom of always ordering the special, if possible. It was fresh, and what the chef felt like cooking. Robert couldn't argue with that. "So, this vision of yours…?"

"When you were in Paris, did you see the Grand Palais?"

"Went past it but didn't stop. Impressive structure."

"It's where the Saut Hermes is held every year. They used to attract *all* the top riders, until the WEF came along. Now, a lot of people compete here instead. Especially Americans, they can avoid traveling to Europe. But Paris is still attracting the creme de la creme that should be ours. We need a venue to rival the Grand Palais; a structure to accommodate classes indoors, so weather won't be a factor."

Spencer reached into his briefcase and pulled out an iPad. He clicked the "on" button and slid it across the table to Robert. Illuminated on the screen was the most phenomenal glass structure Robert had ever seen. He looked up at Ross Spencer. "Quite something. How do you propose to do it?"

"The plans for the building are already complete...down to the unisex bathrooms" Ross smirked. "But there is one problem."

"And what is that?" asked Robert.

"The land. The only parcel of land suitable for this arena, if that's what you want to call it, is owned by Villa Enterprises."

The pieces of the puzzle were finally coming together. Ross Spencer needed Villa's land to build his behemoth, and if their demeanor toward each other at dinner last evening was any indication, the chances of Villa selling to Spencer were none and… none. Robert waited for the other shoe to drop. It dropped.

"So, you see Montrose, ah, Robert, that's where an arrangement between you and I could be beneficial."

"How so?" asked Robert.

"I'm thinking that we put together some sort of partnership. You buy the land. Talk about building an equine healthcare facility...something like that. Then, after the deal is done, we can go about building our *Grand Palais Palm Beach.* Or, if you don't like the idea of being in the horse show business, you can just sell the land to me at a quick, and handsome profit."

"In other words, deceive Villa."

"Hey, all's fair in love, war and business.

CHAPTER SEVEN

Bianca hit the speed dial next to Enrico's name. Well, it wasn't exactly the name *Enrico* showing in her contacts list. She'd entered the name "Erica" instead, just in case Vincente got curious and started snooping in her cell phone. He picked up on the third ring.

"Bianca, darling."

"Don't 'Bianca darling' me! I can't believe what I saw last night. You...all over that Parker woman!"

"No, no baby, you got it all wrong. Sloane is building a polo field on her property in Pennsylvania. She was asking for my advice."

"What kind of advice would she need? A polo field is a polo field."

"Not about the field itself. About assembling a team. She wanted my recommendation on a couple of players she might want to recruit."

"It looked like more than that to me."

"No baby, I swear!"

"Well, okay. When will I scc you again?"

"I don't know. Vincente has me running all over the place trying to replace his string. I must go to Argentina to look at a couple of horses there."

“Are you kidding me?” How long will you be gone?”
“I don’t know for sure, but I’ll be in touch. I promise, baby.”
“Humph. Well, try and get back as soon as you can. I miss you darling.”
“I miss you too, baby.”

Bianca hung up. Argentina? Right now? Something didn’t smell right about that. Vincente had been yammering on about those dead horses and trying to find out what happened. However, he’d said nothing about looking for new ones...yet. True, he didn’t tell her everything that occupied that busy brain of his, but when he was hot to do something, he usually didn’t keep it under wraps. She would have to keep a close eye on the comings and goings of Mr. Enrico Alvero.

She went to her closet and perused her options for the day. She would be chairing the first meeting of a new non-profit that she’d started. *The Equine Wellness Center* would be the perfect project to open those Palm Beach wallets, and another great excuse for a charity ball besides. She selected a Tory Burch hibiscus hued silk sheath and matching jacket.

As she pinned a sapphire brooch to her jacket, she considered the problem of Sloane Parker. She wasn't *completely* buying into Enrico's story about the polo player advice he was giving her. By the look of it, he was giving her more than that...men were such slimy beasts. She knew how to keep tabs on Enrico, even if it meant hiring professional help from time to time. But knowing what Sloane Parker was up to...now that was another ball game altogether. If there was one thing her father taught her, it was to keep her friends close, but to keep her enemies closer. She Googled Sloane Parker for contact information and found an email address through LinkedIn. She crafted a message.

Hi Sloane! Lovely meeting you at dinner last evening. I was hoping to get a chance to speak to you about the new Equine Wellness Center we are planning. It will be the first one of its kind in the country...a groundbreaking innovation. I'd love to tell you more about it. Would it be possible to meet me for a drink...say around six-thirty tomorrow? I'll be in West Palm, so let's meet at IL Bellagio. Please let me know if that's convenient.

Bianca pushed the "send" button, putting the plan in motion.

Dr. Julia Forrest pulled her truck into the driveway of the Sparkling Sands trailer park on the outskirts of Delray Beach. The doublewide that she shared with her sister, Sharon, was rented on a month-to-month lease, giving her the flexibility, they so desperately needed. Ever since they left Kentucky, she was never sure how long she could stay in one place. She lugged the three bags of groceries she picked up at Walmart down the pathway to her mailbox. As usual, she was the recipient of discount store fliers, solicitations for various charitable causes, and political missives, but no check from Uncle Sam. After Sharon's income dwindled to practically nothing but Social Security Disability, Julia had been responsible for her sister financially as well as emotionally. The nervous breakdown that Sharon suffered after the death of her child two years ago, was the impetus for the end of her marriage as well. The tragedy that happened to that family should never happen to anyone.

It was a warm, sunny Saturday afternoon when Sharon asked her husband, Steve, to go to the 7-11 for hotdog buns. He did not see their three-year-old daughter, Carly, as her tricycle careened around the corner and under the moving wheels of his Honda Odyssey. Subsequent months of guilt and blame quelled the Zelinsky marriage. Steve moved back to his hometown of Boise to be with his relatives, and Sharon sought refuge with Xanax. It was another year before she was able to even function...but not without help. Julia picked Sharon up upon her discharge from The Homewood Rehabilitation Center, and the downward spiral of her life began. Although Sharon was still on various medications, and in outpatient therapy, it wasn't good for her to be sitting around the apartment watching soap operas all day. So, Julia found her sister a part-time job near the veterinary clinic where she worked in Paris, Kentucky. That turned out to be a monumental mistake.

Julia banged on the aluminum storm door with the toe of her boot. She didn't feel like setting down the grocery bags to open the door, so she hoped Sharon would hear, and lend a hand. Didn't happen. She put the bags on the stoop, opened both doors, and dragged them one by one into the "living room." How she hated being back in that depressing double wide. They had rented it furnished, which consisted of a mammoth sofa, upholstered in gross brown polyester plaid, and matching loveseat. The accent chair was a tan pleather lounger, with a wagon wheel coffee table anchoring the arrangement. The kitchen featured 70's faux wood cabinets, with heavy brass Mediterranean style pulls, and avocado appliances. The bedrooms were even less stylish, but at least they each had their own, which offered some much-needed privacy in the cramped quarters.

"Sharon! Sharon I'm home! Didn't you hear me banging on the door?"

Sharon walked into the room wearing her robe and fuzzy slippers, even though it was eighty-eight degrees outside. With the air conditioning on full blast in the trailer, how could she have known? Julia visualized an outrageous electric bill next month.

"Hi Julia. No, I didn't hear you. I was in the bathroom."

"Sharon, why aren't you dressed yet?"

"I don't know. What's in the bags?"

"Groceries...food," said Julia.

Sharon padded across the moss green olefin carpeting and started nosing through the bags.

"Please put them away, or at least put them on the counter."

"Why are you always nagging at me? I haven't done anything...except be your damn secretary."

Julia closed her eyes and shook her head. Yes, her sister was right. She hadn't done anything. She hadn't done anything for the seven months that they lived in the trailer. She hadn't cleaned or cooked, or heaven forbid taken any wash to the laundromat. But Julia couldn't complain. The fact that Sharon had done *nothing* for the past seven months just might be their saving grace.

"What do you mean, *secretary?"*

"Well, I've been taking your messages."

"What messages?"

"Like the one over there, under the TV Guide."

Julia lifted the magazine from the coffee table to uncover a scribbled note on the back of a gas station receipt.

Vincente Villa called. He wants you to call him back.

"When did this come in?"
"Oh, a couple of hours ago. Something about his horses. Said he couldn't get you on your cell."
Julia felt sick to her stomach. What was she to do about Villa?

Lloyd Snow slipped onto a bar stool for a quick libation at The Brazilian Court Hotel. He preferred the intimacy and old-world charm of the luxury hotel, compared with the flashier environs of its counterparts on the ocean. Besides, he was much less likely to run into any of his colleagues from the press who were mostly holed up in West Palm. The bartender approached, and Lloyd ordered a Sapphire Martini up. He avoided eye contact which signaled his desire to avoid the customary chit chat. He had a lot of thinking to do and didn't want to waste time making small talk with the "help." He was in Palm Beach, ostensibly, to cover the horse show, but that wasn't the real impetus for his visit to the States. Lloyd Snow had a problem. A very serious problem...and he had to keep Ivy from finding out. He knew it wouldn't be easy. Ivy was so much like her mother...beautiful, charming, kind, and unfortunately...inquisitive. Much too inquisitive. If it hadn't been for that one pervasive quality, none of it would have happened. If Lacey had just stuck to her interior design career, and the raising of her daughter, things could have gone on smoothly in their lives, instead of heralding the chaos that ensued.

The bartender placed an elegant, tall stemmed cocktail glass in front of Lloyd. As he took his first sip of the ice-cold liquor, he sensed a presence behind him. He turned to face Vincente Villa, standing just steps from the bar. Their eyes met, and there was no avoiding a confrontation. Villa approached, invading Lloyd's personal space.

"I'm surprised to find you here, Snow."

"Why? I always stay at The Brazilian when I'm in Palm Beach."

"I didn't know you came here often."

"I've been coming here ever since the first polo match was played at Wellington."

"How long have you been here this time?" Vincente asked.

"A few days. What's it to you?"

"Let's just say I'm curious about anybody who could have been in the vicinity of my stables recently. Besides, I'm surprised you'd have the balls to show up here. Did you know that Ivy was in town?"

Lloyd Snow paused to think. There was a lot riding on how he answered that question.

"Listen Villa, if you think I had anything to do with your dead horses, you're insane. As far as Ivy is concerned, she's liable to show up anywhere in the horse world. You know that as well as I do."

"Stay away from her, Snow. You've brought enough misery into her life as it is."

"What right have you got to say that to me? She's my daughter, and Jaycee is my granddaughter. If anyone should stay away from Ivy, it's you. I think your wife would feel the same way."

Vincente stormed out of the room. Lloyd took another sip of his martini. A good defense is always the best offense. He had to stay ahead of this situation at all costs. The fact that Scotland Yard appeared on his radar screen after all these years came close to unnerving him. Why this cold case was rearing its ugly head after all these years was beyond him, but his cunning, and always reliable instincts told him that the motivation for their sudden interest lay here in the States. The fact that Villa established himself here, and now Ivy and Sloane are showing up? It had to be more than a coincidence.

He finished his drink, signed the tab, and headed for his room. He was wise to stay at the Brazilian rather than the Breakers. He wanted to keep close tabs on Ivy, but from far enough away that she wouldn't realize that he was watching her. He entered his room...700 square feet of luxury, with living space and private patio furnished in the classic Spanish Colonial style. He shed his clothes and headed for the marble jetted walk-in shower. He needed to wash the smarmy Latino smell of Vincente Villa that clung to his Anglican skin

CHAPTER EIGHT

"I can't believe that I agreed to meet him." I said, burying my head in my hands.

Sloane shot a confused look in my direction. "Meet who...for what?"

I told her about my encounter with Vincente in the parking lot.

"Of course, you've got to meet him. Aren't you dying of curiosity?"

"Well, yes, but I can't imagine what he would have to say to me that would make any difference now. It was all so long ago."

Sloane got up from her lounge chair and joined me at the bistro table. "Ivy, seriously, I know that you've moved heaven and earth to put distance between you and what happened in London, but you know as well as I do that there is unfinished business. Unfinished business always circles back...to get finished."

"I know you're right," I said, meeting her eyes. "But as curious as I am, I'm afraid to open up old wounds. I've made some peace with the past, and I've struggled since then to move on with my life."

Sloane poured herself another cup of coffee from the carafe and sat back in her chair. "I'm not arguing with you. I just think that there's a part of you, a big part, that won't be able to move on emotionally until you fully resolve the past. Besides, what about your mother? Think about your mother. Maybe you'll be able to find out what really happened to her. Isn't that worth exploring?"

"You have a point. But there's something else."

"What?" asked Sloane.

"Vincente...his coming back into my life."

"Ivy, you're ashamed to admit it, but the moment you saw him…"

"Ah, yeah, and what about John? And what about the fact that Vincente is married...what about that?"

"Okay, let's deal with one thing at a time...John. Yes, you are attracted to him. The first guy you've been with since Bart. You've been through a lot with him. He's steadfast; he likes the kids. They like him. You live in the same town. You're thinking that maybe you have a future together. All well and good, but then you see Vincente, and... fireworks! Am I right?"

"Shit...why *do you have to be my best friend?* I've been stuck with you since Crystal got married. At least *she* would have kicked my butt at the thought of messing things up with John!"

Sloane threw her head back and laughed. "Of course, she would. Crystal is practical when it comes right down to it. I'm a little edgier. If there's chemistry, there's chemistry...no denying it."

I sat back and let the sun caress my face. "I don't know what to think, but you're right about one thing. I have to meet Vincente if for no other reason than to find out what this is all about."

The ringing of the house phone interrupted us. Sloane jumped up and jogged inside to answer.

"Hello?"

"Ms. Snow?"

"No. This is Sloane Parker."

"Ms. Parker, we have a visitor in the lobby who would like to speak with you."

"Really? Hmm, okay, put them on."

After a momentary lapse, she was greeted by a deep masculine voice with a smooth Latin accent. "Ms. Parker? Sloane? It is Enrico. Enrico Alvero. We met the other night at the Montrose dinner party."

"Yes, of course, Enrico. I remember." Sloane was taken aback at hearing his voice. "What can I do for you?"

"It is I that wish to do something for you."

She couldn't imagine. "Yes, and what is that?"

"I would like to buy you a drink at the HMF…. right now, if it would be convenient?"

"Right now?"

"Yes. I don't wish to inconvenience you, but I was in the area, and I have information on some of the polo players that you were asking about the other night. I thought maybe…"

"Oh, well yes, of course. That's very thoughtful of you. Just give me a few minutes, and I'll meet you downstairs."

"Well, what do you know?" I stood behind Sloane, eavesdropping (she would have done the same.)

She gently placed the receiver back in the cradle. "He says he has info on the players I'm interested in."

I raised my brow. "Really? Players, is it? Some games are being played, but I don't think it has anything to do with polo."

Sloane applied a fresh coat of lipstick and headed for the elevator.

Enrico Alvero planted himself on one of the

comfy velvet lounge chairs that dotted the HMF bar. The waitress, in elegant black and pearls approached, and he put in his order for champagne cocktails for two. A bit over the top? Perhaps, but he had an impression to make on the striking and well-heeled Ms. Parker. She was a woman who knew what she wanted, and he was the man that would get it for her. He knew who was who in the polo world, both here and in Europe and South America. He knew who was on their way up, and who was on their way out. Yes, he was rich in knowledge, but poor in capital. A few unfortunate investments left him in less than desirable circumstances. He was ready to launch his own team. He knew the right players; he knew the right horses. He was sick and tired of putting together strings to bring glory to other men. Now was his time. He had hoped that Bianca would share his vision, but alas, she had not. She still put her resources (and her father's) behind Villa. He'd begun to despair that it would never change. He looked up to see the stunning Sloane Parker staring down at him.

"Ms. Parker...Sloane...champagne?"

"Champagne Mr. Alvero? What are we celebrating?"

"Please call me Enrico."

"Alright Enrico, so what's the special occasion?"
"To my way of thinking, this is the first meeting of a very successful enterprise in the world of polo."
"Really? Are you that confident?"
"Yes, as I said before, my contacts with players and horse brokers alike is unparalleled in this sport. I see the combination of my affiliation with the inner circle, and your passion...and ah resources, to be a winning combination. Together, we can turn polo in North America on its ear."
"Well, I don't know about that, but, as I said, I am interested in exploring the idea of putting together a team of my own. However, I would want to base my activities back in Pennsylvania at my estate, *Heart's Desire*."
"That would be no problem. We could play the northeast in the summer months, and then play here, and perhaps the west coast in the winter."
Sloane took a sip of her champagne cocktail and sat back to consider the possibilities. She noticed that Enrico's gaze shifted to her shapely legs and tugged on the hem of her skirt to lessen the exposure. How bad of an idea could it be, she thought, having her own string, building a

first-class field, competing nationally, and even internationally? It had always been a dream of hers, and this might just be the opportunity she'd been hoping for. However, there was a caveat...Vincent Villa to be precise.

"Enrico, your proposition is enticing, but I must inquire...what about Vincente Villa? You are his manager and trainer. Villa Stables is a world class enterprise, and you said the other evening that Vincente gave you full reign with the management. I'm sure that you are compensated generously. Why would you want to leave a situation like that?"

Enrico paused for a moment to consider his response. He did not want to allude to any problematic issues...although they were numerous, including the increasingly possessive Bianca.

"Does it have anything to do with the recent death of his horses?" Sloane asked. "Has he decided not to replace them?"

"We are waiting to hear back from the vet, Dr. Forrest, with the results of numerous tests. I'm sure whatever the cause, it was accidental."

"Really, and how can you be so sure?"

Here it comes., Enrico thought. Without a readily apparent reason people would begin to

think that he had something to do with it. Had the stable been mismanaged in some way? Was there negligence on his part? But worst of all, the shadow of a doubt. Had he been criminally responsible for the death of those horses? Had he, in fact, murdered them? He knew, well he hoped anyway, that so far Villa was not having such considerations. But the longer the investigation dragged on, the more time to consider a sinister motive in lieu of a simple medical explanation. He sat back, ruminating over the idea that leaving Villa stables now might cast suspicion over him. But the fact that Sloane Parker appeared with the possibility of building his own polo empire...those opportunities didn't come along every day.
"Enrico? Enrico?" Sloane leaned in and tapped his elbow.
"Oh! I'm sorry" he said. I seem to have drifted off into a fantasy world imagining "Parker Polo Stables of Pennsylvania." He hesitated to include *Alvero* in the name. It was too presumptuous at this stage of the game.

Sloane smiled. "First things first. I'd like to see a proposal on paper as to how this dream might become a reality, and how much it would cost."

"Of course. I will commence immediately" he said, intensifying his smooth Hispanic accent. He gently drew Sloane's hand to his lips in a farewell gesture.

"Wow! That guy is something else!" Sloane set her clutch on the hall table and made her way over to the club chair across from mine.

"I've been waiting with bated breath," I said. "What was that all about?"

"I'm not a hundred percent sure Ivy, but he ostensibly wants to put together a polo stable back at Heart's Desire, with his connections and *my* money."

"Makes sense. A young guy like that wants his own slice of the pie; not just working for someone else all his life."

"Normally I'd agree with that, but if you ask me there's something else going on here."

"Like what?"

"Look at the bigger picture. Right now, Mr. Alvero is smack dab in the middle of this catastrophe at Villa Stables, an entity that he is responsible for."

"You're not suggesting that he had anything to do with the death of Vincente's horses?"

"No, not directly, but until the facts are revealed about what really happened, the jury is out. Was it an accident? Deliberate? No one knows for sure. If there are no definite answers, Alvero may be presumed innocent by the public, but he's not home free. It's smart of him to have *Plan B* in his pocket either way. Removing himself to work up north for a while gives things a chance to quiet down. It will be a season, maybe even two before he'd return to the Palm Beach scene, and by then interest would have moved on to another crisis du jour."

"I see...you have a point." I headed over to the bar cart to start shaking up the five o'clock martini ritual. "I have an alternative theory."

"What's that?"

"I suspect that there's something of a more, shall we say, *personal* reason why Mr. Alvero wants to get out of Dodge."

Sloane raised her brow…such as?"

"Such as a romantic entanglement. The way Bianca Villa kept looking over at the two of you having your little tete a tete at Crystal's the other night."

"Oh really? And I thought that Ross's little piece of fluff, Lena, was giving him *that look!"*

"Her? Really? I don't know. I think she gives every guy that 'bedroom eyes' routine. Probably something she's been doing since she was fourteen."

"Maybe, but there were electric currents in the air, no doubt about that! And Ivy, don't think I didn't notice that some of those currents were zipping back and forth between you and Vincente." Sloane flashed a devilish smile.

CHAPTER NINE

I was relieved when Sloane volunteered to drive the girls out to the show grounds this morning. There wasn't much practice time left before their first class, which was scheduled for the day after tomorrow. I wasn't happy about missing this practice session, but they couldn't have a better coach than Sloane Parker, Olympic Silver Medalist. But as much as I thrived on prepping for competition, just like we did in the old days, I still had a magazine to put out. *Equestrian Style* didn't publish itself.

I'm fortunate to have a very competent staff, but inevitably, the buck still stopped with me. Technology certainly made it easier to work from a distance, but the work didn't do itself, and I have deadlines to meet. Being in sunny South Florida instead of frigid Pennsylvania offered a bonus that I wasn't about to pass up. Why stay cooped up in a hotel room (lovely as it was) when I could be basking in rays of sunshine down at the pool. It was still early, and a cool breeze was wafting through the fronds of the Royal Palms that dotted the landscape below.

I slipped into my suit, grabbed my laptop and headed for the elevator. My goal was to finish editing the copy this morning and then review the visuals this afternoon. I headed straight for the pool deck and selected a quiet table in the corner to avoid distractions. The waiter approached, raised the protective umbrella, and presented me with the breakfast menu. Hmm...coffee, no, make that decaf iced tea; I'd already had two cups of French Roast to propel me into action back in my room. The fresh fruit plate sounded appetizing, so I placed my order and opened my laptop. Let's see, first I'll look at the Fashion section, my favorite. The article on the new line from Tailored Sportsman is coming along nicely, just a few changes in the final paragraph. Ariat has a nice new design for formal boots coming out in time for hunting season next fall. Good to get a jump on that for pre-orders.

Suddenly I felt a shadow descend over my keyboard. My goodness, that waiter made a fast job of bringing my breakfast. I adjusted my sunglasses and looked up expecting to see mangos, pineapple and papaya, but what I saw gave me a jolt. It wasn't the waiter's shadow. It

was the shadow of Lloyd Snow falling over me. I gasped! "What are *you* doing here?"
"I thought a little talk between father and daughter would be in order," he said.
"I'm not your daughter."
"Yes, you are, Ivy. Remember, I adopted you when you were just a little girl."
"There may have been some paperwork filed, but you are not my father. My father died in that racing accident in the Poconos." I said with venom.
"But my dear, when I married your mother, I kindly adopted you so that we could be a real family.
I shuttered. "You could never take the place of my real father."
"Perhaps not. But you have to admit that I added quite a bit of value to your young life. I introduced you to horses, and the spectacular world of high-level competition...even to the Olympics."

As much as I hated to, I did have to admit it was true. My mother, however, did pay for all those equestrian experiences with her insurance money, and her earnings from her interior design business. Lloyd's salary with the BBC couldn't support all of that, plus a posh townhouse in Mayfair, and a country estate in the Cotswolds.

"Yes Lloyd, you did introduce me to the horse world, but it doesn't make up for what happened to my mother...and to me."

"Ivy, you can't blame me for all that."

Much to my relief, I spotted the waiter arriving with my breakfast. He approached the table and set the service before me. He glanced at Lloyd. "Will you be having anything, sir?" he asked.

"Well, I... Lloyd began."

"No," I said. The gentleman was just leaving."

Lloyd flashed an icy look my way. "Yes, of course," he snarled.

The waiter retreated to check on his other tables.

"Listen my dear, I've been getting some bad vibes lately from Scotland Yard. They contacted me to ask some questions about your mother's death that they thought I might be able to clarify. I don't like it. What happened, happened a long time ago. It's over and done with, unless there's someone who has not accepted that yet. Someone who is trying to resurrect old ghosts. I'm sure that you wouldn't want Jaycee and Jayson to find out about their mother's sordid past back in England?"

With that, Lloyd pulled back his chair with a grating scrape against the surface of the pool deck and turned to go. *Fuck him. Fuck Lloyd Snow.* Is he telling the truth about Scotland Yard? Were they going to reopen the investigation into my mother's death? The thought of reliving that sickened me. How could I find out if Lloyd was lying? I sure as hell don't want him contacting Jaycee and Jayson. I'm not as concerned about Jayson since he's back up north, but Jaycee… Wait a minute, that gives me an idea! I wonder if John would have any way of finding out if Scotland Yard is poking around? I haven't talked to him in a couple of days. I've been laying low until I get things figured out with Vincente. I don't want to deceive John, but I'm not going to open a can of worms unnecessarily. Lloyd's little visit kind of changes things though.

I retrieved my cell phone from my tote bag, and dialed John's number.

"Hi stranger!" he said.

I couldn't help feeling pangs of guilt. "Hi John. How are you?"

"Freezing my butt off if you want the truth. I've been on a stakeout the last two nights trying to catch this nutcase that made a bomb threat at the high school."

I felt a shiver go up my spine. "Is everything ok?"

"Yes. It was a false alarm, but we think we know who's behind it, and we're keeping an eye on him just in case he tries something stupid."

"Why didn't you tell me about this John? After all, Jayson…"

"It was a prank call. No use getting you all upset over nothing."

"Well, that's what we're living with nowadays." I lamented.

"Don't worry Ivy, if there's any real cause for concern, I'll let you know right away."

"Thanks. I do have a favor to ask, though."

"What's that?"

"Well, I was wondering if you have any connections at Scotland Yard?"

"Scotland Yard? Why?"

"It's about my mother…"

CHAPTER TEN

Dr. Julia Forrest put in yet another call to the lab that was conducting the postmortem on Villa's horses. They moved at a snail's pace, and both Villa and Alvero were on her back every day. They wanted answers, and they wanted them *now*. She couldn't blame them, the longer this dragged on, the more suspicious everyone became. Especially the media. The Palm Beach Post was like a dog with a bone on this story. If the deaths remained a mystery, every owner and trainer feared foul play. No stable felt safe.

She pulled her truck into the trailer park and braced herself for another altercation with her sister. She climbed slowly up the trailer's steel steps and opened the screen door. Sharon must have forgotten to lock it again. She didn't pay much attention to doors, or windows, for that matter. As the heat of the day became more oppressive with every hour, she just cranked up the air conditioning. Why worry about it if you didn't have to pay the electric bill?

"Sharon? Sharon, where are you? I'm home" Julia cried.

Sharon sauntered out of the bathroom, still in her robe and slippers. She stretched and yawned. "What are you doing here in the middle of the afternoon, Julia?"

"I thought I'd come home and grab a bite for lunch. Trying to economize."

Sharon just glared at her through heavy lids. "I think there are still some Fruit Loops left over from breakfast. You should eat those since the milk is about to go sour. Past its expiration date already."

Julia winced. Good God, I'm busting my ass out there in the sweltering heat, and all that's left to eat are Fruit Loops with milk at a precarious state of freshness. Something had to change, and soon.

"Listen Sharon, I don't want to eat Fruit Loops for lunch. Get dressed, and we'll go down to Dick's Diner for a sandwich. You can have meatloaf if you like." It was her favorite.

Sharon turned and shuffled back to her room to throw on some jeans and a t-shirt. Julia went over to the cookie jar and lifted the lid. Maybe there was a leftover cookie or two from Christmas that would help stave off hunger until they got to the diner. She lifted the lid and stuck her hand into the jar. Her fingers rifled through some papers jammed inside, but she found no cookies. She pulled out a wad of papers. They were receipts...taxi receipts! What were these? Receipts of dozens of rides paid for with cash. All destinations were to and from The Palm Beach Polo Club. She examined each receipt and found that Sharon was going out to the polo fields at least three times a week for the past three weeks. What on earth was she doing there? Why would she hide these receipts?

Sharon walked back into the living room flinging her green suede hobo bag over her shoulder. "Ready to go?" she mumbled.

They climbed into the truck, pulled out onto the main highway and headed for the diner. Sharon turned on the radio and fidgeted with the dial until she found her favorite country station. Keith Urban was crooning "You'll Think of Me."

Julia considered how to approach her sister about the taxi receipts. Sharon was in such a fragile mental state that Julia feared setting her off. If she became agitated or thought she was being accused or threatened she might go over the edge. Her once charming, happy-go-lucky sister had become sullen and defensive. Julia found herself walking on eggshells to avoid another breakdown. That was why they left Kentucky. The suspicion surrounding the death of eight Thoroughbreds at Grandview Stables was growing. Getting her sister a job there had been Julia's idea. She was the attending Vet at Grandview, and they were in desperate need of help. Although Sharon had once held a good job as a nurse, she could no longer function in that role effectively, for obvious reasons. She needed something more remote, so cleaning stalls and feeding the horses at Grandview kept her occupied and being around the animals seemed to have a calming effect on her.

When all the racehorses in Stable 10 were found dead in their stalls that horrible morning, Julia was summoned immediately to determine the cause. She signed the death certificates Botulism B, due to contaminated food. How it became contaminated was unknown, but the fact remained that Sharon was responsible for feeding. Julia felt it best that she and her sister relocate in case further disasters were to occur. And now, here they were in Florida, surrounded by more dead horses.

I took a power nap in my room before dressing to meet Vincente at IL Bellagio. I needed to re-group from my encounter with Lloyd, and my ensuing struggle to finish editing the final article for the next issue. I hoped that John's old contact at Scotland Yard could help determine if Lloyd's story about reopening mother's case was true, or part of another one of his schemes. My head was spinning at the thought of reliving that horrid chapter of my life, not to mention the effect it would have on Jayson and Jaycee. It was bad enough that their father was serving time in prison, but to learn that their mother had a black cloud over her head would be devastating. As I was retrieving my cell from the nightstand, I noticed a text message from Sloane. She was dropping the girls off at the hotel on her way to a meeting. She said she probably wouldn't be too late. Hmm? I wonder who she's meeting? Enrico again? I have a feeling that those two were concocting more than plans for a polo field. Sloane had better watch her step. My instincts told me that there's something going on between Enrico and Bianca Villa. Wouldn't that be something if it were true? I would be only too happy to help Sloane kick Bianca's butt.

The buzzer rang, interrupting my fantasy, to let me know that my taxi was waiting downstairs.

Sloane pulled the Range Rover in front of the hotel entrance just as my taxi was departing. "Now you girls order some dinner from room service. Please make it something healthy this time. A steady diet of pizza does not an athlete make!"

The girls chuckled. "Alright Aunt Sloane. Seaweed salad and tofu cakes it is." Jaycee said with a snide smile.

"You don't have to go overboard, girls. A nice piece of grilled salmon and some fresh veggies will do nicely."

"That actually sounds pretty good." Trina said as she stepped out of the cool air-conditioned SUV into the warm tropical air. Jaycee followed, and the girls headed for the hotel lobby, back into the cool processed air. Sloane pulled out her make-up bag and touched up her mascara. Hoping no one was watching, she did a quick change from her t-shirt into a Lilly

Pulitzer floral tunic and reasoned that her white capris would do just fine. A fresh coat of Watermelon Pink lipstick, and she was set to meet with Bianca at IL Bellagio.

She was accustomed to being hit up for all these charity projects and had attended more galas and bought more auction items than she cared to think about. But she did care about supporting worthy causes, and since this would benefit horses, it might just be worthwhile. Besides, Bianca sent a follow-up text confirming their meeting, and mentioned that Crystal Montrose was getting involved in the project. That came as kind of a surprise. Crystal had never expressed any particular interest in equestrian activities, except to cheer Jaycee and Trina on in the showring. Bianca can be quite persuasive, and Crystal and Robert are interested in becoming involved with the Palm Beach community. Sloane wondered if Crystal would be joining them.

Her cell phone rang, and she saw that it was Enrico calling. Humm? Already? He was persistent.

"Hi Enrico. How are you?"

"Maravilloso! I can't wait to tell you about the exciting news I had today!"

"What's that?" she asked.

"Ah...I cannot tell you over the phone. This kind of news requires a champagne toast."

"Well, that does sound exciting Enrico, but I'm afraid that I'm quite tied up right now."

"No fear. We can meet later."

"I'll be in West Palm. As a matter of fact I'm headed there now. Someplace called IL Bellagio." She immediately regretted telling him that.

"Oh yes, I know it well. We can meet there later."

"I don't know how long I'm going to be. We'd better make it another time. I'll talk to you soon, Enrico."

"But Sloane…"

She hit the end button and pulled the Range Rover out onto the highway.

Ross Spencer was getting nervous. He hadn't heard anything from Robert Montrose about his proposal for *Palais Palm Beach.* He was concerned that the land he needed, the land currently owned by Vincente Villa, would soon be developed by Villa Enterprises to expand his polo empire. Ross needed that land. It was the perfect spot for his indoor show facility...close to the existing show ring. He knew that the only way he could get his hands on that land was through a third party; someone just like Robert Montrose. Right now, Villa was all wrapped up in the forensic investigation of his horses, and probably building up a new string. That will keep him occupied for a while, but eventually he will turn his attention back to empire building. His focus has been in Europe for the past few years, but now that he was here, in the thick of things, he was likely to screw things up.

He decided that it was time to get in touch with Montrose again. It had been a few days since their luncheon, and he didn't want the idea going cold. Or worse yet, Montrose finding another project to invest in. He didn't want to come on too strong, so he decided to include the ladies to soften things up a bit. He picked up the phone and dialed Robert's number.

"Hello Robert? Ross Spencer here."

"Oh, hello Ross. What can I do for you?"

"Well, I was just thinking that we might get together for a drink later...have the ladies join us."

"You mean tonight?"

"Yes."

"I don't know if that will work. Crystal has some sort of meeting about a charity project. I think it's over in West Palm...IL Bellagio."

Ross took a deep breath. "Yes, I know it well. We could meet there, and Crystal could join us when she's finished with her meeting."

"I'll have to check with her. I'll call you later." Robert hung up the phone.

Ross wished that Lena would get involved with some of these society women. It would be good for business. But maybe she wasn't the kind of woman he could count on...for that sort of thing.

Crystal stared at the rack of dresses hanging in her walk-in closet. She sighed as she pulled out a flamingo pink Tory Burch shift. She wasn't feeling particularly excited about the meeting that Bianca Villa talked her into. She'd never been one of those "committee women," organizing charity functions and fundraising events, but she and Robert were new to the area, and it was one way to make contacts. Robert thought it would be beneficial for future business ventures, so she agreed to go.

She walked out into the bedroom and found her husband sitting there in his wheelchair, staring into space.

"Penny for your thoughts" she said with a smile.

Robert snapped out of his trance. "I was thinking about Ross Spencer," he said.

Crystal frowned. "What about him?"

"I just got off the phone with him. He invited us to meet him and Lena for a drink this evening."

"Did you tell him I was busy?"

"Yes, but he suggested that we get together at IL Bellagio after your meeting. I'm interested in finding out more about Spencer's plans for expansion. What do you say, honey?"

"Okay, I guess. Tell him to make a reservation for dinner, I'm sure I'll be famished by then."

Robert smiled and picked up his phone to call Ross.

CHAPTER ELEVEN

Bianca arrived at Il Bellagio twenty minutes ahead of the others so that she could secure a secluded table for her meeting with Sloane and Crystal. She didn't want her plans for the equestrian wellness center to be overheard. Daddy had agreed to jump start the project with a generous donation, so she was already well on her way to making it a reality. Bianca didn't want anyone mucking up her plans for using that tract of land near the showgrounds and the polo fields...not even her husband, who had his own plans for it.

She ordered a pitcher of Sangria, Beef Carpaccio and Flatbread, and sat back to wait for her guests. Sloane was the first to arrive, having lucked out finding a convenient parking space. Bianca stood to greet her as she approached their table. With outstretched arms she embraced Sloane and grazed her cheek with a "social kiss." Sloane hated that but smiled broadly anyway.

"So glad you could meet with me" Bianca said in a sickeningly sweet tone.

Sloane immediately regretted agreeing to this meeting. What was she getting herself into? Her mood brightened a bit as she saw Crystal heading their way.

"Sorry I'm late, ladies," Crystal said.

Bianca planted one on her in the same fashion she had Sloane, obviously her "signature greeting." At least there was no close contact embrace involved. Getting stabbed with Bianca's huge jewels posed an ominous threat.

"You're not late at all," Bianca cooed.

Crystal and Sloane shot each other with a quick glance that said it all. They sat down as the waiter approached with Bianca's order. At least we're being fed, thought Crystal. Ross's dinner reservation wasn't for another hour and a half.

I paid the cab driver and gave him a generous tip for a smooth and silent ride. It gave me time to think about how I would handle this meeting with Vincente. I knew that when I agreed to meet him that he was looking for an opportunity to rehash our past and try to explain why things turned out as they did. I always thought I'd want closure between us, but now it seemed moot, except for Lloyd's newfound suspicion that Scotland Yard was reopening Mother's case. That would be news to Vincente, I'm sure. I wondered how he would take it. I knew that he wanted justice, but I also knew that he hated Lloyd, and would not welcome the idea of being involved with him again under any circumstances.

I must have opened my compact at least a dozen times since leaving The Breakers...at least it seemed that way. I thought I still looked decent for my age, but Vincente was one of those men who got better looking as they matured. His once coal black hair was now an elegant salt and pepper, and his handsome features held their chiseled appearance over the years. Maybe I should rethink that facelift I'd been contemplating.

I stepped out of the cab and entered the restaurant. The Maître d led me to an alfresco table where Vincente was already seated.

"Hello Ivy. You look lovely" he said.

I smiled. He oozes charm, but not in a smarmy way; just refreshingly sincere.

"Hello Vincente. It's good to see you." I meant it. As soon as I laid eyes on him, my trepidation disappeared. He looked handsome and sexy in his crisp white shirt and mango hued linen sports coat. He held my chair, and we placed orders for Stoli martinis. "Have you been waiting long?"

"No, I just arrived moments ago. I left the house early, before Bianca got back from wherever she was."

I was guessing that he avoided her so that he wouldn't have to lie about meeting me. I wondered how he would explain his absence later, but maybe they've just come to the place where neither of them cared much anymore.

"Thank you for agreeing to meet me," he said.

"Of course. We've both been through a lot. You know, we don't have to revisit our past and open old wounds. You're married to Bianca now, what was between us is water under the bridge."

Vincente looked deep into my eyes "Not as far as I'm concerned" he said.

I felt my heart pounding as though it would jump from my chest. What was he telling me? Did he want to resume our relationship? Was he considering divorcing Bianca, or did he think I would consent to being *the other woman*?

"Vincente, you need to know that I have someone in my life."

"I didn't know. Is it serious?"

I wasn't sure how to answer. "It's becoming more serious as time goes on."

The waiter brought our martinis. Vincente took a sip, and the smile re-appeared on his face. "I was foolish to think that you would not be involved with someone" he said with a touch of irony in his voice.

I took a deep breath and thought it might be a good time to change the subject. I told him about Lloyd's visit at the pool. The news was not well received.

He furrowed his brow. "Do you believe him about Scotland Yard?"

"I'm not sure. The man that I'm involved with is a police detective. He's checking it out with some of his contacts in London."

Vincente frowned, "What's your gut feeling?"

Well, opening cold cases is becoming more commonplace these days, with the advancement of forensic science. Maybe new information has come to light...or maybe Lloyd is trying to shake me up."

"Shake you down is more like it." Vincente said. He considered the ramifications of reopening the case. So many lives had been turned upside down when Ivy's mother died, including his own.

I looked at the handsome man sitting across the table from me, and I suddenly felt sorry for him. My thoughts drifted to the past...we had been so much in love back then…

I tracked my mother down in the basement kitchen of our Mayfair townhouse. She was standing over the Aga boiling water for yet another cup of tea. She'd readily adopted the British panacea for all difficulties that life can throw one's way. She was looking elegant, as usual, dressed in slim black pants and a black turtleneck sweater accented with a colorful Hermes scarf. In the ten years that we'd been in London, mother had become one of the city's hottest interior designers. She brought her cutting-edge New York sensibility to freshen up the elegant, but tired traditional English decor.

"Morning Mom," I said.

"Good morning sweetheart. What else do you have planned for today?" Lacy asked.
"Vincente and I are going to Harrods to do some shopping, and then have a bite of lunch."
"That's nice," she said, her voice barely audible.

I didn't think mom sounded too thrilled at hearing my plans. Sometimes I think that she doesn't care much for Vincente. I'm mad about him though. I can't believe my good luck meeting him at the polo match last summer. He is without a doubt the most handsome, charming man I've ever known...well, next to dad that is. Funny, but there are times that I can hardly conjure up a picture of my father's face in my mind. It's been years since his accident, but in some ways, it feels like he's still right here with me. I know for sure that he's looking down at me from heaven. I suppose I can't blame mom for marrying Lloyd. She's not the kind of woman who's happy being single. I just don't know if she's happy being married to *him.* Lloyd was okay at first, but I'm seeing a lot of chinks in the knight's shining armor. He's short tempered so much of the time. Mom seems to be walking on eggshells when he's around.

The doorbell rang and I went upstairs to answer it. I could see Vincente's image through the leaded glass door. My heart skipped a beat. "Hello handsome," I said, pulling him into the vestibule.

He kissed me on the lips and handed me a package that he had hidden behind his back.

"What's that?"

"Just a little something for my Love" he said in his sexy Argentine accent.

I tore off the paper and opened a book of poetry by Keats, my favorite. Mom appeared in the doorway. I showed her the volume, and she glanced at him, smiling wanly.

"Good morning, Lacy," he said.

"Good morning, Vincente. I understand that you're taking Ivy shopping?"

"Yes. She's helping me to select some new ties. Your daughter has excellent taste. Just like her mother" he added with a smile.

"Enjoy yourselves" Lacy said as she turned to go back down to the kitchen.

"She's been in a rather strange mood lately. I don't think that she and Lloyd are getting along too well" I whispered.

He shrugged his shoulders. "I'm sure they'll work it out" he said unconvincingly as he helped me on with my coat and headed out the door.

We had a lovely morning selecting a dozen new ties for Vincente. He'd just gotten a promotion at the bank and extended his plans to stay in London indefinitely. He relocated after breaking off his engagement to heiress Bianca Garcia. Bianca was well known in upper crust social circles in Argentina, Europe, and the United States. Well known as a bitch of the highest order, that is. After getting to know Vincente, I couldn't imagine them together. What had he ever seen in her in the first place? True, she was rich beyond imagination, but Vincente wasn't the gold-digging kind. She must have really toned down when she was with him.

I looked over at Vincente as he held up one tie after another trying to decide which looked best. He's so handsome no one would even notice his tie after looking into his velvety brown eyes. Well, the women wouldn't anyway. "Honey, definitely go with the red Hermes, it says *power tie!*"

He smiled and picked up three others as well. "Let's get something to eat Ivy, I'm starving."

We headed for the Ritz, his favorite hotel, where lunch was just starting to be served. He took my hand as the maître' d led us to a corner table in the Palm Court. As I perused the tempting menu, Vincente ordered champagne. "Are we celebrating something?" I asked. He reached into his pocket and pulled out a small blue box...Tiffany blue. He opened it and handed it to me. I was shocked to see the brilliant stone set in platinum. "Vincente...I..."
"Say yes Ivy, say you will marry me."
My heart leapt! "Yes! Of course, yes!"
He removed the ring from the box and slipped it onto my finger. The champagne arrived, and we toasted our new life together. "I can't wait to tell my mom!"
"Ivy, she already knows. I asked her for your hand last week. I thought it would be better than asking Lloyd."
"You were right about that! No wonder mom has been acting so strange. She never was very good at keeping secrets. She must have been bursting to tell me."
"I imagine so, but I needed time to plan and buy your ring."

I was so excited I could hardly eat. He led me to the elevator and up to the Green Park Suite, where we made love for the remainder of that glorious afternoon. It ended all too soon. Vincente's cab dropped me off in front of the townhouse as the sun began to set. I burst through the door and called for my mom, but there was no answer. The townhouse was four stories tall with the kitchen in the basement, the parlor, dining and billiard rooms on the first floor, and bedrooms and bathrooms on the top two floors. Sound did not travel readily through the structure. I headed downstairs to see if she was making dinner. I walked into the kitchen, and gasped! Mom was lying in a heap on the floor next to the stove. I rushed over and touched her arm. There was no movement. I gently turned her body over. She was completely still...dead still.

"Ivy...Ivy?"

I snapped out of my daydream when Vincente called my name. "I'm so sorry," I said.

"What were you thinking about?'" he asked.

I couldn't answer. I felt shaken, traveling back in my memory to that horrible day. I had a feeling that Vincente knew exactly what I was thinking about.

He took my hand. "I'm sorry...so sorry that this has come back to haunt you" he said tenderly. "I detest Lloyd Snow. I'd hoped I'd never see him again after I moved back here. Now, he's turned up to wreak havoc, as always. He was all too happy to let me take the blame for my mother's death. He fed the police anything he could to implicate me. How I'd been the last to see her alive. How I knew that she started each morning with a cup of tea...the tea that contained the Belladonna that killed her."

Vincente remembered how the media had dubbed her "Poison Ivy." He knew in his heart that she wasn't guilty. Unfortunately, Lloyd had an airtight alibi for that day. He'd been on assignment with the BBC in Liverpool. He was eager to hand over Lacy's diary to authorities; the diary in which she professed her love for Vincente Villa. Vincente never knew that Lacy was secretly in love with him. He took her aloof manner as one of indifference, not as a mask to hide her true feelings.

Tears welled up in my eyes. I thought back to all those long days and nights I spent in jail awaiting trial. I was obsessed with thoughts of how my own mother was in love with my fiancé. I detected her growing disdain for Lloyd, and I felt terrible for her. After her happy marriage to my father, she found it almost impossible to tolerate Lloyd's cold neglect. I couldn't help but think that her fantasies about Vincente were just her way of coping with emotional abandonment. I believed that she would never have acted on any of it. She would never have hurt me. I had to hold on to that belief.

"I'm amazed to this day that I didn't stand trial. That solicitor you hired for me was a godsend. How he unearthed that suicide note, I'll never know."

Vincente took a deep breath. It was time for Ivy to know the truth. "I have something I must tell you. That solicitor ...I could never have afforded to hire him back in those days."

I was confused. "But you did hire him."

"Yes Ivy, but not with my money."

"Well, how then?"

"It was Bianca's money, or more likely her father's."

"What? What are you talking about Vincente?"

"Bianca saw the mess we were in, and she came up with a plan. She said that she would give me the money to pay for your defense, if I would leave you and marry her."

I stared at him... unbelieving.

"I couldn't let you rot in prison, or worse yet face the gallows."

I was stunned. "But if I had been found guilty and sentenced to life, or worse, you would have been free."

"Bianca knew that I would never marry her of my own accord. She had to hold power over me to coerce me into marrying her."

Vincente got up from his chair and came around to my side of the table. He put his arm around me and gently kissed me. We sat in silence as the sun began to set. When we looked up, we saw Bianca staring down at us, with Sloane and Crystal standing behind her.

CHAPTER TWELVE

Robert glanced around the bar at IL Bellagio looking for Ross and Lena. They'd decided to have a drink there first while waiting for Crystal to finish her meeting with Bianca and Sloane. Ross picked up on Robert's suggestion to make a dinner reservation, which suited his plans perfectly. It would give him more time to entice Robert into his scheme, and Crystal and Lena would get a chance to know each other better. He hoped that it was a good idea. If Lena did anything to mess this up, he would...well, he'd better not go down that road.

Ross spotted Robert in the doorway and caught his attention. He'd selected a table near the bar where there was more room to maneuver a wheelchair. "Hello Robert. So glad you were able to join us" Ross said.

"Yes. It worked out quite well after all. Crystal is in her meeting, and we can relax with a cocktail while we wait for her."

Lena ordered a Pink Lady, while the men ordered Scotch on the rocks.

"How are you enjoying Palm Beach?" Ross asked Robert. He thought it wise to start off with a little small talk before getting down to business.

"I like it very much," Robert said. "I'm happy not dealing with the snow up north this winter."

Lena asked how Robert got around in the snow with his wheelchair. Did they have snow tires for that, or did he have to put on chains?

Everyone laughed.

Robert wasn't much for small talk, so he thought he'd cut right to the chase. "So, Ross, how are your plans for *Palais Palm Beach* coming along?"

"Coming along great. Have you given any more thought to my proposition?"

Lena had no idea what they were talking about. Ross rarely shared his business goings on with her, except to rant and rave when things weren't going his way. What was this palace that they were talking about? Was Ross going to build a palace? She was curious, but she kept her mouth shut. Ross told her that he didn't appreciate her "two cents." She was learning.

"Yes, I've been considering it. I'd be interested in hearing more. What's your time frame on this project?" Robert asked.

Just then, Crystal came buzzing into the lounge, breathless. She plopped down on a chair between Robert and Ross with a heavy sigh.

"Darling, what's the matter?" Robert asked.

"Nothing," she said. "I need a drink."

Ross signaled the waitress to their table.

"I'll have a Stoli martini. Make it a double, please."

Robert took his wife's hand. "Crystal, you're as white as a sheet. What's wrong?"

She nodded her head toward the al fresco dining tables. They all craned their necks to see what was happening... and what they saw stunned them. Bianca Villa was throwing a Margarita in Vincente Villa's face, while Ivy and Sloane looked on in horror. Lena squirmed in her seat. No one said a word. The maitre' d approached. "Your table is ready. Please follow me."

The four of them settled in at a table near the entrance to the room. An uncomfortable silence was finally interrupted by Lena, who thought she was broaching a safe subject to break the ice." So Crystal, how was your meeting?"

Ross cringed. Lena could be so dense. Didn't she know how to finesse a conversation? He should have jumped in before she had a chance to open her big mouth.

Crystal took a hefty gulp of her martini. "Oh, it was fine...just fine." Secretly she felt uncomfortable around Bianca and women like her. The social movers and shakers who influenced everything from business to politics in their realm. She was afraid that she'd never fit in. She was just a small-time real estate broker in a town full of wealthy power brokers. But she knew that it was important to Robert that they make their way socially, and in business in Palm Beach. She didn't want to let him down. "As a matter of fact, Bianca has some wonderful ideas about improving the equestrian community here."

Ross raised his eyes from pursuing the wine list and focused his gaze on Crystal. What had she just said? "Crystal...I'm sorry?"

"I said that Bianca has come up with a great idea to benefit the horses here."

"You've piqued my curiosity. What sort of idea?"

"Well, I don't think it's a secret any longer, or it won't be since she's been able to raise most of the funds to support a state-of-the-art equine wellness center."

Robert chimed in. What would that entail, exactly?"

"I don't have all the details yet, but it would provide a world class surgery center, a rehab facility, plus everything necessary for day-to-day veterinary care. There's also a plan for a vet school...eventually."

Ross's palms were getting sweaty. "Really? And where would this super center be located?"

"Right on that tract of land near the showgrounds and the polo club."

Ross could feel the blood draining from his face. No one said anything for a moment, then Lena piped up. "That sounds just fantastic! I would love to be involved with that!"

Ross shot dagger eyes at her. What had she said that was wrong now? She knew that he wanted her to get involved with the social scene here. He wanted her to become friendlier with Crystal Montrose. Why was he giving her dirty looks?

Ross realized that Crystal and Robert were staring at him. He quickly adjusted his countenance with a smile. "You know darling, you have so many projects right now as it is. Do you think adding another is a good idea?"

"I don't know Ross. I'll have to think about it."

Lena looked confused. She didn't have any *projects* going on, except trying to keep Ross happy, which wasn't easy nowadays. The waiter arrived with the menus.

Saved by the bell, thought Crystal.

Sloane grabbed me by the elbow and ushered me out to the parking lot before any of Bianca's flying cocktails drenched my face. "God Ivy, what the hell is going on?"

"That woman is crazy!"

"We *know* that. The question is what were you *doing* with Vincente at Il Bellagio?"

"He didn't know that Bianca was going to be there. It was pure coincidence that he asked me to meet him at the same restaurant!"

Sloane stopped. "Are you sure about that, Ivy?"

"What do you mean? Vincente told me that he didn't know where Bianca was this evening. You don't think he'd choose this restaurant deliberately...knowing she would be there? Do you think he has a death wish?"

Sloane looked away. "I don't know. It just seems suspicious if you ask me."

"Why would he do such a thing?"

"Well, I don't think that the Villa marriage is one made in heaven. Maybe he's trying to provoke her. He might be looking for a way out, forcing her to pull the divorce trigger."

"That's not the only trigger she might pull. I hope that Vincente wouldn't use me in that way. As a matter of fact, I *know* he wouldn't. Not after what he told me about how things went down in London all those years ago."

"What are you talking about, Ivy?"

I described the series of events that led to my release from police custody.

"Wow! You've got to be kidding me. Why would he tell you that after all this time?"

"Because of Lloyd."

"Lloyd? What does he have to do with it?"

I realized that I'd never had a chance to fill Sloane in on my encounter with Lloyd at the pool. When I told her about his concerns that Scotland Yard might be reopening the case, she just stood there staring at me. It was a lot to digest.

A red Miata pulled into the parking lot and slipped into a space right next to our Range Rover. I glanced over to see Enrico Alvero hop out of the driver's side.

"Sloane...look who's here!"
She turned around, and their eyes met. "Oh no. I can't believe he came over here" she said.
"How did he know you'd be here?"
"I accidently told him. Damn."
"Hola ladies," Enrico shouted, waving his arm to get our attention.
"I don't want to talk to him now," Sloane whispered.

It was too late. Enrico bounded toward us flashing his Colgate smile. There was no denying that Enrico was a handsome man, as many polo players are. I'd often wondered why? It appears the "good looks gods" favored polo players over other athletes...percentage wise, that is.

"Hi Enrico. I'm surprised to see you here" Sloane said.
I detected a hard edge in her voice.
"I thought I would take a chance, since you told me that you were coming to this place."
"What can I do for you?"
"It's not what you can do for me, it is what I can do for you, dear lady."
"And what might that be?"

"Surely you have not forgotten our discussion the other evening? I am as good as my word, Sloane Parker."

Sloane looked over at me, obviously confused.

"I told you that I would find the perfect ponies for our string...and I have." Enrico grinned from ear to ear.

"What do you mean? We've only started to discuss assembling a team." I thought that you were developing a plan. It's too early in the process to be acquiring ponies."

"But Sloane…"

"And really Enrico, shouldn't you be looking to replace Vincent Villa's string right now? After all, you are still working for him, are you not?"

"Well, yes." Enrico shifted his weight from one foot to the other, his eyes downcast. "But this kind of opportunity doesn't occur every day. It could take months to source superior mounts such as these."

Sloane took a deep breath and exhaled with a heavy sigh. "Enrico, this is neither the time nor the place for this discussion. I will be in touch when I'm ready...*if* I'm ready to move forward."

Enrico met her gaze. There was something steely simmering in his deep chocolate eyes. Something that Sloane couldn't quite read.

"Of course, Ms. Parker," Enrico said in a monotone. He turned on his heel and headed back to the Miata.

"Well, what do you think of that?"

"It sounds to me like he's trying to hustle you into putting this 'plan' into action before there's even a real plan" I said.

"That's what I'm thinking too! I wonder if Vincente knows what he's up to?"

"The disloyalty is really kind of disgusting, isn't it?"

"Yes, and if he's doing it to Vincente, then you bet he'd do it to me in a heartbeat."

CHAPTER THIRTEEN

My phone's ringtone rang out Blondie's *Call Me* just as Sloane and I entered our suite back at The Breakers. It was John. "Hi" I said tentatively, trying not to reveal the guilt in my voice. I don't know why I hesitated to tell John that I'd met with Vincente? Well, to be honest with myself, I did.

"So, how are you?" he asked.

"Great! The girls are doing well schooling, the weather is beautiful, and the hotel is pure luxury."

"Ah...that's good Ivy. Haven't heard much from you lately."

"You know how it is getting ready for a horse show." He didn't know, since he was never into horses.

"I wanted to let you know that I did hear back from my contact at Scotland Yard."

"You did? What did he say?"

"It's not he, it's a *she.* Detective Fiona Wescott."

"Oh...I hadn't realized...?"

"Fiona gave me some pretty interesting news."

"Really?"

"Yes. It turns out that Scotland Yard is reopening your mother's case."

I was stunned. Lloyd said that they *might* be reopening the case. He must have known that they did exactly that, or why would he come all the way over here to disrupt our lives.

"They have a new Cold Case Division. Fiona is heading it up, as a matter of fact. She said that they'd brought Lloyd in for an interview two weeks ago. She was not happy to hear that he'd left the country."

"I'll bet! Just this afternoon, he came over to the hotel to see me, and he didn't say anything about an interview. He said that Scotland Yard called to ask a few questions. What do you think his end game is, John?"

"I think he's going to try and pin it on you again."

It was as though I'd been plunged into Arctic waters. I'd dare not say a word.

"Ivy? Are you still there?"

"Yes, yes I'm still here. Sorry."

"The problem is that the suicide note is missing."

"Missing?"

"Yes. Fiona went through the old boxes containing all the documents and case files, but no suicide note was found. Apparently, it disappeared, and without that note there's no way to tell if it was original or forged.

I felt myself starting to tremble.

"Oh, and Ivy, there's something else."

"What? "I could tell from his tone that this wasn't going to be good news.

"Fiona read some of the testimony from the investigation to me. It was testimony given by Vincente Villa...your fiancé at the time. I thought you told me that you didn't know Villa."

"Oh John! I'm so sorry. It was stupid of me. I panicked. I never told you about Vincente because it was part of my past that I'd buried forever. I couldn't bear the thought of reliving it. Jaycee and Jayson know nothing about any of this, and I hope to God that they never do. When I came down to Florida and learned that Vincente was here when his horses mysteriously died, I planned on steering clear of him."

"But that's not what happened, is it Ivy?"

Jaycee felt her cell phone vibrate in the back pocket of her jeans. She put her muck fork aside and pulled the phone seeing the little text balloon on the screen. She swiped it open and saw a strange number. She frowned; her brows narrowed. Who was this? The area code was unfamiliar. She read the message that said "Jaycee, you look very beautiful today." She poked her head out of the stall, looking left and right down the aisle. There was no one there. Trina had gone in search of cold drinks to quench their thirst in the dusty barn. Her mom and Aunt Sloane were perusing the vendor booths in search of the Katherine Page sandals they were dying to try. Jaycee found herself chillingly alone even as the heat of the day was rising. She listened carefully to see if she could hear anyone moving about. The barn was eerily silent, except for the usual sounds of the horses snorting and pawing in their stalls. Although she couldn't hear or see anyone else, she felt a presence. Who texted her this anonymous message...and why? Was he (or she) trying to scare her? Did she have a secret admirer? She popped back into Pirate's stall, put the phone back in her pocket, and picked up the muck fork. She had to finish her work, and the muck fork would make a good weapon if she needed one.

"Hey!" The voice breaking the silence startled Jaycee practically out of her skin. She whirled around to see Trina's outstretched hand offering a bottle of iced tea.

"Trina, you scared me!"

"Why so jumpy?"

Jaycee pulled out her phone and showed Trina the text message and the strange number.

"Do you have any idea who sent that?" asked Trina.

"No. I don't recognize the number. I don't even know what area code it's from."

Trina grabbed the phone. "Let's Google it." She brought up the search engine and punched in the number 817.

"I don't know anyone from Texas. Do you?"

Trina thought for a moment. "No. Nobody."

"Whoever it is knows my name" Jaycee said under her breath.

The two girls looked at each other, not knowing what to do.

"Maybe I better tell my mom, but I'm afraid it'll just worry her. You know how she is."

"Yeah. It's probably just a joke anyway. One of the grooms fooling around, or something" Trina said. She picked up a fork and helped Jaycee finish mucking out the stall.

The atmosphere at Casa Verde had been thick with venom since the incident earlier at *Il* Bellagio. Vincente moved into the guest room, and Bianca all but sequestered herself in the master suite. Vincente turned crimson with humiliation every time he replayed the scene with Bianca tossing that drink in his face. Bianca was rigid with rage over finding Vincente with Ivy Snow. She had to step up her plan to send Ivy packing back to Pennsylvania.

Bianca took a cool shower to help calm her nerves and popped a Valium. Her landline rang, and she picked up the receiver of her Princess phone. "Hello darling." Bianca knew it was Enrico, even though the vintage phone had no caller ID. He was the only one that had her number.

"Hello my love. I heard what happened at Il Bellagio."

Bianca briefly considered asking how Enrico found out, but she quashed that question. Word travels fast in Palm Beach. How he found out didn't really matter. There were more important questions at hand. "Vincente deserved it! All over *that woman...*and in public!" She sensed her rage rising to the surface again. Enrico felt the bad vibes traveling down the phone line. He had to get control of the situation.

"Don't worry about Vincente. You will have your revenge soon" he said.

Bianca was silent. This was unexpected. Just how could Enrico manifest her revenge? "What do you mean darling? "she asked.

"It will be perfect. Vincente prides himself in being the king of polo here. His big plans are to make his polo enterprise dominant in the United States as well as Europe and Argentina. I will foil those plans."

Bianca was stunned. She didn't think that Enrico had it in him to operate on such a grand scale.

"And how do you propose to do that, my darling?"

"The wheels have already been set in motion. The death of his current string has left him "horseless" so to speak."

"He is counting on me to build up his stable to its former glory...and beyond, but I have another plan."
"And what is that?"
"Sloane Parker."
"Sloane Parker? What do you mean?"
"No, no, it's not what you think. I have no interest in Ms. Parker, except for what her money can buy."
"I don't follow..."
"I told you, my beautiful Bianca, Sloane wants to build a world class polo operation at her estate in Pennsylvania. I've already been sourcing a marvelous string for her. It's a string that Vincente would die for, but he doesn't have my connections, or the time to pull it all together for that matter. It's one of the reasons that he hired me in the first place."
"Why do you need this Parker woman? I could finance your operation."
Enrico considered this statement. Bianca was never willing to finance him until Sloane Parker came into the picture. No wonder he felt that he could never really trust her. "No darling. Ms. Parker is the cover we need to succeed in this plan. I'll be building up the string in

Pennsylvania while still working for Vincente. He'll never know what hit him."

Bianca thought about it. She liked that element of surprise. The look on his face when he thinks that the world's best horses will be his, and then discovering that they belong to Sloane Parker. Another bonus is that her name, and her money, would be kept out of it altogether. Vincente never needed to know that she was privy to Enrico's plan. "How can I trust you? I know that you are attracted to this woman."

Ha, thought Enrico...how can *she* trust *me?* "No, no my love. It's just that I must *charm* her into helping me."

"Okay, but if I find out..."

"No worries, my love. I'm doing this all for us!"

Bianca wondered briefly if Enrico had anything to do with the death of Vincent's horses...but no, surely not! She hung up the receiver of her Princess phone.

Vincente hung up the extension that he'd recently installed in the guest room.

CHAPTER FOURTEEN

Ross Spencer was having a meltdown. At least that's what it looked like. "Ross honey, what's the matter?" Lena asked.

They'd just returned from the dinner with Robert and Crystal, and he was fit to be tied.

"What's the matter? What's the matter? Can't you see? I'm no closer to getting Robert Montrose into this deal than I was two weeks ago. All this bullshit with Crystal and her friends, Ivy Snow and Sloane Parker. They are fouling it up with Bianca Villa and her hairbrained scheme to create an "Equine Wellness Center" on the land that I need to build Palais Palm Beach. Equine Wellness Center, my ass!"

"Ross, I had no idea what you were talking about with this palace thing. What is it anyway?"

Ross gave Lena a brief description of his vision. A vision that was fast slipping away from him.

"Oh, I see. Why didn't you tell me about this before?" Lena asked.

"I didn't think you'd be interested. What he really thought was that she probably couldn't grasp such a grand concept in that pea brain of hers.

"Well, I don't get it silly. Why did you say that I was too busy to be on their committee? I could go to all the meetings and find out what they're up to, then I'll come back and tell you! You can mess up all their plans," Lena said with delight.

Ross was silent. His eyes shifted back and forth in his head. What a splendid idea. He was impressed with the little bimbo. He crossed the room and took Lena in his arms. He kissed her hungrily on the mouth while fumbling for the zipper of her black silk Zac Posen sheath.

I pulled out one of the lounge chairs neatly stacked on the beach at The Breakers. It was a beautiful night in South Florida. I could almost see myself making a home here one day. Not that I'd leave Little Paddocks permanently, especially since Sloane just bought Hearts Desire next door. It would, however, be a wonderful place to spend the winters, especially with Jaycee coming along so well with her riding. I could feel the tears well up in my eyes. What was I thinking? Ever since I came down here, I've been confused. Finding Lloyd here...what a nightmare that is. Then, reuniting with Vincente, and now look what I've done to John. I lied, and for no good reason...I think? I know I hurt him. Hurt our relationship and probably our chances for ever getting together for good. What's wrong with me? Maybe it's the sun. After living in England and Pennsylvania, the exposure to sun day after day must be having an effect on my mental faculties. I smiled despite myself.

I gazed up at the stars above, so beautiful, so ancient. I love thinking about the idea that all of our ancestors looked at the same stars. People all over the world look at the very same stars!

"Penny for your thoughts?" whispered Crystal.

I turned around to see Crystal and Sloane standing behind me. "How did you know I was here?"

"We *are* your best friends. Give us some credit," said Sloane.

I smiled. If ever I needed friends, it was now.

"So, what's going on?" Crystal asked.

I told them about my phone conversation with John. They just looked at each other. I was sure they were doing mental eye rolls.

"Ivy, you've got some serious thinking to do. You were getting along so well with John, then everything went haywire when Vincente entered the picture again after all these years. I understand how you must feel, but it's all in the past...and he's married now," said Sloane.

"I know. It's more than Vincente. Lloyd showing up again. I hate the idea that he's back in my life, and I'll do anything to keep him away from Jaycee and Jayson. At least Jayson is back home. I'm not as worried about him. But Jaycee is right here, and I don't want Lloyd anywhere near her. I found out from John that Scotland Yard did reopen my mother's case. I have a feeling that Lloyd is here to put me back in the 'hot seat' again."

Sloane sighed. "I think you might be right. I haven't seen any interviews or reports on the show that he is supposedly doing for the BBC. It wouldn't surprise me if it's all just a lie to cover why he's really here."

I turned my head to stare back at the cresting waves in the moonlight. "And what about

Bianca? Boy, does she have it in for me now...after catching me with Vincente tonight."

They all knew that was a cause for concern. Bianca Villa had a reputation for being quite vicious when she wanted to be. At least being on her Equine Wellness Center committee would give Crystal and Sloane an opportunity to keep an eye on her.

"Well, you guys, what should I do?"

Crystal held out her hand and pulled me out of my lounge chair. "Let's sleep on it!"

That sounded like a good idea. At the mention of the word *sleep* I realized how exhausted I really was. Sloane and I walked Crystal to her car, and then headed back to the suite. I found Jaycee and Trina watching Netflix. "Why aren't you girls in bed yet?"

Jaycee grinned sheepishly. "We're just finishing *How to Lose a Guy in Ten Days*."

"Oh...that is a cute movie. It better be over soon though. You have an early day tomorrow." I went to my room and changed into my nightgown. The pink silk slipped easily over my body and felt luxurious. As I rubbed anti-wrinkle cream into my face, I caught Jaycee's reflection behind me in the bathroom mirror. "What is it honey?"

"Mom, I've been debating all afternoon whether I should tell you about something that happened this morning at the barn. I don't want you to worry."

"Of course, you should tcll mc. What is it?"

"I got a text from a number I didn't recognize. It said *Jaycee, you look very beautiful today.* I got a really weird feeling when I read it."

I knew better than to dismiss Jaycees's *weird feelings.* "Let me see." I looked at the message on her phone. It creeped me out too.

"Mom, I looked all around, inside and outside the barn, but there was no one there. I figured it must be one of the grooms just fooling around, but I'm kind of spooked about the *beautiful* comment, and using my real name. I feel like that's something that a stalker would do."

"I don't like the sound of it either. What area code is it from?"

"Texas. I don't know anyone in Texas, do you?"

"No. Let's not get too concerned just yet. Maybe it's an isolated incident."

"Okay, Mom."

"Jaycee, if you get another text like that, let me know *right away!*"

"I will. Maybe John could find out what's going on" Jaycee said.

"Yes, maybe. Good night honey. Six AM wake up tomorrow." Yes, maybe John could find out...if he ever speaks to me again.

I took two sleeping pills and crawled between the smooth cotton sheets. I said a prayer for a peaceful night for all of us. It was doubtful for me now that I was worried that Jaycee might have a stalker. And John...John isn't...Lord, what have I done?

CHAPTER FIFTEEN

Lloyd Snow looked down at his phone and saw that he had voicemail. Someone must have called while he was in the shower. The number was international...London calling. He pressed the icon to hear the lilting accent of Detective Fiona Wescott.

"*Mr. Snow, I recently learned that you went to the United States. You hadn't mentioned that you were leaving the country. I have some additional questions that I would like to ask you since the interview. Please call me at your earliest convenience.*"

What did that bloody bitch want now? Lloyd felt a flush of heat rising from his neck to his cheeks, even though he had the air conditioning in his hotel room cranked up to the highest level possible. He walked over and sat on the edge of his bed. Hmm, he had to think this through. He had to come up with every possible question she might have, and how he would answer. He was sure she'd want to know why he came to the US. He'd have to make that answer a good one since she knew that there was no love lost between him and Ivy, and that he'd never met his grandchildren. The BBC story wouldn't stick...too easy to check up on that.

He hoped that she didn't know that Vincente Villa was in the States. She'd put two and two together for his motive there. Think...maybe it was best to put that on the back burner for now. He could use the time difference as an excuse for not getting back to her right away. What *was* it that she wanted to ask him that she hadn't already? She said something about questions she had after his interview. Perhaps she gathered more information. Who else would she be talking to? Villa? Ivy? That's the only possibility, unless some unknown person has come forward with information he knew nothing about.

He walked over to his closet and selected a periwinkle polo shirt and ivory chinos. A dapper Panama hat completed his ensemble. He looked quite handsome for a mature gentleman. Handsome enough to take Bianca Villa to lunch.

John heard the phone ringing on his desk as he unlocked the door to his office. He reached it just in time to hear Fiona's voice on the other end of the line.

"Hello John. Glad I caught you."

"Hello Fiona. How are you?"

"I'm doing well. And you?"

"Ah, yeah, fine...sure."

Fiona caught the hesitant tone in John's voice. She knew that tone. It took her back twenty years. Twenty years ago, when she was a young rookie cop attending a seminar in which a handsome detective from the NYPD came over to Scotland Yard to educate the newest members of the force on American police procedures. She'd been attracted to him with a force so great that she hardly heard a word he said in the lecture. She was dumbstruck when he posed a question to her on the subject at hand. She felt like a fool as she stuttered and stammered to concoct a plausible answer to a question she hadn't heard. There were snickers among the other rookies, and Fiona ran from the room, humiliated.

That auspicious beginning was the prelude to the greatest romance of her life. John had been so kind. He caught up with her after the lecture and tried gallantly to sooth her bruised ego by taking the blame for the fumbled Q&A. He insisted that he hadn't asked the question properly, and that anyone would be confused as to how to answer. He applauded her for being brave enough to rise to the challenge of responding. As for the others? He doubted that they would even make an attempt. After her tears dried, John invited her to join him for a drink. He asked her to take him to an "authentic" English pub (as if there were any other kind) and initiate him in the fine art of ordering a pint.

As they waited for their *Theakston's Old Peculier,* John inquired about the top cases at Scotland Yard. Fiona filled him in on their current nemesis...a cat burglar that was heisting baubles and bangles from every well to do matron in Mayfair. It appears the slippery bugger had an innate talent for knowing when households would be empty, and where the combinations to the safes might be hidden. It was all beginning to look just a little too slick. The fact that many of the victims were members of the same social set would make it convenient for someone operating on the inside. But so far Scotland Yard was stymied.

John thought about it as the barkeep set their pints before them. He took a sip of the bitter liquid and licked the foam from his lips. "Fiona, how long have these robberies been taking place?"

"Well, they started about a year ago, but they're intermittent. There would be a rash, and then a somewhat long period of time when no robberies occurred. Then suddenly, *bam,* another batch."

"Hmm, that's odd."

"We think so too. When the robberies stopped, we reasoned that the thief had moved on to greener pastures. We had a watch out in other affluent communities to see if there was an uptick of robberies anywhere else with a similar M.O., but nothing surfaced. Then suddenly our phones were ringing off the hook with reports of stolen jewelry in Mayfair again."

"Do you have any clue as to where he might be fencing the stuff? I mean maybe he lives the high life until the money runs out and then strikes again."

"We thought of that, but nothing has shown up in the market."

"I assume that the victims are well insured?"

"Of course. These are all high-profile people we're talking about. They are savvy enough to be insured to the max, with all their valuable possessions."

John considered. "Fiona, I like your theory about an inside job. I'd follow up with that if I were you. Find out who the victims have in common, and when they might be away on holiday, or at their country houses."

"Yes, I see."

"The common denominator, that's what to look for. And in this case, it might be one of those *right under your nose* kind of things."

Fiona smiled.

"So, anything else?" John asked. "We Americans love a good grizzly murder just as much as you Brits."

"Well, there is a rather sordid murder that we're investigating right now, and it happens to be in Mayfair as well."

"Oh?"

"Yes, and as a matter of fact the victim is an American."

"Really? What's that about?"

"It involves the murder of a beautiful and successful interior designer from New York."

"What happened?"

"The lady was found on the floor of her basement kitchen dead from a hefty dose of Belladonna."

"Ah, poison! How very Agatha Christie! And the suspects?"

"We're primarily interested in the daughter, although the husband is definitely in the running."

"And what about the motives?"

"According to her diary, the lady was secretly in love with her daughter's fiancé."

"Whew" John let out a low whistle.

"Both the daughter and the husband swear that they had no idea. And there is an insurance policy involved. The husband took it out on the wife. A million pounds, and he's the sole beneficiary."

"Strong motive."

"Right. But we're holding the daughter" Fiona said.

"Why?"

"Turns out she did know about the "love triangle." According to the charwoman, they had a real *row* over it earlier that morning."

"Hum...any other evidence?

"We're checking into that now. There's a hole in her alibi. Apparently, she spent most of the day shopping with her fiancé, and then lunch at the Ritz. That's been verified. But they parted company late that afternoon, and she can't prove where she was at the time of death. And she's the one that *discovered* the body."

"What about the husband?"

"He has an alibi, of sorts. He works for the BBC as a reporter. His assignment that day was the Tattersalls Sales at Newmarket. There are witnesses that vouch they'd seen him there."

"Pretty good alibi," said John.

"Yes, but there's more. A suicide note has turned up. But there seems to be a question as to the authenticity of the note. The daughter believes it's genuine, the husband says it's forged, and he's pointing his finger directly at the daughter."

"I'm not sure I follow that," said John.

Fiona took a sip from her pint. "You see, if the note is genuine, then that means that the lady did commit suicide, therefore there would be no payout on the policy. If the note was forged, then it's murder, and the husband cashes in. We're working on that."

"So, where does it stand now?"

"It's not looking good for the daughter. She's the one that found her mother, and the charwoman swears that she heard them arguing earlier that morning. The daughter says that it had nothing to do with her fiancé, and it wasn't even an argument. She says that the charwoman is a busybody, and a troublemaker."

"Any other suspects?" John asked.

"None has turned up so far." Fiona said.

"The husband does have an alibi."

"It has its flaws. He could have done his report earlier and gone back to London later that day to commit the murder. It's only about an hour and a half traveling time. He could have gone back for more footage, and had it edited to confuse the timeframe. It's a 'highlights' piece."

"Is there any way to prove or disprove that?"

"We have a special team working on it right now."

"It's a very interesting case, Fiona. Are you directly involved?"

"Only on the sidelines...getting the leading investigators their tea!"

They both laughed. As they finished their pints, John looked longingly at the beautiful young rookie. He asked her for her number.

CHAPTER SIXTEEN

Dr. Julia Forrest lay in her bed staring at the ceiling. She hadn't slept properly since she'd discovered Sharon's taxi receipts in the cookie jar. What was her sister doing at the polo grounds? Why didn't she mention that she'd been going there? Whatever was going on, Julia was sure that it would come to no good.

Sharon was secretive about a lot of things lately. Hiding things and pretending not to know where they were. Julia wondered if Sharon was deliberately trying to "Gaslight" her. And Sharon's health was of deep concern. She ate too much junk food. Julia couldn't imagine where she was getting it, or how she was smuggling it into the trailer. But the candy wrappers and empty potato chip bags under Sharon's bed don't lie. Her unhealthy food choices, along with the heavy medication that she's on aren't doing her any favors.

She knew that something had to be done about Sharon, but what? The lab report came back today with the test results for Vincent's horses. Toxic poisoning. Vincente was beside himself with anger and grief. Enrico was mortified that such a thing could happen on his watch. The source of the toxins and how they got into the horse's systems was unknown. The only clue they had was that it was a natural substance, not a synthetic. Next steps involved having everything at the Villa Stables tested. Food, supplements, topical treatments, water, bedding etc. Julia agreed to assist with gathering and transporting the samples to the lab.

Enrico's cell phone rang. It was his boss. He took a deep breath. "Good evening, Vincente."

"Not for me it isn't. Since that report came in, I can think of nothing else."

"I know. I don't understand how this could have happened."

There was an uncomfortable silence on the other end. Finally, Vincente spoke. "I put the care of my horses in your hands when I went to Europe. This happened under your watch. I expect you to explain how this came about."

The heat began to rise in Enrico's tawney cheeks. Was Vincente suggesting that he'd been careless, or that he'd purposely done something to the horses? "I will be meeting with Dr. Forrest at the stable tomorrow morning to gather samples of everything that the horses were exposed to. Everything will be tested."

"I suppose that's all we can do for now. Let me know as soon as you hear something."

"Of course, Vincente."

"Enrico, there is something else."

"What is it?" Enrico said, catching his breath.

"I received a call last evening from Argentina."

The heat in Enrico's cheeks turned ice cold. "Who called? What did they want?"

"Apparently you have been eyeing new polo ponies that are for sale."

Enrico's mouth was arid. "Well, yes. I assumed that you would want to start building up your string again as soon as possible. I took the initiative to start searching."

"Funny, it seems as though *my* name has not been mentioned."

"I assure you, Vincente, I was only looking out for your best interests. If I mention your name, the prices go up at least twenty-five percent!"

Vincente felt the bile rise in his throat. "Very well, but may I suggest that you use caution in your relationship with Sloane Parker. She is a very lovely woman, but I heard that she is considering putting together a string of her own in Pennsylvania. She may very well be a competitor of Villa Stables in the future."

"Vincente...I don't know what you are talking about."

"Yes. I suppose that you had more provocative topics of conversation to explore during your champagne cocktail hour at HMF the other day. Have a pleasant evening, Enrico."

Enrico hung up the phone. How did Villa know anything about his meeting with Sloane Parker at HMF? It must have been Ivy Snow, that nosey bitch!

As she crept across the green shag carpeting toward the kitchen, Sharon saw a sliver of light under Julia's bedroom door. She must still be awake...or she fell asleep with the light on again. It seems that keeping track of her sister was becoming a full-time job. She felt trapped in the trailer. Julia's ever watchful eye followed her every move. What business was it of hers if she enjoyed a bit of chocolate now and again?

Just because Julia was a health food nut didn't mean that everybody else had to be.

She knew what Julia thought of her...lazy, fat, incompetent, crazy. Well, that was just too bad. They were sisters. Julia had an obligation to take care of her, especially after what she'd been through. Oh sure, Julia was the big-time veterinarian, acting so smug. Doctor this, and Doctor that! Never mind that it practically broke their parents financially to put her through vet school. Did she ever offer to pay them back one single cent? Hell no! She just took off for Kentucky to seek her fortune in the Bluegrass. It's a damn lucky thing that their parents were dead now, and they couldn't see what a greedy selfish narcissist that Julia had become. Very strange about that brake line going bad so soon after they had their Chevy Impala inspected. What was it...a month? Something like that. Right after Julia's last visit home, and right before she stopped at our house in Ohio to check up on Steve, Carley and me before making her way back to Kentucky.

Sharon opened the refrigerator door hoping that Julia was asleep and wouldn't hear her. There would be hell to pay if she was caught. Humph, of course there's nothing good in here.

Yogurt, *yuk.* Whole wheat this, low fat that. Talk about taking the pleasure out of something so simple as a midnight snack. She checked the freezer. No ice cream either; figures! The pantry yielded some Saltines and a jar of peanut butter. It would have to do. She made herself a plate of peanut butter crackers, then carefully put the foods back on the shelf exactly where they had been. She wiped off the spreading knife and placed it back in the drawer. She made her way back to her room, silently opening and closing the door, just in time to miss seeing the light in Julia's room fade to darkness.

CHAPTER SEVENTEEN

Lloyd Snow considered his lunch with Bianca Villa to be a great success. He fluffed the down pillows on his king-sized bed at the Brazilian and stretched his body out smiling like the Cheshire Cat. His mind mellowed out into a replay of their meeting.

She'd already been seated at a corner table at Eau Palm Beach. The resort was a good meeting place because it catered mostly to the tourists. It was unlikely that anyone they knew would spot them there together. She was dressed impeccably, as usual, in a lemony voile sundress that complimented her copper skin and raven waves. Her signature "statement" jewelry didn't disappoint. A heavy Etruscan gold suite of earrings, necklace and bracelet. Her left hand sported only her simple gold wedding band...she knew when enough was enough. She evoked the image of a Sun Goddess. She was drinking a glass of Chardonnay. The waiter approached, and Lloyd ordered a Sapphire Gin Rickey to join her in a pre-luncheon cocktail.

"You look lovely, my dear."

"And you...so dapper. As only the English can" she smiled, her teeth dazzling white.

They spoke of the weather, and the increased traffic on the island as they scanned the menu, each opting for the lobster salad. When the waiter placed their chilled plates before them, Lloyd got down to brass tacks.

"You may be wondering why I asked you to meet with me, Bianca."

"Yes, the thought crossed my mind."

"Personally, I loathe when the past is regurgitated, but unfortunately Scotland Yard has seen fit to reopen the Lacy Snow case."

Bianca froze mid-forkful. "What did you say?" Her words came out in a whisper as she lifted her eyes to meet his.

"I said that Scotland Yard has reopened the investigation into the death of my wife."

It took only a split second for Bianca to regain her composure, but he knew he'd struck a nerve.

"They have a new Head of Cold Cases…Inspector Fiona Wescott."

"And why do you think that would be of any interest to me? It's ancient history."

"Not any longer. I'm sure that you'll recall that Vincent was engaged to our daughter, Ivy, when Lacy died.

"Well, yes, but I haven't thought about that for years. Once Ivy was released from police custody, he broke their engagement. He was honorable enough to stand by her in her hour of need, but in the end, he realized that the two of us would make a better match."

"And you were right there to assure that he saw the light?"

"I don't know what you're getting at Lloyd?"

"Bianca, isn't it true that you were engaged to marry Vincente before he met Ivy?"

"Yes, but I broke it off that time because he was moving to London for his career, and I wished to remain in my home, Argentina. I thought he would reconsider, but he didn't...not until he realized that he did not belong in England, or with Ivy. I'm not sure what any of this has to do with me now?"

"Perhaps nothing," Lloyd flashed a smile. "But there is the matter of a key piece of evidence missing from the police files."

"What evidence?"

"The police found a suicide note among Lacy's things. There was debate as to its authenticity."

Bianca took another sip of her Chardonnay. "I don't believe I recall…"

“It was a key piece of evidence, Bianca. It’s what forced the police to release Ivy. Surely, if you think back, you’ll remember.”

Bianca was silent.

“Of course, I believe that the note was a sham, and eventually the insurance company had to consider it as such. They paid me as the beneficiary.”

“I see, and what about Ivy?” asked Bianca.

She maintains that the note is real. I suppose in a way, you can’t blame the poor girl. It’s what got her off.”

“I still don’t see what any of this has to do with me. Bianca said.

“I have a theory. I suspect that your husband knows the origin and the whereabouts of that note. That he’s been concealing it from the police all these years. My concern is that he may consider it necessary to use that piece of evidence in a nefarious way to manipulate the investigation.”

“That’s rather far-fetched if you ask me!” she said.

“Think about it Bianca. As custodian of that note, Vincente wields great power. Whether or not he knows of its authenticity, it's really up to him to produce it or not, thus controlling the outcome of the investigation. I believe the note not to be in Lacy's own hand, of course. But what if, by some slim measure, I'm wrong? Then it will be up to the authorities to look for proof. With the advances in forensic testing in the past twenty years, DNA testing, and the like, they have a much better chance of putting the question to rest once and for all. Who knows what the fallout could be from that?"

Bianca stared at her lobster salad, unable to take another bite. What if Vincente does have the note? Depending on how the investigation proceeds, would he come forth with it again? She knew that Vincente would throw her under the bus if it came down to a choice between her and Ivy. She felt as though a noose was tightening around her neck. She had to think this through carefully.

"Lloyd, what is it, exactly, that you are asking of me?"

"I want you to learn the whereabouts of that note. If it were to be destroyed, then I doubt that Scotland Yard's investigation will yield anything new. It's best to let sleeping dogs lie at this point!"

"I agree," said Bianca. She walked away from the table leaving a barely touched salad, and a very satisfied Lloyd Snow. She hopped into her Maserati and headed back to Casa Verde. She could feel the wine churning in her empty stomach...she thought she might be sick. She despised the thought of teaming up with Lloyd Snow in this horrible nightmare, but she didn't know what choice she had. If he was right, Vincente held a sword over them both. She'd always preferred to believe that Ivy killed her mother. But what if she was wrong? What if Lloyd did it and tried to frame Ivy. Was he still trying to frame Ivy now? What if Lacy's death really had been a suicide, and she hadn't left a note? No matter what the circumstances of Lacy's death were, she was certain of one thing. That note had to be found...and destroyed...*if* it still existed!

She entered the house through the garage door. The click clack of her Manolo's echoed across the tiled floor of their massive kitchen. She called for Vincente, but there was no answer. They hadn't spoken since the flying cocktail incident, but a truce was imperative if she were to find the note. Her maid, Marisol, poked her head around the corner, and informed Bianca that Vincente left the house an hour ago.

He did not tell her where he was going, or when he would return.

Bianca found it hard to believe that Vincente would hide the note here at home...too risky. Perhaps in one of his foreign offices, or a secret safety deposit box? With that, there would have to be a key. She decided to take this opportunity to search the guest room where Vincente had been sleeping since their blow-up. She climbed the stairs and crept down the hallway of the east wing so as not to alert any of the other servants. She didn't trust any of their servants, except Marisol, whom she'd personally hired and brought to Palm Beach from Argentina. The others were hired locally, and she'd always felt that their allegiance was to Vincente, since he was the one that signed their checks. If only they knew where the *real* money came from.

She approached Vincent's room and quickly opened the door, silently stepping inside. The door closed with a gentle click. Good hardware always paid off. Her black eyes swept around the room, taking in the lustrous hunter and crimson color scheme she chose. It was very different from the rest of the house. Very un-tropical, but suitable for a horseman. She'd cared in those days. It was no wonder that

Vincente chose to retreat here to lick his wounds. She approached the nearby mahogany Highboy, and began ruffling through the drawers, looking for the note...or a key. She found nothing. The nightstand drawers were a wash as well.

She looked around the room, and her eyes brightened as they rested on the kidney shaped writing desk in front of the windows. Of course! If Vincente were to hide anything, he would hide it in the desk. She walked across the room, and as her gaze scanned the surface, she spotted it. The *extension phone!* She froze as ice ran through her veins. Vincente had been listening in on her conversations with Enrico! How long had he known about their plans? She was devastated. He had the upper hand now!

She went straight to her room, panic setting in as she paced the floor. What would Vincente do to her? To Enrico? She had to warn Enrico that Vincente was wise to them. She could use the landline since Vincente wasn't home. She picked up the receiver and dialed Enrico's number. It went straight to voicemail. She flung the vintage pink Princess phone across the room.

CHAPTER EIGHTEEN

Jaycee finished cleaning Pirate's tack after her morning schooling session with Sloane. Trina was now in the ring putting Dynamo through his paces. She heard the stable door slide open and stuck her head out of the tack room to see Dr. Forrest shutting the gate behind her. Jaycee wondered what the vet was doing here. Hopefully none of the horses were sick. She stepped out into the aisleway. "Good morning, Dr. Forrest."

"Good morning," the vet said tentatively.

Jaycee got a strange vibe. "Is everything okay?"

"Yes, fine" she said as she continued briskly down the aisleway.

Jaycee frowned. Her gut told her something didn't seem quite right. She noticed that Dr. Forrest was not wearing her signature white lab coat with the veterinarian's practice logo on the pocket. Instead, she wore a tattered cornflower blue polo shirt, loose fitting khakis and cowboy boots. Her curly gray hair fell loosely around her shoulders, which was also odd. Dr. Forrest always had her hair tied back in a ponytail to keep it out of the way while attending to the horses.

Jaycee watched as the vet bypassed every stall without even looking in and then left the building at the other end. She went back through the tack room and entered the parking lot to wait for her mom. She expected to see Dr. Forrest's truck, but the lot was empty. She circled around to the back of the stable just in time to see Dr. Forrest cross the road, heading to the polo field. Jaycee noticed something fall from the vet's pocket. She shouted out to alert her, but Dr. Forrest just kept walking on. Perhaps she didn't hear her calling? She hurried across the lot as a gust of wind blew the paper into a pile of leaves under a Walnut tree. Jaycee riffled through the leaves, finally capturing the elusive scrap. She stuffed it in her backpack when she saw her mom's Range Rover pull up. She quickly hopped into the passenger seat.

"Hi mom!"

"Hi honey. Did you have a good ride?"

"Yeah, it was great. Pirate set the record for his time, and not one pole down."

"Excellent!"

"Mom, did you happen to see Dr. Forrest any time this morning?"

"No, I didn't. Is anything wrong?"

"I don't know. I saw her come through the stable a little while ago, and she was acting kind of strange."

"How so?"

"Well, she hardly spoke to me at all. She seemed totally preoccupied, and she didn't even stop to look in on any of the horses. She always does *that*."

"Honey, I'm sure she had a lot on her mind with that business over at Villa Stables."

"Has there been any news about what happened there?"

"I understand that the horses died of toxic poisoning, but they don't know how it got into their systems."

Jaycee became very quiet. Every time she thought about those poor horses, she had to fight back the tears. "Mom, I have a bad feeling. Something evil is going on around us."

"Honey, it might have been an accident. Maybe they got into something that they shouldn't have. You know how horses are...an accident waiting to happen."

I sat by the side of the glistening blue pool at The Breakers, thinking about what happened this morning. None of it made any sense. Why was Dr. Forrest at the stable this morning? The horses were all fine, and none of the other riders or grooms were there for routine services or consultations with the vet. It was unlike her to be short with Jaycee. True, she is embroiled in the Villa Stables mess...I'm sure it's nerve wracking for her, but still, Jaycee is convinced that there's more going on than meets the eye, and she's never wrong about these things. Over the years, I've learned to trust her instincts, psychic intuition, or third eye...whatever you want to call it. Ever since she was a little girl, she had this uncanny sense of what would happen before it ever did. Whenever she senses something and tells me, I keep my radar up. Humm, what do we really know about Dr. Julia Forrest? The veterinary practice she belongs to was highly recommended down here, but what do we know about Dr. Forrest herself?

I looked up to see Jaycee headed toward me with a tall glass of iced tea in each hand. She looks so adorable in her pink bikini and floppy straw sunhat. She's growing up so fast. Before I know it, she'll be driving!

"Hi honey! Thanks for the tea. I'm sweltering."

"Why don't you get in the water then?"

"I will before I go back to the room. You know how I hate sitting around in a wet bathing suit."

Jaycee laughed. "Oh mom, you'll never change!" She reached into her beach bag, pulled out a ragged slip of paper, and handed it to me.

"What's this?"

"It's a taxi receipt."

"A taxi receipt? Where did you get it?"

"It's the piece of paper that Dr. Forrest dropped when she left the stable this morning."

I studied the receipt and saw that Dr. Forrest was picked up at Sparkling Sands Drive in Delray Beach at 8:25 AM and was driven to the showgrounds in Wellington. The twenty-nine-mile trip took thirty-seven minutes. Her driver was Roy, and she paid with cash.

"How odd. I wonder if her truck broke down?"

"I don't know Mom, but there's not much that she can do without it...the supplies and all."

"Maybe her business wasn't medical."

"Maybe. I guess even vets have a life besides treating sick animals. Mom, I forgot to tell you, I got a call from Jayson this morning. You're not going to believe this, but he landed the lead in the school play this year!"

"You're kidding! I can't even believe that he tried out."
"Well apparently the new drama teacher at the school is a hottie, and Jayson has a crush."
"What play are they doing?
"That old fashioned musical "Oklahoma."
"Don't tell me he's playing Curley?"
"Yup. Unfortunately, we'll be back by then, and we're going to have to sit through it. Mom, I'm going to take a dip before lunch."
"Okay honey...not too long, I'm getting hungry."

I watched her do a perfect dive into the deep end. Yes, it won't be too long before we head back home. I've yet to figure out what to do about John. He hasn't called since that last terrible conversation we had when he told me that he knew about Vincente. I know how it must look. I denied knowing Vincente, and then John goes and finds out that I was once engaged to him. I suppose that my subconscious dreaded raking up all that ugliness from the past.

If John and I were to make a commitment to each other, of course I would have to let him know that I was once accused of murdering my mother. I know that he would believe that I didn't do it, but when in a budding relationship is it the right time to tell someone something like that? If it weren't for that awful Lloyd, none of this would have happened. I hated to admit it, but in the back of my mind I always thought that Lloyd had something to do with my mother's death. Sure, it looked like he had a solid alibi, but did he really? After all, Newmarket is only just a little over ninety minutes from London...and a million pounds is a lot of money.

I was so frightened at the time, being the number one suspect (thanks to him), grieving over my mother's death, and finally having to accept the fact that Vincente and I were not going to marry. It was just too much for me. All I wanted to do was get as far away from London as I could, only to end up in Philadelphia in the arms of Bart Skelton.

I took a deep breath. Things are different now. I'm not that scared, naive little twenty-two-year-old anymore. I'm a grown woman with a lot of turbulent water under the bridge, and two teenage children to protect. If Lloyd Snow did, in fact, have anything to do with my mother's death, I'm going to find out about it this time...with or without the help of Detective John Garrett

CHAPTER NINETEEN

Enrico Alvero tossed and turned in his king-sized bed at his condo overlooking Lake Worth. He hadn't had a decent night's sleep since the confrontation with Vincente Villa. He knew that Bianca was trying to reach him, but he dared not answer her call. He prayed that Vincente hadn't found out about their affair. Surely, he didn't know! He said nothing during the confrontation, and if he did know he would have threatened murder, or at least fired him on the spot. No, he did not believe that Vincente was aware of the affair...at least not yet.

Enrico knew that he was in a very inopportune, if not dangerous position. He saw his dream of having his own polo team slipping away. If Vincente were to hold him responsible for the death of his horses, he would surely lose his job...if he found out about the affair, he may very well lose his life. Surely Bianca would realize that if Vincente learned of their affair, he would be only too happy to divorce her. Due to his success in business, he no longer relied on her for the money to fund his passion for polo. And it was evident at the Montrose dinner that the heat between Vincente and Ivy Snow, if ignited, would burst into flames. Enrico knew that if Vincente ever dumped her, Bianca would not come running to him. He had neither the bank account nor social standing she required. She would hunt in greener pastures.

He must address this problem one step at a time. He stared at the ceiling until the red glare of the rising sun streamed through the chink in his bedroom curtains. And then, an idea struck him. The first order of business was to prove to Vincente that he had no culpability for the death of his horses. He would thereby secure his position with Villa Stables. He would deal with Bianca and Sloane later. His job, and his standing in the polo community was priority number one.

He jumped into his Miata just as dawn fully broke. The traffic was light heading for the polo grounds. Rush hour, such as it was in Wellington, had not yet gotten under way. He pulled up to Villa Stables to see Dr. Forrest's truck already parked outside. Hmm...the early bird! He made his way through the orderly tack room. Gleaming saddles and bridles hung neatly against the walls, and the mammoth mahogany and glass case sparkled with lustrous sterling trophies. The room smelled of leather polish and the musky scent of Vincente's cologne.

There was no one about, so Enrico made his way to the rolltop desk in the far corner, where the stable management logs were kept. There were logs detailing cleaning schedules, routine vet services, exercise schedules, feed and bedding deliveries and equipment purchases. Employee records and financials were kept in a locked filing cabinet, for which Enrico had no key. He wasn't sure exactly what he was looking for, but it was a place to start. He got out his cell phone and took photos of the pages from each log for every day of the week leading up to the day of the horse's death. That way he would know who was on sight, what they were doing there, and the outcome of their visits. That is, unless there were persons unknown and unseen that were there with evil intent.

He'd just finished returning the last logbook to the shelf when Dr. Forrest came through the door. She was dressed in her signature white lab coat and was carrying a huge cardboard box. Enrico was startled at the sound of the door opening but recovered quickly and took charge of the situation.

"Dr. Forrest, good morning," he said, flashing his one-hundred-watt smile.

Julia was surprised to see Enrico at the stable at that time of the morning.

"Good morning, Enrico. Early start to the day?"

"Yes, much to do."

"There certainly is. Senor Villa asked me to conduct research to determine how his horses died."

"I understand they were poisoned," Enrico said.

"That was the cause of death. How the poison got into their systems...that has yet to be determined." Julia set the heavy box down on a nearby table and fixed her stare into Enrico's coffee-colored eyes.

"And how do you expect to do that?" he asked.

"To start with I'm collecting samples of all agents that the horses may have been in contact with. Everything will be tested at the lab for toxicity."

"Dr. Forrest, do you have any idea as to how the poison was administered?"

"No. There are too many variables at this point. It will be a process of elimination. However, I don't think it was an accident."

Enrico shifted his eyes from hers. "Why do you say that doctor?"

Julia continued to stare at him with laser intensity. “In my opinion, someone with a great deal of knowledge about horses and equine anatomy had a hand in this. Someone who stood to gain monetarily...or in some *other* way. A lot depends on the outcome. The insurance investigation, and if it is determined that there’s been foul play, a police investigation as well.”

Enrico was desperate to shift attention away from himself, if that was what Julia Forrest was getting at.

“Surly doctor, you are not suggesting that Senor Villa had anything to do with it?”

“No. Not Vincente Villa” she said.

Julia headed for the exit, heavy box in tow. Enrico rushed ahead to ingratiate himself by opening the door. Was it his imagination, or was Dr. Forrest implying that *he* killed Villa’s horses? Had Vincente Villa said something to her? Of course, he must have! They were working together to pin the blame on him...but they won’t get away with it!

CHAPTER TWENTY

I woke up both excited and nervous. Today is the big day. Jaycee and Trina will be riding in their first competitions. It's the reason we came to Florida in the first place, and the girls have worked so hard...they deserve to do well. I'm glad that Sloane suggested we record their classes, so that we can share with everyone back home. Back home...where John is. I still haven't heard from him. Should I call him? Does he hate me? Is this the end?

The monkey chatter in my brain was interrupted by Jaycee as she burst through my bedroom door. She rushed over and threw herself on my bed, tossing her cell phone in my direction. I caught it mid-air.

"What's up?" I asked.

"Mom, look at that text message." *Good luck today, Jaycee. Bring home the blue!*

No name. Only the mysterious number that appeared in earlier texts.

"Who could this be, Mom?

"I don't know honey, but I'm going to look into it. If the person sending you these messages thinks it's a joke, they are sorely mistaken."

It would be so much easier to find out who's behind this if John were around to help. But he wasn't, and it's all my fault.

"Don't worry honey, we'll get to the bottom of it. Now, go get ready, and we'll head for the showgrounds." It would be easy to fall into fear mode, but that wasn't an option. I had to be strong to inspire Jaycee's confidence. We all grabbed some fresh fruit and climbed into the Range Rover. I could tell that the girls were nervous about their rides this afternoon, and Jaycee's mysterious text wasn't helping.

"Jaycee, show Aunt Sloane the text messages you got from that strange number."

Jaycee handed her phone to Sloane and watched while she scanned the messages. *You look pretty...good luck.* They all seem innocent enough. It's not knowing who sent them that's creepy."

"Do you know anyone from Texas Aunt Sloane?"

"Can't say that I do. Except maybe Ross Spencer and Lena, his girlfriend."

"You think that these messages might be from Ross or Lena?" I asked.

"I doubt it. Why would either of them communicate with Jaycee...anonymously?"

We pulled into the grounds, and Jaycee and Trina headed for the tack room to collect their saddles and bridles. Sloane went to check on the horses, and I headed for Crystal and Robert's box in the stands. Crystal looked fresh and sporty in her Lilly Pulitzer capris and Jack Rogers sandals. The transformation was amazing...from small town Boho girl to elegant Palm Beach lady. I know she worked hard to pull it off, with the stacks of *Vogue* and *Town & Country* on her nightstand. But no matter the outward appearance, Crystal was still Crystal. Irreverent, quirky, lovingly scatterbrained, and perfectly marvelous. It was a joy to see how happy she and Robert were in their new lives.

"Well, you two, I see you've come prepared. Binoculars, Nikon, and Veuve Clicquot."

"Absolutely" said Crystal, handing me a flute.

"This is a special occasion," said Robert, raising his glass.

"I probably shouldn't drink this. I have a coaching job to do for Trina."

"Oh! It's just one glass. It'll steady your nerves."

I took a sip. Crystal's orders.

"You're coaching Trina? I thought you'd be coaching Jaycee?"

"Nonoo...mother coaching daughter? Not a good idea. Too personal. It works much better if I coach Trina, and Sloane coaches Jaycee. More focus, less drama."

Crystal pulled a tray of prosciutto with melon and dilled shrimp hors d'oeuvres from her cooler. "I never had any kids, but from what I've seen, teenagers are none too happy to take advice from their parents. And with this, there's so much at stake!"

I savored a delectable shrimp. "Nice spread, Crystal. Did you make it yourself?"

She rolled her eyes, and we both laughed.

"Trina and I do work really well together. She's such a sweetie, and cool as a cucumber."

"Are they riding in the same class?"

No. We all thought it best if they didn't compete directly. They are best friends, and...it just wouldn't be a good idea."

"I get it. How about Jaycee? Is she nervous?"

"A little...and we've got a *situation* that's adding to her stress."

"What's that?"

I told Crystal and Robert about the mysterious texts that were sent to Jaycee.

Robert sat up at attention. "You say that you traced the area code to Texas?"

"Yes. Dallas."

"I'm assuming that Jaycee doesn't know anyone from Texas?" asked Crystal.

"No, she doesn't."

"You either?"

"No, except for Ross Spencer, and his girlfriend, Lena. I just realized that I don't know Lena's last name."

"Neither do I" Crystal chimed in. "Do you know honey?"

Robert shook his head. "Spencer didn't say her last name when I invited them to dinner. He just asked if it was okay if he brought his girlfriend. Speaking of Ross Spencer, I've got to give him a call. He's been after me to invest in this project he's working on, and I've decided to opt out."

"What project?"

"He wants to build a huge indoor riding arena like the Grand Palais in Paris."

"No kidding? You mean down here?"

"Yes, near the showgrounds. Turns out that the piece of land he wants to build on is owned by Vincente Villa."

I didn't try to mask my surprise. "That might pose a problem for Ross. I take it that there's no love lost between him and Vincente."

"Not only that," said Crystal. There's another fly in the ointment."

"What's that?"

"Bianca has her own plans for that land. Remember the meeting we had that fateful night at IL Bellagio?"

"Yeah…"

"The meeting was all about planning an Equine Wellness Center on that very spot. That really complicates things for Ross."

Robert poured another glass of champagne. "I think it best if I stay away from it all together. Besides, I don't like the plan that Spencer cooked up."

"What plan?" Crystal and I said in unison. We laughed...some things never change.

"He wants me to tell Villa that I'm going to buy the land for a luxury condominium development, and that I should offer him double the land's valuation. He said that it would appeal to Villa's greedy nature."

I was indignant. Vincente's greedy nature? What about Ross Spencer? It was like the pot calling the kettle black.

"What about Spencer's plans for the arena? How is he supposed to manage that if there are condos on the property?

“That’s just it!” Robert said. There were never any real plans for building condos on that land. Spencer wanted me to do a deal with him to build the arena facility.”

“Well, basically he wants you to double cross Vincente.”

“That’s about it in a nutshell.”

“How underhandedly disgusting!” said Crystal. If I’d known what was going down, I never would have agreed to sit down to dinner with them. And that Lena...talk about an obvious social climber...and gold digger to boot!”

“How does Bianca fit into all this? “I asked. Crystal filled us in on Bianca’s plans for the Equine Wellness Center.

I finished my champagne. “Given that, she’d never permit Vincente to sell the land.”

“Something just doesn’t ring true about her motives either,” said Crystal.

I asked her what she meant.

“I thought it was odd that she invited me to be on her committee. I don’t have the right connections down here. And then to invite Sloane? Bianca knows that she’ll be heading back up north soon, so why involve her? And I’ll tell you, when Lena found out about the committee, she didn’t waste any time in letting me know that she'd be oh so happy to volunteer."

"Really? Very interesting."

Spencer didn't seem too keen on the idea" said Robert.

"No. But he must have changed his mind about that. I got a text from Bianca about the next meeting, and Lena's name was on the roster of those attending. And guess who else will be joining us?"

"I can't imagine."

"Dr. Julia Forrest."

"What?"

"Yeah, I guess Bianca figures that it would be a good idea to actually have a veterinarian on board," said Crystal.

"That does make sense, although Julia doesn't exactly seem like the committee joining type."

"Right, but who knows...maybe the practice is urging her to join. It would be a great opportunity for them to be involved."

"There's something strange about Dr. Forrest…" Just then my phone buzzed. It was a text from Trina. She had Dynamo ready to go in the warm-up ring and needed me ASAP.

"I've got to go. It's showtime folks!"

CHAPTER TWENTY-ONE

Delta flight 729 landed at Heathrow Airport early Monday morning. Detective John Garrett made his way through the crowd and headed for the baggage claim. It didn't matter what airline, airport, or baggage claim was involved; John always stood in trepidation that his bag would not be sliding down the ramp onto the moving carousel. In his mind, "lost" was always the precursor to "luggage." Why he felt that way was a mystery to him. Never, in all the years that he'd been flying, did he ever suffer the fate of lost luggage.

As he contemplated this anomaly, he witnessed his bag tumbling down the ramp, and he swiped it before it could be carried away in a whirl. He pulled out the retractable handle, coaxing the bag to roll along behind him toward Ground Transportation. As he walked through the automatic sliding doors, a burst of chill air assaulted him. He zipped up his maroon down filled jacket and reached into his pocket to retrieve a soft knitted gray cap to protect his head. It was nearly as cold in London as it had been in Philadelphia when he flew out yesterday. It was different though, Philadelphia was a crisp cold, London, a soggy one.

John hailed a cab and took in the sights of the countryside as he sped toward the heart of the city. What was it that Samuel Johnson said? *If you're tired of London, you're tired of life?* Something like that. London had always offered up a paradox for John. A place that held untold possibilities, but that was always just out of reach.

He repeated the address of his final destination, reminding the driver that he was very familiar with the city, thus avoiding the temptation to take the long way around. He slipped the cabbie a generous tip as the fellow retrieved his bag from the "boot" of the cab. Funny, how even though we all speak English, we could come up with so many different euphemisms for so many different things. How did the "boot" of an automobile in England become the "trunk" of a car in America?"

John took a deep breath of cold damp air and began walking the streets of Mayfair looking for a particular townhouse...the townhouse that Lacy Snow died in so many years ago. Ah, yes. There it was. He knew the number 336, although the exterior was now a sandy stone color, not grayed from ancient soot as it had been when the Snow family lived there. The new owners must have cleaned the facade. John spent hours poring over the photos Fiona sent him from the case files. Photos that told a cryptic story of the people that had crossed the threshold back then. Those that wove the unfinished tale of what really happened that fateful Fall morning when Lloyd Snow ostensibly traveled to Newmarket, and Lacy Snow drank a cup of tea.

Lately, when John worked a case, he found it beneficial to spend some alone time at the scene of the crime. He let the atmosphere permeate his senses, as though he could learn the answers to his questions through osmosis. Although that was unlikely, the vibe he got from being in close proximity made everything seem much more *real* to him. It was as though he could almost witness it. Perhaps it came from hanging around Jaycee. Hmm...Jaycee, Jayson, Ivy. They seemed further away than ever before. He looked up at the tall upstairs windows. They reflected a blank stare back at him. He hailed a cab and headed for Scotland Yard

Detective Fiona Wescott stood to greet John as he approached her desk. She held out her hand in welcome. It felt strange, but what could he expect? After all, they were in a police station.

"John, welcome! It's a pleasure to see you" Fiona said in her soft English lilt. "How was your flight?"

"As good as can be expected in coach."

"I know what you mean. For once I would like to fly first class...see how the other half lives" she smiled.

"I'm afraid you'd be spoiled."

"Have you checked into your hotel yet?" she asked.

"No. I came straight from the airport. Oh...I take that back. I did make one stop, but I'll tell you about that later."

John locked his gaze on Fiona's eyes, hoping to find a message in them. He marveled at how little she'd changed. Her hair, still a shiny golden blonde. Her complexion, still dewy and flawless. Her lips, full and sensual, enhanced with shimmery pink gloss. She was much too beautiful to be on the police force. She should have been a model, or an actress. A profession that didn't hide her beauty away from the world.

Fiona shuffled some papers on her desk. “It’s almost lunch, John. Why don’t we find a spot at Nicholson’s, and I’ll fill you in on what’s been happening with the case.”

“That’s what I’m here for,” he replied.

Lloyd stood on the corner and stared at the text message that Detective Wescott left on his phone. He’d better answer soon, or she might think he was avoiding her. Worse yet, that he’d fled London for good. If only Bianca would come up with that suicide note, and soon! He would feel much better if he could be sure that no one would ever see it again. His nerves were frayed. He hated the idea of not being in control. How did he know for sure that Bianca hadn’t found the note already? If that were the case, why hadn’t he heard from her?

A terrible thought crossed his mind. What if Bianca already found the note? What if she was holding out on him? Why would she do that? Of course! Blackmail. She could blackmail him. Maybe not for money, she’s got enough of that, alright, but she'd have him by the balls. Doing her bidding...doing her dirty work for fear that she'd expose him. How naive of him to take her into his confidence...to try and enlist her help. It was *she* who wrote that note. It was *she* who knew the truth. What a fool he'd been. If she found that note...and she probably had by now, it was she who held his fate in her hands!

CHAPTER TWENTY-TWO

Vincente pulled his Land Rover up to the entrance of Villa Stables. He'd received a message from Dr. Forrest earlier that the results came in from the lab. They now knew what poison killed his horses, and how it got into their systems. Who was responsible? That was now the question. He called a meeting with Dr. Forrest and Enrico Alvero for two that afternoon.

The three of them sat at the copper topped table in the center of the tack room. The mood was somber as Julia pulled the documents containing the lab reports from her briefcase and read the report. Vincente's horses died from Black Walnut poisoning. They came in contact with it in the shavings used to bed their stalls. The poison seeped up into their systems through their hooves, causing severe laminitis, and ultimately death.

Vincente's jaw dropped open. Of all things he never expected to hear...how could it be? He never knew that black Walnut was poisonous to horses. How did it get in their bedding? Julia explained the facts about Black Walnut, while Vincente and Enrico sat in stunned silence. "And so that solves the mystery," she said.

Vincente stood up and walked around the table. "Not entirely. We now know the cause of death. The question remains...who is responsible?"

Julia looked at Enrico as he fidgeted in his chair. His eyes shifted to the ground as he felt the heat rising in his face. It was as he'd expected, they were going to pin the blame on him.

Vincente walked over to the roll top desk and retrieved the stable management logbook. Enrico already knew what Vincente would find. The photos that he took of the pages in that book yielded no new, or unusual information about the comings and goings at the stable. Each entry of deliveries of grain, supplements, equipment and shavings were checked by him. He didn't remember anything unusual about the shavings themselves. They appeared to be the same as always.

"Alvero, you were responsible for the welfare of my horses. It was your responsibility to keep them healthy and safe."

Enrico's eyes flashed with anger. "You are blaming me for this?" He saw Julia smirk out of the corner of his eye.

"I must be going now. I'm already late." She put her lab coat on, picked up her briefcase, and headed for the door.

"Yes. I am blaming you! I don't know if it was pure negligence, or a vicious criminal act."

"Why would I do something like this on purpose?"

"Because you want your own stable with Sloane Parker. You knew that you could never compete with me. Not with those horses. You would never achieve the greatness you desire, or you wish to crush me by taking everything away."

"You're crazy Villa."

"Am I? I know about your affair with my wife."

Enrico took a deep breath and held it. His fears had been realized. His skin turned ashen.

Vincente opened and closed his fists. "How long Alvero? How long have you been screwing Bianca?"

"I... I don't know what..."

"Don't lie to me. I heard it with my own ears. You are fired Alvero! Get out!"

Enrico stomped across the room toward the door as he heard Vincente shout "You'll hear from my lawyer!"

Enrico jumped into his Miata and sped away from the stable. He struggled to grip the steering wheel; his hands were shaking so violently. He had to reach Bianca. She was the only one that could help him now. He didn't have the money to hire a lawyer to defend himself. He pulled over to the side of the road and pushed the speed dial button on his phone.

"Hello Enrico. So, you finally decided to return my calls."

"I'm sorry darling. I have such trouble!"

"What kind of trouble?"

"Your husband knows about us."

"I'm aware of that. It's why I have been calling you" she said icily.

"I didn't know. I just met with him. He said that he heard about us with his own ears?"

"That's true. He had an extension phone installed in the room he's been sleeping in. He's been listening in on our conversations."

Enrico felt his stomach heave. "Bianca, he is holding me responsible for the death of his horses. I swear, I had nothing to do with it. He's threatening to sue me."

"That doesn't surprise me. You'll be lucky if he doesn't do worse."

He couldn't believe his ears. He thought Bianca was in love with him. He counted on that to gain her support.

"You've got to help me. If I'm exposed to the court system, I'll go to jail, or be deported."

"Deported? What do you mean? I thought you had a Green Card?"

"I did, but it expired months ago."

"Well, why didn't you have it renewed?"

"I couldn't. My renewal quota was depleted. I would have been sent back to Argentina, lost my job, and missed the polo season here."

Funny, thought Bianca. The one thing he didn't mention was missing *me.* "Yes, you would have missed the opportunity to undermine Vincente, using me, and looking for the chance to start your own polo team with someone like, ah...Sloane Parker for instance."

"What does Sloane Parker have to do with this?"

"Don't take me for a fool, Enrico. I know that you've been chasing Sloane Parker for more than just her money to build a polo team. You planned on moving up north with her and leaving me behind."

"No, never my darling!"
"Don't 'darling' me. As far as I'm concerned Enrico, you're on your own."

That bitch! Enrico could picture her standing in the middle of her lavish bedroom suite wrapped in black silk and holding the pink receiver of her Princess phone with her diamond clad fingers. How dare she turn her back on him! He'd practically been her lap dog, bowing and scraping to her every whim. As she slammed down the receiver, he pounded his fist on the steering wheel. She would be sorry she turned her back on him. Very sorry!

CHAPTER TWENTY-THREE

I half walked; half ran to the practice ring to meet Trina. She and Dynamo were walking around the rail, warming up for her class. She looked so elegant. Her show coat was a rich loden green, which set off her milky complexion. Too bad her helmet concealed so much of it. She smiled brightly when she saw me and trotted over to the gate when I entered.

"Hello Trina. You look beautiful, and I don't think I've ever seen Dynamo's coat so shiny."

"Thanks. I worked all morning to get it that way!"

"Are you nervous?"

"Yes, a little."

Trina was the kind of girl who would never want to admit to fearing anything. "Well, who wouldn't be?" I said.

"Even though we walked the course, I'm still afraid I'll get confused. That's my biggest worry."

I stood at the rail and pointed out each jump on the course in order.

"Okay, I've got it," Trina said.

It was a class of twenty-two riders, and the competition was stiff. Even though it was a youth division, most of the riders had competed in this ring at least once before. It put Trina at a bit of a disadvantage, but she was an excellent rider on a great horse. It was almost enough to level the playing field...almost.

Her name and number were called over the loudspeaker. She entered the ring, walked around, and then got into position. The buzzer sounded, the clock started, and off she went. My heart was in my mouth. I held my breath as they approached each jump. They sailed over, with room to spare, except for the last one. The tip of Dynamo's rear hoof touched the rail. No! I dropped my head, anticipating the worst. It shook back and forth for what seemed an eternity, but then settled back into the cups. Whew! They were finally finished. Her time was not the fastest so far, but no rails down.

I met her as she came back through the gate.

"Excellent Trina! Great ride!"

"Thanks. I'm glad it's over."

Me too, I thought, but I wasn't going to say it. I helped her dismount. Her legs were shaking. No matter what she said, she had to have been nervous. We waited until all the riders had their turn in the ring. The results were in. Trina and Dynamo came in eighth out of twenty-two. We were elated! We jumped up and down, patting each other on the back. Dynamo just looked at us as if to say "What about me? Where's my treat?

We walked Dynamo back to the stable, and found Jaycee and Sloane grooming Pirate, and getting ready for her class later in the afternoon. Jaycee had a rather solemn look on her face. As soon as she saw Trina, her countenance changed. She was all smiles.

"How did it go?"

"Great! I came in eighth out of twenty-two. I can't believe it!"

"Well, I can," said Jaycee, hugging her friend. "I'm so happy for you!"

I studied Jaycee. Underneath the smiles and jubilation, I could tell that something was wrong. I don't want to ruin the moment, so I just caught Sloane's eye with a quizzical look to convey *what's up?* Sloane tilted her head to the left, indicating that I should follow her. The girls were deep in conversation and didn't even notice that we slipped into the tack room.

"Alright, what's going on with Jaycee?"

Sloane shook her head. "She got another one of those text messages."
"Oh no. What did it say?"
"Just *Hope you win today"* Sloane said.
"Humm. Whoever is sending these is clever. They know that Jaycee must be creeped out, and that's probably their intention. Maybe it was one of the other competitors in her class, trying to get her rattled. But, if they are ever identified, they can't be accused of doing anything wrong. The messages are innocuous enough, pleasant even. They could always say that they assumed Jaycee knew who was sending them."
"Yeah. You can hardly accuse someone of being too nice."

Sloane pulled out her cell. "I did some investigating. The number is attributed to a burner phone, so no luck there. Is this something that John might be able to help with?"
"Probably. The thing is, I haven't heard from him in days. Not since he found out that I wasn't completely truthful about knowing Vincente."
"You can't really blame him. Have you tried calling him?"
"No. I haven't the slightest idea of what I would say. I already apologized. I have no idea why I

said that I really didn't know Vincente. It just came out. I suppose there's some deep psychological reason."

"I think you should do something. Call, or text him. This silence will just drive a bigger wedge between you two."

"I guess you're right. I'll call him later. It's Jaycee I'm concerned about right now."

"Okay. Let's get back in there and put the finishing touches on Pirate. It's almost time to warm up."

We tacked Pirate up and helped Jaycee dress. She looked so grown up, so elegant. I could feel the tears welling up in my eyes. Before too long she'd be off on her own, as would Jayson. I wasn't looking forward to an empty nest. Sloane escorted Jaycee to the warm-up ring, while Trina and I headed for Crystal and Robert's box where we would have a great view, and perhaps a little more champagne.

As soon as we entered the box, Crystal threw her arms around Trina. "Congratulations honey, you were marvelous!"

"Thank you," Trina said, blushing.

Robert, bursting with pride, squeezed her hand. "That's my granddaughter!".

"Oh, and Ivy, you must be so nervous. Jaycee is next!" said Crystal.

"Ah, you could say that." I mimicked shaking hands.

Robert glanced at the program. "Looks like she's up against eighteen others."

"Yes. And she's slated to go in third."

We took our seats at the window and watched the first two riders jump the course. Not bad times, but the first rider knocked down the last rail, and the second rider knocked down two rails overall. It was a tough course.

I could barely see Jaycee as she stood waiting readily at the gate. They were next. Sloane stood by her side, and I could tell that she was giving Jaycee last minute instructions...and encouragement. As Sloane moved away, I could see Jaycee bow her head. She was praying. The gate opened, and they went in. I couldn't tell if they were in the ring for a minute, or an hour. My brain was traveling at a pace of its own.

I watched as Pirate's hooves sailed over each jump and held my breath at each approach. At last, they were finished. I glanced up at the board. Wow! Her time was great. She's in the lead, with no rails down. Unfortunately, there are fifteen more riders to go. This class will last an eternity.

I turned to see Crystal, who was practically in a trance.

"That went quite well," I said. I was trying to hide the fact that my nerves were in shambles. I could never fool Crystal though.

"Quite well? They were fabulous. I'll bet they win!"

"There're fifteen more riders to go. I don't think I can stand it."

"Here Ivy, have another glass of champagne. It'll calm you down."

"Knock me out is more like it." It was my third glass.

"That daughter of yours must have nerves of steel," said Robert.

"She does. She's been through a lot for her young age. I do think this text stalking is getting to her though. She doesn't like to let on that it bothers her, but who wouldn't be rattled? It would creep anyone out."

Crystal handed Trina an iced tea. "You must be exhausted honey...here, sit down and relax."

"I don't know if I'm tired from my ride or watching Jaycee with my heart in my mouth!"

"I'd say both. Trina, you don't have any idea who would be sending these texts to Jaycee, do you? I mean like someone we'd never think of."

"No, I can't imagine."

"I mean, do you think it could be some guy that has a crush on her, and is too shy to let her know?" asked Crystal.

Trina pursed her lips. "It's possible. There are always a lot of guys checking her out, but I can't think of anyone in particular."

I walked over and sat next to Trina. "You know honey, Crystal may have something here. Try and keep an eye out for that. Be aware of any guys hanging around acting suspicious. You'll let us know, won't you?"

"Of course, I will. It just never occurred to me."

"Okay, thanks."

We finished watching the remainder of Jaycees's class. When all was said and done, she ended up coming in fifth. The day was successful beyond our wildest dreams.

"Let's celebrate tonight! Who's up for dinner at *Hot Pie Pizza?"* I shouted.

Everyone raised their hands.

"Trina, would you please tell Sloane and Jaycee to meet us there in an hour? I have a call to make."

"Sure. I've got to change too. I'll go with them and meet you there."

I signaled Crystal that I was stepping out to make the call. Sloane was right. Not talking to John solved nothing. It just created more distance between us. I took my cell phone out of my bag and hit John's number in the speed dial. The call went straight to voicemail. I had no idea of the insurmountable distance that was already between us...both literally and figuratively.

CHAPTER TWENTY-FOUR

Detective John Garrett felt his cell phone vibrate in his jacket pocket. He'd shut the ringtone off so that it wouldn't interfere with his time with Fiona. They'd just entered the restaurant, and Fiona went to the ladies' room to freshen up, while John secured a table. She returned, looking lovelier than ever. That boxy policewoman's uniform couldn't hide her tauntingly voluptuous body no matter how hard it tried.

The atmosphere at Nicholson's was authentic Brit through and through. Dark wood paneling, etched glass partitions, gleaming brass accents throughout. John cursed himself for staying away from London for so long. It was a place he truly loved.

"The fish and chips are very good here," Fiona said.

John closed his menu. "That'll do for me."

"I'm officially off duty now. Shall we have Pale Ale as well? They make their own here, you know."

"I didn't, but I'll let you be my guide," John said with a smile.

They ordered lunch, and when the waiter left, an uncomfortable silence fell between them. Fiona cleared her throat. “John, would you like to tell me what brought you here?”

“My visit isn’t official Fiona.”

“I know that. You would have needed the proper clearances.”

“I'm here about the reopening of the Lacy Snow case.”

“Really? And in what capacity, may I ask?”

“Someone involved in the case is very close to me.”

“Who might that be?”

“Well, it’s Ivy Snow. Lacy’s daughter. It’s kind of a long story, but after I left the NYPD, I joined the Pennsylvania State Police. I’m stationed out of a barracks near the town where Ivy lives. We met a few years ago on a murder case.”

“A murder case? Was Ivy accused of murder?”

“No. She found the body. Things got complicated from there.”

“That’s quite a coincidence, John.”

“Yes, thinking about it now, I suppose it is,”

“So why did Ivy Snow send you here?”

“She didn’t. I came of my own volition.”

“I’m confused,” Fiona said.

"Understandably. So, you remember when we first met? Scotland yard was investigating Lacy Snow's murder."

"Yes, I was involved in a limited capacity. Ivy Snow was the primary suspect. Her stepfather, Lloyd Snow, was convinced that she'd killed her mother. We were on that line of investigation when Ivy's fiancé, Vincente Villa came up with a suicide note supposedly written by Lacy. We didn't have enough to hold Ivy, so the case went dormant."

"Exactly. But now the case is being reopened. Why is that Fiona?"

"I'll tell you why. It's because Scotland Yard doesn't like unsolved cases. That's why they put me in charge, so that there will be as few of them as possible."

"Yes, but there must be so many cases."

"There are, believe me, but this one's got a lot of loose ends. After reading through the case files, I'm not entirely convinced that Ivy Snow didn't kill her mother."

"Fiona, that's just preposterous!"

"John, did you come over here to convince me to stop investigating this case? What is your relationship with her?"

Just then, the waiter arrived with their food. The fish and chips were delicious, and the ale was a refreshing respite, one that Fiona sorely needed as she felt the heat rising in her cheeks.

John ignored her question. "Alright, what about Lloyd Snow? He had a lot to gain from Lacy's death...a million pounds, I understand."

"That stone is not being left unturned, believe me. As a matter of fact, I questioned him as soon as the case was reopened. He has since left for the United States. I've been trying to reach him, but he's not responding."

"That doesn't surprise me. He's been too busy harassing Ivy."

"What? He's with Ivy?"

"Well, let's just say that they're in the same vicinity. Palm Beach, Florida."

"What's going on? Why are they there?" Fiona asked.

"Ivy took her daughter down for some horse show. Suddenly Lloyd Snow shows up, and coincidentally, so does Vincente Villa."

"You're joking!"

"No. I wish I were."

"You didn't answer my question, John. What is your relationship with Ivy Snow?"

"To be honest with you Fiona, at this moment, I truly don't know."
"Really, John. It seems to me that you are so often confused when it comes to relationships."
"What do you mean?" He knew exactly what she meant.

Fiona looked at him long and hard. She took a drink of her ale. "If you will recall, some twenty odd years ago, when we first met and started up, you were engaged to a woman back in the States. Her name...Angelique."
John hung his head, remembering back to those shameful days. "I...um...there's no excuse. I was young and foolish."
"Not that young. And quite clever, as I recall. You kept that hidden from me, until I just happened to answer the phone in your hotel room while you were in the shower. Have I jogged your memory?"
"I know what I did was wrong Fiona and believe me I paid for it dearly."
"How's that?"
"Angelique and I didn't have the happiest of marriages. We struggled along though, for the sake of the kids. Just as our youngest was about to go off to college, Angelique came down with

a case of early Alzheimer's. She's spent the last five years in a nursing home."

"Oh, I'm sorry to hear that. For her sake. Obviously, you are not inclined to tell me about your relationship with Ivy Snow, but that's okay. It wouldn't make a difference. I'm going to continue to investigate the death of Lacy Snow."

"But Fiona…"

Her cell phone rang, and she looked down to the caller I.D. The name Lloyd Snow appeared.

CHAPTER TWENTY-FIVE

Lloyd hit the *call end* button on his phone. He was quite satisfied that he handled Detective Fiona Wescott's inquiries satisfactorily, even though all his responses were lies. He had bigger fish to fry now, and top priority was handling the Bianca Villa problem. She was a loose cannon as far as he knew, and he wasn't about to give up control of the situation, let alone control of his very life to her.

He vacated his barstool at Ta-boo and hailed a taxi back to the Brazilian Court. He could have walked, but the punishing Florida sun threatened him with heat stroke every time he slipped out of air conditioning. The Brazilian was his haven, and a luxurious one at that. Unfortunately, luxury comes at a price, and a million pounds didn't last forever, especially factoring in his limited success at the racetrack. He would have to start replenishing the coffers soon, or Motel 6 it would be for him!

Hmm...that gave him an idea. He'd been so wrapped up in the fear that Bianca Villa would have him over a barrel with that forged note, that he hadn't realized that tables could be turned.

Bianca had just about enough of all of them. Who did these peasants think they were, trying to intimidate her? She was, after all, Bianca Bazan of Argentina, and the beau monde of Palm Beach. Who did that Lloyd Snow think he was, sending her on a fool's errand to find that suicide note? And what about her own husband? What right did he have to hide that note, planning to hang it over her head when the time was right? After all, what happened years ago was his word against hers.

Perhaps the most disappointing of all is Enrico. After all she had done for him, he turned his back on her for that slut, Sloane Parker. Protesting his innocence in the death of Vincent's horses. Perhaps he doth protest too much. And what about that bitch, Ivy Snow, going after Vincente again after all these years.

Bianca walked to her desk and opened her laptop. She sent a group email to her Equine

Wellness Center development committee, calling for a breakfast meeting the next morning. There was much work to be done.

Lena read the email message sent by Bianca. "Oh Ross! A meeting tomorrow morning" she squealed. My first *society* meeting."

"Don't get yourself all in a twist trying to impress these bitches. Remember, your job here is to find out what Bianca Villa is up to, and report back to me."

"Sure Ross, I remember. Help me decide what to wear."

Here we go again, he thought. Lena was like a child. She looked to him for everything, could never decide on her own, and had a limited relationship with the English vernacular. If she wasn't so hot and sexy under the sheets, he wouldn't keep her around. But wait, maybe that kind of thinking was a little hasty on his part. After all, he could persuade her to do a lot for him. She was so dense, she'd never realize that she was a patsy, not until it was too late, that is.

No question though, something had to be done to make her fit in better with high society, or they might both be blackballed. If only she were a little more suave, more sophisticated, like Bianca Villa.

"You know, Lena, there is something else you could be doing to help me...and yourself."

"What's that Ross? Anything!"

"When you're in these meetings, associating with Bianca...Sloane Parker even. Pay attention to how they express themselves. Look to them for guidance."

"What do you mean Ross, express themselves?"

"I mean how they talk. The words they use. The things they talk *about.* You know?"

"Ah, sure Ross, I'll pay attention to that."

He walked to the closet and pulled out a simple silk suit, the color of saffron. It had a Carolina Herrera label inside and was one of the more expensive items he'd purchased for Lena to wear. He considered it an investment. One that would not be liquidated if and when she ceased to be an asset.

Lena took the suit into their immense bathroom, and held it up to her body, gazing at her reflection in the full-length mirror. She turned from side to side, viewing the garment from all angles. *Look to Bianca Villa for guidance,* he said. Yes, look to Bianca Villa…she would certainly do that!

Crystal dragged herself out of bed stretching and yawning, as she made her way across the thick ivory carpeting to the bathroom. One thing she had insisted on in their new apartment was shades of lilac and lavender in their bedroom suite. They were her signature colors, and they reminded her of home. Her *old* home, that is.

Robert was still asleep, and snoring, bless his heart. Fortunately, it didn't bother Crystal. She slept like the dead. Leave it to Bianca to call a breakfast meeting. Yuk...Crystal's idea of breakfast was dark roast coffee...black. But here she was, dressing for the occasion. Hmm, Bianca invited them all to meet at her home. That would be interesting. She'd only seen *Casa Verde* from the outside, and it was fabulous. A landmark Palm Beach residence for sure. She licked her former real estate chops! She missed selling real estate. It was in her blood. Maybe she should talk to Robert again about opening an agency down here, especially since he wasn't going to be involved in the Ross Spencer project.

She selected a simple Prada white linen sheath. She spiced it up with gold gladiators from Manolo, so that Bianca couldn't fault her for not putting in enough effort. Humm, maybe she should add the diamond tennis bracelet that Robert bought her on their honeymoon. Yes, it was just the right amount of bling. She went to the bedroom wall safe hidden behind the Frank Stella painting that Robert loved. Crystal thought it interesting, but it wouldn't have been her first choice. She turned the dial to the numbers that she so carefully memorized, and "open sesame" ...she was in! She removed her jewelry box and scanned the gorgeous pieces that she never dreamed would be hers. Robert was so generous. Hmm? Where's her diamond tennis bracelet? She began re-arranging the jewelry, hoping that it was just hidden under one of the other pieces. No! She searched the bottom of the safe with her hand, thinking that perhaps the bracelet had somehow fallen out of her jewelry box. But no, the bracelet wasn't there.

Crystal felt a growing discomfort in the pit of her stomach. Where was that bracelet? She got down on her hands and knees and searched the thick carpeting on the closet floor. No bracelet. The discomfort was turning to panic. Where could her bracelet be?

"Crystal!"

It was Robert calling her.

"What dear?"

"I called George to bring the car around for you."

"Oh. Thank you. I'll be right there."

She returned the jewelry box to the safe, and slammed the door shut to secure it behind the painting. She would look for the bracelet later. Robert would be so disappointed if she'd lost it.

Sloane winced when she heard the alarm go off. She blinked her eyes open, and her first thought was *I'm tired.* How could she be tired? She'd just slept eight hours. Oh well, yes, yesterday was a banner! The girl's first class at the festival, and then the celebration at *Hot Pie.*

It was so much fun! She hadn't remembered when she had so much fun. Just her, Ivy, the girls and Crystal and Robert.

She stretched her lovely limbs, and then planted her feet in the soft blush carpeting. The sun was just peeking through the blackout curtains (she must remember to close them all the way) and she could see that they were in for another glistening day in sunny South Florida. It was a welcome change from the gray frigid Pennsylvania winter. She mentally checked her schedule for the day. Ah, yes...she remembered the email from Bianca calling for a breakfast meeting this morning. It was more like a command performance than an invitation.

The girls were not scheduled to ride in any classes today, so Ivy insisted that they take a break and spend the day at the pool. She may as well hit the shower. After all, it was a good idea to keep her eye on Bianca Villa. She was sneaky and unpredictable. The old adage popped into her mind: keep *your friends close, and your enemies closer.*

She dressed in a tawny linen skirt and crisp white cotton blouse. She added a Hermes scarf in a riot of sherbet hues for a fun accent. Large gold hoop earrings, and Stubbs and Wootton flats embroidered with snaffle bits completed the outfit. She called for the Range Rover, and then quietly slipped out of the suite so as not to disturb the other sleeping beauties. This promised to be an interesting morning.

Julia Forrest sighed as she poured steaming black coffee into a Dollywood souvenir cup with a chipped rim. Honestly, one of these days she would cut her lip, or other body part on the chipped, cracked and broken glassware that Sharon carelessly jammed into their kitchen cupboards. She didn't want to attend the meeting at Bianca Villa's this morning. She dreaded sitting around the table with those women. The practice insisted that she accept Bianca's invitation to join the Equine Wellness Center's development committee. They would be vying to provide most of the veterinary care at the center and having one of their team members on the development committee would provide a solid "in." Besides, Vincente Villa was an important client, and would surely have a say as to the veterinary group chosen to supply the clinic.

She had nothing appropriate to wear. They would all be in designer clothes and expensive jewelry. She didn't fit in. Best to just show up in her standard white coat with the practice logo on the pocket. No one could accuse her of being inappropriate in professional garb. She went to the front closet to retrieve it and stood in stunned silence to discover it missing. Oh no, Sharon's taken it again! She felt a wave of panic run through her body. What was her sister up to now? She didn't have time to figure it out. She pulled a white polo shirt over her head, tucked it into her Wranglers, and headed for her pick-up truck. She had to hurry, or she would be late.

The women all arrived at Casa Verde at the same time. Well, that wasn't quite true. Crystal arrived first, but had her chauffeur wait around the corner until she saw the others pass through the gates and pull into the driveway. She didn't want to spend any time alone with Bianca before the other committee members got there. She had the chauffeur drive up as the others got out of their cars. They gathered at the massive front door, and Sloane rang the bell.

A butler, dressed in the traditional tailcoat answered. He led them through a cavernous foyer to the morning room, which featured a table set for five. Bianca sat at the head, with a stack of blue folders to her left.

"Ladies, thank you for coming this morning. Please have a seat."

A small dark maid wheeled in a cart laden with tropical fruit and pastries. A sterling coffee and tea service adorning the buffet was large enough to accommodate a multitude. Crystal gazed around the room. Casa Verde didn't disappoint. The color palette of pinks and greens were tropical, yet soft. The fabrics were of the highest qualities, and the furnishings gleamed with a well-worn patina. There was nothing faux or garish about *Casa Verde.*

"Please help yourselves." Bianca gestured to the cart. They each chose among the delectable pastries.

"Can I get you something?" Lena asked.

Crystal smiled to herself. If Lena were any more

ingratiating her nose would be permanently brown.

“Yes, the beignet” Bianca snapped, as she passed around the blue folders. Each sported a logo combining the Caduceus floating above the image of Pegasus. Sloane thought it a rather convoluted design.

The folders contained the agenda for the meeting, and Bianca wasted no time getting down to business. The project would start out with a media blitz announcing its inception, followed by a ball at Mar-A-Lago to raise additional funding. Bianca assigned each member their duties for pulling this off. The women looked at each other cautiously. Julia Forrest squirmed uneasily in her massive chair. No one said a word. It was clear that this directive was not open for discussion, but that each member would execute their assigned part of the plan precisely as presented. There was no room for democracy here!

CHAPTER TWENTY-SIX

Ross's *Eye of the Tiger* ringtone jolted him out of his daydream. The caller ID announced Robert Montrose.

"Hello Robert, good to hear from you" he said, forcing a smile into his voice.

"Hello Ross. Sorry it's taken me so long to get back to you, but this horse show business has me all tied up." It was a lame excuse, and Robert knew it.

"You're preaching to the choir," Ross said, trying to hide his annoyance.

"Listen Ross, I've given your proposal very serious consideration, and after looking at all the facets, I'm going to have to pass."

Ross stood frozen. He thought his brain was going to explode.

"Ross, are you there?"

He struggled to compose himself. "Yes, I'm here. I'm just a little stunned, wondering why you would pass up a great opportunity like this."

Robert had thought this through very carefully and prepared an answer to this question he knew would be asked. He saw Ross Spencer's scheme for what it was, just as Crystal had. When you add up all the components of his plan, it was not only unethical, but it was also the kind of thing that would surely land him in court. Vincente Villa was not a man to be crossed.

"Well Ross, it turns out that I'm going to be much busier than I expected. Crystal's decided that she wants to get into the luxury real estate market down here. Real estate is what she did in Pennsylvania before we got married."

"Really? I had no idea that Crystal had such plans. She never mentioned it."

"I know. It's something she's been kicking around for a while. She figures that after Ivy and Sloane go back up north, she'll be bored."

"I thought she was working with Bianca Villa on that half-baked idea about an equestrian wellness center."

"She's attended a couple of meetings, but Crystal is a very energetic gal. She thrives on having a lot of irons in the fire."

"I see," said Ross. He hung up the phone abruptly.

Just then Lena came bounding into the room "Oh Ross, it was so cool! That house of Bianca's is awesome! There's a real butler, and everything!"

He looked at her with contempt. “So, what did you find out?”

Lena handed him the folder with the meeting agenda. “I’m going to be in charge of getting the prizes for the silent auction. Isn’t that exciting?”

Ross scowled and turned away. *There isn’t going to be any silent auction. There isn’t going to be any equine wellness center either,* he muttered under his breath.

Jaycee and Trina grabbed their beach bags, cell phones, and earbuds. They both liked Pandora, but not the same songs. Jaycee was more into Taylor Swift, and Trina was more of a Keith Urban kind of girl. They’d slept in late, so they were both hungry, although they’d opted for the large “everything” pizza at *Hot Pie* last night. Breakfast was served at the pool, so that problem was solved!

Trina scanned the pool deck and pointed to an umbrella shaded table with two lounge chairs nearby.

"Perfect!" said Jaycee. I'm ready for a break, and so is Pirate."

Trina put on her sun hat. "Me too. I'm glad that your mom suggested it."

"I'm kind of surprised that she did."

"How come?"

"She's been really pushing me a lot lately."

"Jaycee, this is a big deal down here, and your mom was, is, a fierce competitor. What did you expect?"

"I don't know. Maybe I'm just feeling it more since Jayson isn't around. She doesn't have to divide her parental supervision."

"True, but I wouldn't want to be in Jayson's shoes. With my mom in charge of him, he's like a prisoner. Know what I mean?"

"Yeah, but your mom's not so bad, and Jayson's all wrapped up in that play. I can't picture it. Jayson singing "Surry With The Fringe on Top!" Both girls broke out in hysterics.

Jaycee heard the phone buzz in her beach bag. OMG, the number that was texting is now calling! She swiped to answer. "Hello?"

"Hello Jaycee."

She gestured to Trina *IT'S HIM.* She froze, her eyes glued to Jaycee's phone.

"Who is this?"

“I’m an old friend of your mother’s...back when she lived in England.”

Jaycee put her hand over the phone, and whispered to Trina, *he said he’s an old friend of mom’s.* Trina’s eyes grew wide.

“I don’t know much about my mom’s friends in England. What’s your name?”

“My name is Lloyd.”

“Why are you calling me instead of my mom?”

“Your mom doesn’t know I’m in Florida. I want it to be a surprise.”

“Oh well, I’m sure she’ll be happy to see you.”

“I’d like to set up a surprise meeting at a restaurant. Maybe lunch, or dinner?”

“That sounds nice, but how are you going to get her there without her finding out?”

“That’s where you come in, Jaycee. I’m calling to ask for your help. Would you be willing to help me?”

“Uh, I guess. What do you want me to do?”

“Is there somewhere we could meet, and come up with a plan?”

Jaycee shot a glance at Trina. *He wants to meet up,* she whispered.

“Um...okay, we can meet at my stable on the show grounds. I’ll be over there in the morning.

Mom won't be there. She has a hair appointment, or something."

"That would be perfect Jaycee. Thank you. Would 10am be alright?"

"Sure. 10am."

Jaycee hung up the phone. "That's really weird. Mom never mentioned anyone named Lloyd. She doesn't talk about those days."

"I'll tell you one thing Jaycee, you're not meeting this guy alone. I'll be right behind you. I didn't just fall off the turnip truck, you know!"

They picked up their menus and perused the pastry selections. Pineapple danish and fruit smoothies hit the spot. The waiter arrived, and the girls placed their orders.

"You're right Trina. There's something weird about this. The hair is standing up on the back of my neck."

"I'm getting bad vibes too, and I'm not even psychic!"

Bianca's plan was unfolding. She was getting those women under her control, one step at a time. She now had to turn her attention to Lloyd and Ivy Snow. Lloyd was so hot to get his hands on that suicide note to protect himself from the Scotland Yard investigation. Too bad for him that it will prove to be a forgery. Too bad for Ivy as well. There's no statute of limitations on murder in the UK. No double indemnity either. Looks like history just might be repeating itself, but with a different outcome this time. She forged the note once, she could do it again.

She climbed the stairs to her bedroom and entered her dressing room. She removed the Chagall, and carefully twisted the lock on the safe. Left, right, left, right. The door swung open, and Bianca began removing the contents. Her jewelry box first, of course, then a copy of her will and other important legal documents, and finally a plain manila envelope. She opened it, and carefully removed a folder containing sheets of heavily embossed linen stationery, with the monogram LSE...Lacy Evangeline Snow.

Bianca mentally patted herself on the back for having the foresight to save the stationery used to write the original forgery. She'd had her friend, Sonia, order it from a stationer in New York, and shipped it to England where Bianca could intercept it at General Delivery. Sonia had paid in cash, so as not to leave a trace. No worries now since the stationers were out of business for the past ten years. Neither authenticity nor origin could be proved.

Now, there was the question of ink. Bianca dared not use a pen readily available on today's market. It might be traceable. What to do? Ah, she remembered a pen that she purchased years ago while touring cities in South Africa after the safari. Yes...it was long ago, and far away, virtually untraceable. She opened her desk drawer and rummaged to the back. Fortunately, it was still there. She began to write…

To Those I Love,

I'm sorry. I cannot live with this pain any longer. I hope you will forgive me and remember only the good times.

Lacy

Although she'd written it long ago, she remembered every word of that note. It was burned in her brain. She kept it short and simple so that expression, or manner of speech would not influence judgment of authenticity. She folded the note in half and returned it and the manila envelope to the wall safe. She pushed the pen to the back of the desk drawer, where she found it.

Lloyd Snow wasn't a stupid man. He knew that once Scotland Yard had their teeth into this, they weren't going to let go. They were bound and determined to get to the truth about Lacy's death no matter how much time had passed. She'd heard of a new head of Cold Case Investigations, a policewoman who'd been part of the original investigation as a rookie. She would have a vested interest in making sure that this case never went cold again. Fine. Bianca was up to the challenge. She rather liked the idea of toying with Scotland Yard. She sent a text message to Lloyd, letting him know that she "found" the suicide note.

CHAPTER TWENTY-SEVEN

Lloyd pulled his gold Jaguar rental car into the parking lot next to the stables. Good! There were no other cars in the lot. Jaycee must have taken a cab or maybe Uber. He took a quick look around to see if anyone was about. No, it looked like he and Jaycee would be alone. He opened the door to the tack room, which was empty, and proceeded to the stall area. He walked down the aisle way alerting every horse of his presence. One by one they stuck their heads out of their stalls, making horsey noises, hoping it was feeding time. He walked along slowly. There was something eerie about the place. Just then, Jaycee poked her head out of Pirate's stall. Lloyd gave her a little wave, and she stepped outside.

"Hello Jaycee. I'm Lloyd. Lloyd Snow."

"Jaycee's brow furrowed, as she tilted her head to one side in obvious confusion. She realized that the stranger on the phone yesterday had not given his last name, only his first, saying that he was a friend of her mothers.

"I don't understand. Who are you really?"

"I know that this may come as a shock to you my dear, but I am your grandfather."

Jaycee shook her head. She was totally stunned. Her voice caught in her throat. She reached out and grabbed the stall door to steady herself.

"What did you say?" she whispered.

"It doesn't surprise me that your mother never told you or your brother about me."

"I don't believe you. My mother would never keep a secret like that. Why would she?"

"I'm afraid that it goes to the heart of the matter my dear." He reached out to touch Jaycee. She recoiled.

"You'd better explain yourself."

Lloyd proceeded to tell Jaycee his version of what happened in London so many years ago. She listened to his words in silence, feeling the bile rising into her throat.

"You are telling me that my mother was accused of her mother's death?"

"I'm afraid so. It was only on a technicality that she wasn't convicted."

Jaycee took a deep breath. "So why are you here? Why are you telling me this now?"

"I'm here to protect you, Jaycee."

"Protect me from what?"

"Abandonment, I'm afraid."
"I don't follow."
"You see dear, Scotland Yard has reopened the case involving your grandmother's death. It is very likely that they will extradite your mother back to England and put her on trial for murder."

Jaycee tightened her grip on the stall door. She felt lightheaded. Afraid she might faint. They stood in silence, for what seemed like an eternity. Finally, she pulled herself together.
"I don't believe you. I don't know who you are, or why you're here telling me these lies."
Lloyd reached into his pocket and pulled out a newspaper clipping, yellowed with age, and handed it to Jaycee. It showed a photograph of her mother trying to shield her face from a crowd. The headline read "POISON IVY."

As Lloyd made his exit through the tack room. Trina came out of Dynamo's stall where she's been hiding, listening to every word.
"Oh my God Jaycee!" She put her arm around her friend's shoulder.
Tears were streaming down Jaycee's face. She handed the newspaper clipping to
Trina. Both girls just stood there, not knowing what to say.

Finally, Jaycee broke the silence. "What should I do?"
"Honestly Jaycee, I don't know. I mean how do we know that everything he said is true? I guess some of it is, because of this picture, but his story is *his* story. I suppose that the only thing you can do is go to your mom and tell her about all this. See what she has to say."
"Right. I wonder if she knows about Scotland Yard reopening the case, and that she might be extradited to stand trial?"
"We have no proof that any of that is true. He may be making it all up."
"Well, he was lying about something. He was surrounded by the black aura...a sure sign of deception."
"If you say so."
Trina looked down on the ground and spotted something shiny. She stooped down to pick it up. It was a coin. 50 pence. Lloyd hadn't realized that he dropped it. Trina handed the coin to Jaycee. She looked at it carefully, running her fingers over the surface. She put the coin in her pants pocket.
"Thanks Trina. This might come in handy."

I told the girls that I'd pick them up at noon so that we could grab some lunch and do a little shopping on Worth Avenue. After all, what's a trip to Palm Beach without it? Crystal and Sloane were waiting for us at Cafe Via Fiora's garden patio. Um...I was longing for good Italian.

Vincente said he had something important to discuss with me and asked that I stop by Villa Stables before getting Jaycee and Trina. I haven't seen Vincente since that horrid scene at Il Bellagio. I'm trying to limit my communication with him, and John, giving myself time to think, and sort out my feelings. Vincente just sounded so stressed out when he called, I couldn't say no.

I pulled the Range Rover into the parking lot expecting to see Vincente's car, but he hadn't yet arrived. I noticed Dr. Forrest's truck. Why was she here? There were no horses stabled here now. I decided to wait for Vincente in the cool air conditioning of the tack room. Even though it's still morning, temperatures were already on the rise. I was glad that I chose my ice blue linen blouse to keep cool. I proceeded to make myself comfortable on the cushy tan leather sofa, delighted to see the current issue of *Polo* magazine on the coffee table, set to entertain me while I waited for him. I began thumbing through the pages when I heard loud voices coming from the anteroom. Women's voices. I crept nearer to the door and recognized the taut tones of Dr. Forrest's voice. She was arguing with another woman whose raucous voice I didn't recognize. I bent forward, listening closely, trying to make out what Dr. Forrest was saying.

"Sharon...I told you to stay away from this place."

"You can't tell me what to do. Who do you think you are? Just because you have "Doctor" after your name, you think that you can boss everyone around."

"Somebody has to keep you in line. Especially after what happened in Kentucky."

"Oh! Now you're going to try and blame that on me, are you? And how is it that you know so much concerning my whereabouts? Are you spying on me?"

"No. I don't have time to follow you around. I found the_taxi receipts in the cookie jar."

"Snooping around, as usual."

"Listen Sharon, let's cut to the chase. I suspected all along that you had something to do with the death of Senor Villa's horses. What I want to know is how you did it?"
"How isn't as important as why. I found the perfect way to destroy his string, and hopefully teach you a thing or two. Bet you didn't know that Black Walnut shavings mixed in with the other bedding would be fatal? Yeah, it seems that the toxins are just sucked up through the horse's hooves, and then BAM, bye, bye ponies! Doesn't exactly make you look like the vet of the year, does it Julia?"
"You insane bitch!"

I couldn't believe my ears! What on earth? *BAM...BAM.* Oh my God! I threw open the door to see Dr. Forrest lying in a heap on the floor, a gun next to her body. I rushed over to her, grabbing her wrist to feel for a pulse. Yes, there it was, thank God! I looked around the room. The other woman "Sharon" was gone. Where did she go? I hadn't time to think. I saw the blood flowing from Julia's body, slowly soaking the shirt under her rib cage...so close to her heart. I tore off my blouse and wound it into a tight ball. I pulled up her shirt and pressed the fabric onto the wound, hopefully compressing it. I dialed 911, waited for the ambulance, and prayed. Where the hell was Vincente?

CHAPTER TWENTY-EIGHT

Vincente breathed a sigh of relief now that Ivy had agreed to meet with him. His sharply honed instincts told him that the noose was tightening around her neck, and he had to warn her of what he feared Bianca had in mind. He was aware that his wife had been sneaking around his room, searching for something, and he knew what that something was. But he also knew that she'd never be able to find it there. Bianca was transparent to him, and he was keenly aware that once she put her mind to something, there was no stopping her. She was hell bent on destroying Ivy, and anyone else that got in her way. Scotland Yard's reopening of the case gives her the perfect opportunity to come full circle. Finally, an opportunity to get rid of Ivy Snow for good. She must be in her glory.

Vincente finished dressing, adding one of the silk Hermes ties that Ivy helped him choose at Harrods so many years ago. He'd kept every one. He was to meet Ivy at his stables at eleven, so he had some time to kill before leaving the house. Perhaps it would be worth it to confront Bianca and let her know that he was wise to her scheme. No matter how she reacted, she had to know that their marriage was over. Maybe she would chase after Enrico. She'd finally be free to finance his polo team. He secured his Windsor knot and headed for his wife's ensuite.

Marisol Martinez finished clearing the table, putting away the leftovers, and washing up the breakfast things. She was exhausted, even though it was still morning. She'd been up since five am to get the service ready for Ms. Bianca's breakfast meeting. Everything had to be so perfect, from the freshly baked pastries (which fortunately were her specialty) to the freshly cut flowers from her garden. The silver service and cutlery had to be polished between each use, and the linens freshly laundered and starched. Thank heaven there were no more than four guests.

Missy Bianca was hard to please, but life in Palm Beach beat anything she had back in Argentina. Perhaps someday she could gain citizenship and freedom. She brewed a cup of tea and took a short break before changing into a fresh uniform to meet with her boss, and receive further instructions for the day. She slowly climbed the wide marble staircase and padded down the hallway to her mistress's room. She noticed that the door was ajar, which was unusual. Missy Bianca was almost a fanatic when it came to her privacy.

Marisol pushed the door open and tentatively entered the lavish room, finding it empty. Maybe her mistress had gone out without telling her. That would also be unusual, since she rarely left the house without handing Marisol a list of tasks to be completed before her return.

She called out Bianca's name as she entered the bathroom. She caught her breath and froze before letting out a shrill scream. There was her mistress, lying on the floor motionless...Mr. Vincente standing over her body.

As I waited for the ambulance, I tried Vincente's cell. No answer. He insisted that I meet with him...something important. It wasn't like him to be late. It wasn't like me either, so the girls must be wondering where I am. I took a deep breath and hit the speed dial for Jaycee. She answered immediately.

"Where are you mom? We've been waiting!"

"I'm sorry honey, but there's been an ah, emergency.

"What kind of an emergency?"

"It's Dr. Forrest. She's been taken ill." I didn't want to upset the girls. There would be plenty of time to explain later.

Jaycee shot a sideways glance at Trina. "So, what should we do?"

"I'm going to the hospital with her, so why don't you and Trina call for a ride and meet up with Sloane and Crystal at the restaurant. I'll join you as soon as I can."

"Okay mom but hurry up. I really need to talk to you."

"I'll be there as soon as I can honey."

I'd just hit the *end call* button when the ambulance arrived. Relief flooded through my body. The medics carefully lifted Julia onto a stretcher and slid it into the back of the ambulance. I introduced myself and said I would follow them to the emergency room. They turned on the siren, and we snaked through traffic to Wellington Regional Medical Center. As soon as we arrived, they rushed Julia to Triage, and I helped with registration as best I could. It was obvious at this point that I wasn't going to make lunch, so I sent Jaycee a text telling them to go on and eat without me.

I don't understand why Vincente hasn't returned my call. I'm getting a strange feeling that something is very wrong.

"Ms. Snow? I'm Dr. Clements."

I turned to greet the handsome owner of the deep southern accent. A young doctor who could not have been a year or two out of medical school.

"Yes, I'm Ivy Snow."

"Registration told me that you brought Dr. Forrest in."

"That's right. How is she?"

"Stable, but I'm afraid we'll have to operate right away. The bullet is lodged directly under her heart, and the sooner we get it out, the better."

God was with us. The surgery went quickly, and successfully, so I was advised to go home. Julia would not be awake for quite a while, and there was nothing more that I could do. It was late in the afternoon, so I called Sloane and said I would meet them back at the hotel.

By the time I arrived at our room I was exhausted. I didn't know whether to be worried or annoyed that Vincente hadn't returned any of my calls. I hit the bar cart and fixed myself an Absolute martini to calm my nerves. I slouched down on the creamy chenille couch and flicked on the TV just in time to catch the local news. What I saw nearly shocked me to the core. There in high definition was a police crime scene set at the entrance to Casa Verde. I followed the announcer's every syllable.

"We are here at Casa Verde, the palatial Ocean Drive home of socialite Bianca Villa, and her financier husband, Vincente. Police were called at 10:15 am by Mrs. Villa's maid, Marisol Martinez, who found Mrs.Villa unresponsive, lying on the bathroom floor. Mr. Villa was present and has been taken into police custody for questioning."

At that point, my brain shut her out. Bianca was "unresponsive" ...a euphemism for *dead.* Vincente was taken in for questioning. The husband is usually the prime suspect. Vincent would never kill Bianca. Divorce her...maybe. But kill her? Never! I wonder how she died? The reporter said nothing about a weapon, but maybe the police are keeping that quiet. The fewer details they give to the press, the better. The real killer might reveal him or herself by knowing facts about the murder not revealed to the public.

All I know is that I've got to help Vincent...but how? If only John was here. Wow! I can't believe that thought came into my mind. Asking John to come to Vincent's aid after creating a rivalry between them. Surely, it would be too much to ask. Besides, John hasn't called in over a week. For all I know, it's done between us.

I heard the door to the suite open and close. Sloane, Crystal and the girls rushed into the living room.

"Ivy, we heard about Bianca on the radio! It's awful! And Vincente's in police custody! They always suspect the husband."

"I know Sloane, and they're usually right."

"You don't think that Vincente killed her, do you?" said Crystal.

"Of course not. They were living in the same house. He must have discovered her body moments before the maid came into the room."

Crystal headed for the bar cart to fix more drinks, while Sloane sat on the couch next to me.

"I wonder how Bianca died?" she said.

"I don't know. That seems to be the big question. How did she die? Not *why* did she die? Bianca had a lot of enemies, both here, and back in Argentina. The motives for killing her could be many. She ran roughshod over so many people, including me, and Vincente. At one point, he even speculated that she was behind the death of his horses, but then rejected that theory. She resented the time, energy and money that he put into his stables, but not enough to destroy them. After all, it did give her time for her *extracurricular activities.* If she thought she was fooling anyone with her *loving wife* act, she blew it the night she threw her drink in Vincente's face."

Sloane nodded. "By the way, have you noticed the absence of one Enrico Alvero since that night?"

"Yes, I have, and I know why. Vincente told me that he discovered their affair, and he fired

Enrico. Bianca probably dumped him, for fear she'd lose her husband."

"His hot temper would make him a particularly dangerous jilted lover," said Sloane.

Crystal brought around a fresh tray of drinks. "There's no shortage of suspects. Take Ross Spencer, for instance. Bianca's plan for the Equine Wellness Center was in direct conflict with his plans for an indoor riding stadium. According to Robert he was willing to go to great lengths to get that land away from the Villas."

"Hmm, you've got a good point Crystal. No Bianca, no Equine Wellness Center. Spencer would still have the opportunity to secure that land with his plan, and another, more willing partner than Robert. Ross Spencer is not a man to give up easily."

By now, we could see the sun setting through the glass doors to the balcony. Time to get some food. I scanned the room service menu and ordered an extra-large tray of sushi that we could all share. After dinner, the girls wanted to watch a movie, Sloane had some work to catch up on, and Crystal headed for home. I dimmed the lights and sat in semi-darkness…thinking.

CHAPTER TWENTY-NINE

Early the next morning, Jaycee found me sitting on the balcony savoring a cup of French Roast coffee. "Hi honey, how did you sleep?"

"Not very well mom. I need to talk to you. I would have last night, but everyone was so freaked out about Mrs. Villa's murder, that it just didn't seem like the right time."

"What is it honey? What's wrong?" She handed me a scrap of yellowed newsprint. I unfolded it to see an old photo of myself back in London. My stomach turned as I read the headline.

"Oh Jaycee!"

She proceeded to tell me about her meeting with Lloyd yesterday morning. I was stunned. That bastard! I couldn't believe the ruthlessness of the man! Actually, yes, I could. Why would he leave Jaycee alone just because I told him to. He was hell bent on causing trouble, and insidious enough to use my child to achieve his ends.

"Is what he said true mom?"

"Yes Jaycee, some of it. The part about reopening the case is true, but there has been no move to extradite me."

"Mom, I can't believe all that stuff happened to you and you never told me. Did you tell Jayson?"

"No, I didn't tell Jayson. Honey, it all happened so long ago. Way before you children were even born. I just wanted to stop living in the past, and create a bright future for all of us. Can you blame me?"

Jaycee sighed. "No Mom. I don't blame you. I blame that terrible man. He says he's my grandfather!"

"He's not your grandfather. Adoption papers were filed, but in my heart, my *real* father is my *only* father. He's your grandfather, and he died in a race car accident when I was just a little girl."

"I remember you're telling us that story, but you said that your mom got sick and died."

"She did. She was poisoned."

Tears welled up in Jaycee's eyes. She put her hand on mine. "How terrible for you Mom. What's going to happen now?"

"I'm not sure, honey, but there was a suicide note brought into evidence back then. They couldn't prove whether it was authentic, so they had to let me go. They didn't have sufficient evidence to hold me."

"What about Lloyd?"

"Lloyd was supposedly out of town on a work assignment when mother died."

"What do you mean *supposedly?*"

"He said that he was at the Newmarket Sales, covering a story. There would have been enough time for him to go back to London, commit the crime, and then go back to Newmarket at the end of the day. The sales were packed that year, and people moved around. Several of his colleagues said that they saw him there, but that doesn't mean he was there the entire time."

"Mom, do you believe that your mother could have committed suicide?"

"No Jaycee, I don't."

"Do you think that Lloyd killed her?"

"I hated to think that, but after everything we've been through, I wouldn't put it past him. It seemed, at the time, that he was doing everything in his power to pin the blame on me. After I was released, and the investigation ended, I just wanted to come back here and put it all behind me. My mother was dead, and nothing was going to bring her back."

"I understand Mom, but now that the case has been reopened, it looks like Lloyd is going to throw suspicion on you again."

"As far as I can tell, it's still a stalemate. The suicide note disappeared, and unless the police find it, I doubt that there's any new evidence."

"Then why is Scotland Yard reopening the case?"

"I'm not sure, but I do know that there is a new officer in charge of cold cases, and she is very focused on solving as many of them as possible."

"Mom, what should I do about Lloyd?"

"Nothing. Stay away from him. If he contacts you again, tell me right away.

Jaycee nodded. She slid her hand into the pocket of her robe and ran her fingers over the 50p coin that Lloyd had dropped in the stable.

I stepped out of the shower, and into a cocoa brown Ralph Lauren linen sheath. I wasn't in the mood for festive tropical colors. I was searching for my tan espadrilles, when my cell phone rang and I saw Vincent's name on the caller ID.

"Oh my God...Vincente!"

"I know. Listen, I need to talk to you, but we can't be seen together," he said.

"Of course."

"Meet me at the far corner of the parking lot at Publix in 15 minutes. I'll be driving my BMW."

"Okay."

I hung up the phone, grabbed my straw tote, and left a note for Sloane and the girls telling them that I had to go out, but I'd be in touch. I had the valet bring the Range Rover around and headed for Publix. As I pulled into the parking lot, I spotted Vincent's white BMW at the back of the lot. I pulled in next to him, and he hopped out of his car and into mine. He looked haggard, and in need of a shave.

"Vincente, what's going on?"

"I just left police headquarters. They questioned me all night. They think I had something to do with Bianca's death."

"Did you call your lawyer?"

"No. I have nothing to hide. I was afraid that if I 'lawyered up' at this point they would think I did."

"Did Bianca have heart trouble? Any health issues that could have caused her death?"

"Not that I know of. They don't even know for sure that it wasn't natural causes...heart attack, stroke? You know? For now, they're calling it *suspicious."*

I scanned the parking lot to be sure we weren't being watched. "Tell me everything that happened."

"I was at the house getting ready to meet you at the stable, when I went to Bianca's room to confront her."

"Confront her about what?"

"I knew that she was snooping around for something in my room. I figured that the *something* was the missing suicide note."

"Why would she do that?"

"It would give her power over you, over Lloyd Snow, and over me."

"Oh! That makes sense. It would explain what Lloyd said to Jaycee."

"What do you mean?"

I told Vincente about Lloyd's conversation with Jaycee suggesting that I might be extradited to London and charged with my mother's murder.

Vincente's eyes narrowed. "How would he know anything about that?"

"He and Bianca must have been working together."

Vincente stared straight ahead through the windshield, trying to process what I'd just said. "Well, her plan would not have worked. The letter would not be found at Casa Verde."

"Vincente, what happened at the house?"

"I looked for Bianca in her room, but she wasn't there. I went to check the bathroom and found her lying on the floor. Seconds later Marisol was behind me screaming. I told her to call an ambulance, and I tried to resuscitate Bianca. It was no use. She was dead."

"Oh Vincente!"

"The ambulance arrived, followed by the police. They met with Marisol in the kitchen to get her statement. She apparently told them that she found me standing over Bianca's body, and since we were the only two people in the house, they took me downtown."

"What about Gerald, the butler?"

"He left right after the breakfast meeting. He had the rest of the day off."

"That's right, the breakfast meeting Bianca held for her committee. Let's see, there was Sloane, Crystal, Lena, and Dr. Julia Forrest" I said.

Oh no! Dr. Forrest! I'd nearly forgotten about her. I told Vincente about the shooting at the stable yesterday. I needed to get an update on Dr. Forrest's condition.

"Oh God, Ivy. A shooting at my stable, on top of everything else."

"Vincente, when will we know how Bianca died?"

"Soon. They're doing an autopsy this morning."

Lloyd handed the keys to his Jaguar to the valet and sauntered through the doors of the Brazilian. He was smiling to himself. He felt good...good for the first time in a long time. He took the elevator up to his room, and slipped off his jacket, extracting an ecru linen envelope from the inside pocket. He deftly removed the single sheet of stationery…

To those I love,

CHAPTER THIRTY

John took a sip of acrid black coffee from a paper cup as he sat at the gate in Heathrow Airport. His flight was running on time, so they should be boarding any minute. He closed his eyes and let his mind wander over the events of the past few days. It was difficult seeing Fiona again. He bristled at the thought of how he'd hurt her so long ago. It was obvious that she'd never really gotten over it. Maybe that's the reason she never married. She was still bitter, which made it impossible to convince her to drop the Lacy Snow investigation. He only made things worse by getting involved.

He thought about Ivy. He hadn't heard from her in over a week. He really couldn't blame her after the way he behaved. Abruptly ending their last conversation after learning the truth about her and Vincente Villa. But who was he to judge her? After all, look at his own behavior. Taking up with Fiona Wescott while engaged to Angelique. She threatened to break their engagement when she found out, but he knew that a life with Fiona in London would never work out long term. He begged her to forgive him, and she did, but even though they went through with the wedding, nothing was ever the same between them.

John pulled out his iPad and hit the Google icon to check on the news. Oh no! Unbelievable! The headline announced the death of prominent Palm Beach socialite, Bianca Villa. Cause of death...yet undetermined. The article followed up with a photo of the beautiful Bianca, dripping in diamonds. There was a picture of her home, Casa Verde, and of her husband, Vincente Villa being escorted to a police car. John took a deep breath, headed for the reservation desk, and changed his ticket from Philadelphia to Fort Lauderdale.

I assured Vincente that I would do everything in my power to help him, although I had no idea what that might be. We would just have to wait for the results of the autopsy to know what we were dealing with. I told him that for now, he just needed to go home and get some rest. I had to go to the hospital to see how Julia Forrest was doing.

The sun was shining brightly, as usual, and the temperature was climbing steadily, so I cranked up the air conditioning to keep from wilting. I texted Sloane to let her know where I was and suggested that she and the girls call for a ride out to the stables and get some practice in before the heat became unbearable. It was unusually hot in Florida for this time of year. I set my GPS for the hospital and pulled out of the parking lot. I couldn't stop thinking about Bianca. Surely, she must have had a heart attack, or an aneurysm, or something! It was horrible to think that she might have been murdered...but who was I kidding? Bianca had a lot of enemies. If it was murder, the police would have no shortage of suspects, including Vincente...including *me*. But fortunately, I did have an alibi. I was with Julia Forrest at the Villa Stables calling for an ambulance when Bianca died. But wait, we don't yet know exactly when she died. If the time of death was much earlier in the day, my alibi wouldn't hold water. I've got to stop thinking like that. Right now, I need to be concerned about Dr. Forrest.

I stopped at registration and learned that Julia Forrest was in room 412. I took the elevator to the fourth floor and stopped at the nurse's station. A red headed nurse in a white uniform and colorful smock sporting palm trees told me that Dr. Forrest was still in and out of consciousness. However, she thought that a short visit...a v*ery* short visit would be okay. She pointed me in the direction of room 412. I walked down a long hallway, permeated with the odor of antiseptic and bleach. I opened the door as quietly as possible, in case Julia was asleep. But she wasn't. She was sitting up in her bed and gave me a peculiar look as I approached her.

"Hello Dr. Forrest. How are you feeling?" She just looked at me, brow furrowed. "You've been through quite a lot," I said.

"Who are you?"

"It's me. Ivy Snow."

Julia shook her head slowly from side to side. "I don't know you."

"What do you mean, you don't know me? I'm Ivy, Jaycee's mom."

"Jaycee?"

Oh no, I thought. She has amnesia! "Dr. Forrest, you know me. Please try to remember."

"I'm not Dr. Forrest," she said.

I felt sick to my stomach. The poor woman didn't know who she was.

"I don't know any Dr. Forrest. My name is Sharon Zelinsky. What are you doing in my room? Get out of here!"

I backed away from the hospital bed toward the door. I pulled it open, only to practically collide with a tall sandy haired man with huge biceps. "I... I'm sorry" I said, looking up into his pale blue eyes.

"No problem. Is this Dr. Forrest's room?"

"Yes…"

"I'm Detective Anderson."

"I'm Ivy Snow. I called the ambulance that brought Dr. Forrest here."

"You were at the scene of the shooting?"

"Well, yes, and no. I was at the stable, in the tack room. Dr. Forrest, and the woman who shot her were in the next room, with the door closed."

"She was with another woman?"

"Yes, I heard them arguing, and then gunshots. I rushed through the door to find Dr. Forrest on the floor. She was wounded."

"Did you see the other woman?"

"No. She vanished out the back door."

"Do you have any idea who she was?"

"No. I didn't see her at all."

"How is Dr. Forrest?" he asked.

"Not well, I'm afraid. I think she has amnesia or something. She didn't know me. We see each other almost daily at the showgrounds. My daughter is showing her horse at the festival, and Dr. Forrest is our vet, yet she says that she doesn't know who I am."

Detective Anderson rubbed his hand over his smooth-shaven chin. "Humm, maybe it's not so unusual. She's been through a lot of trauma. I'll have to check with her physician team about the extent of her injuries. She may have suffered a concussion when she fell to the floor."

"Yes, that would explain it, I suppose, but the strange thing is that she thinks she's someone else."

"What do you mean?"

"Isn't it true that most amnesia patients don't remember who they are?"

"I guess. I don't have much experience with amnesia" he said.

"Neither do I. Maybe you could mention it when you talk to her doctors."

"I will. I'll get a comprehensive report. Does Dr. Forrest have any family nearby?"

"Not that I know of."

"We're checking out her home in Delray, and the vet clinic where she works. Ms. Snow, is there anything you can tell me about the woman in the room with Dr. Forrest? Maybe an unusual sounding voice...accent...anything?"

"No, I'm afraid not. Wait! I did hear Dr. Forrest call her *Sharon.* I don't know anyone named Sharon."

Anderson jotted some notes on a small pad.

"So, you have nothing to go on? No one saw a woman leaving Villa Stables at that time?"

"No. Whoever she is, she's gone," he said.

We exchanged cards. "Detective, please let me know what you find out."

"Alright. If you do think of anything else that might help us, call me."

I climbed into the Range Rover and started for the showgrounds to help Sloane coach the girls. It was the only useful thing that I could think of to do."

Ross Spencer ran his tongue over his lips, savoring the last salty grains from the rim of his Margarita glass. He couldn't believe his good fortune. The news of Bianca's death blew through the mansions, clubs, and watering holes of Palm Beach like a Mistral. It was the topic du jour on every wagging tongue. How did she die? Was she murdered? Who did it? Was it the husband, Vincente Villa? Wasn't it always the husband?

Ross enjoyed the buzzing of those busy bees. No matter what the outcome, the Villa name would never be the same in Palm Beach. A shadow had been cast...and he could work that to his advantage. True, the land was not yet available to him, but with Bianca dead, so was the dream of the Equine Wellness Center. And Villa himself? If he were to be found guilty of his wife's murder, it would mean life in prison, or better yet, the death penalty. There were no children to take over, the business would erode, and assets liquidated. Certain assets, perhaps liquidated to him. He smiled to himself.

"What's so funny Ross?"

He looked up to see Lena standing over the table. "Lena, I didn't expect to see you here."

"I've been looking for you all over town."

She sat down across from him and pulled her white pashmina over her shoulders. The air conditioning was blasting in the Leopard Lounge. The waiter came over, and she ordered a Cosmopolitan. Ross did a double take. It was a step up from her usual Pink Lady. Maybe she was learning something after all.

"I guess you heard about Bianca Villa," she said.

"Yeah. I heard."

"Kind of convenient for you."

Ross looked at her, his eyes narrowed. "What do you mean by that?"

"Oh, come on, you know, now that she's dead, she won't be building the Equine Wellness Center. You're one step closer to Palais Palm Beach."

"That may very well be, but there's still Vincente. Now that she's dead, he'll have complete control."

"I've heard talk that he might be charged with her murder," said Lena.

"Talk? Where did you hear that?"

"I don't remember, just around."

Even Lena's tapped into the local grapevine, he thought. "Just keep your ears open, baby."

Maybe Lena could still be of use to him, even

though there would no longer be a committee. She's getting her information somewhere. Who knows? Salons, spas, wherever these women go.

"Of course, Ross. We're a team, right?"

"Right, baby."

The waiter arrived with Lena's Cosmo. She picked up the graceful, stemmed cocktail glass with her perfectly manicured hands, painted Jungle Red. Ross noticed a Cameo ring that he'd never seen before.

"Lena, a new ring?"

"Oh Ross, I forgot I was even wearing this." She removed it and dropped it into her clutch. "I know how jealous you get when you think of me with another man. It was a long time ago. I never think of him anymore. This ring just matches my dress so well...that's all."

Ross decided to let it go.

Enrico Alvero stood on the balcony of his high-rise apartment overlooking Lake Worth. He stared at the sunlight as it danced over the gentle lapping waves. Bianca was dead. He thought back to the many hours of passionate lovemaking they'd shared right here. It was hard to believe that she would turn on him in the end. After all their hopes and dreams of creating a world class polo team of their own. How she could abandon him was unfathomable, especially since she knew his secret. He was no longer legal in the United States, and she was the only one he'd ever told. He trusted her. That was his mistake. She held that secret over his head like the blade of the guillotine. She'd made subtle threats to expose him, but to his knowledge, she took his secret to her grave.

CHAPTER THIRTY-ONE

Our buzzer rang. I opened the door to find Crystal with an armful of coffees and pastries from Starbucks.

"Oh, yum, you read my mind."

She set everything out in the kitchenette, tempting Sloane and the girls out of their rooms with the fresh aroma of Breakfast Blend.

"You're up bright and early, Crystal."

"I figured I may as well get up and out. I hardly slept a wink last night with Robert's snoring."

Sloane took the lid off her cup, and gingerly sipped the steaming liquid. "Maybe he's got sleep apnea. Has he ever been tested?"

"No. He refuses. He doesn't want to accept the fact that he snores like a buzzsaw. I think he's afraid that he'll have to wear one of those CPAPs. I know they're not very comfortable, and they're ugly as sin, but hell, at least there would be some peace at night."

I nabbed the Bear Claw (my favorite) before anyone else could get their hands on it. "Into each life a little rain must fall." Crystal stuck out her tongue. "But seriously, he should get checked. Sleep apnea can have some pretty serious health consequences."

"I know, I'm working on it," she said.

The girls got their coffees and pastries and went out onto the balcony to enjoy breakfast in the sun.

"Has there been any news on the autopsy?" Crystal asked.

I shook my head. "No. Not that I've heard."

Sloane picked up the remote and turned on the morning news. There were several stories on robberies, auto accidents, and storms brewing off the coast, but no mention of Bianca Villa.

I paced across the floor. "I'm on my last nerve. I can't imagine how Vincent must feel. It's like his whole life hangs in the balance."

Crystal shot a sideways glance at Sloane. "Ivy, are you feeling like your whole life is in the balance too?"

"What do you mean?"

"Have you heard from John lately?"

"No. If he wants to talk to me, he has my number. I don't want to call him."

"Do you think that's wise? After all, you are adults. You can't let this stalemate of silence go on forever. What would Dr. Frick say?"

I thought back to my many sessions with my shrink, the formattable Dr. Frick. The wise old owl, who always had a way of helping me sort out my feelings. I could use a session with Dr. Frick right now. "I'm not sure what he'd say, except that this is a fine kettle I've gotten myself into now." We couldn't help but smile at that.

I heard my cell's ringtone and reached into the pocket of my robe to answer. It was Vincente.

"Good morning. How are you?"

"Not so well, I'm afraid."

"What is it?"

"I heard from the police. The autopsy results are in. Bianca was poisoned."

"Oh no! No Vincente."

"The police want to talk to me as soon as possible. They're sending a car."

I glanced up at Sloane and Crystal, their faces frozen in anticipation. I shook my head back and forth. They both looked down at the floor.

"What can I do to help?"

"Nothing. I'll be in touch when I know more. Please don't worry, Ivy."

He hung up. Don't worry! How can I not worry? This is a nightmare.

"What happened?" Sloane asked.

"Bianca's autopsy...poison."
"Good Lord," said Crystal. "What happens now?"
"The police are taking Vincente to the station for more questioning. That's all I know."
"They always look at the husband first, and most of the time, they're right."
"Well, not this time. There's no way Vincente would do such a thing."
"Okay Ivy, I'm sure you're right, but *someone* poisoned Bianca," said Sloane.
"I know, and I've got to find out who."

I needed more information. Type of poison, time of death, the crime scene...information that the police would have. But how will I get it? I don't have any contacts down here. Wait! What about Detective Anderson, the guy I met at the hospital yesterday? He gave me his card. I grabbed my straw tote, and started rummaging through it, looking for the card. Ah! Yes, here it is. I pulled out my cell and punched in his number. He answered on the third ring.
"Hello. Anderson here."
"Hello Detective Anderson. It's Ivy Snow."
A momentary silence. "Oh yes, Ms. Snow, we met yesterday."

“Yes, at the hospital. Is there any news about Dr. Forrest?”

“I haven’t been back to see her, but I’ll check with the hospital later. We’re conducting a search of her residence. It's a trailer in Delray Beach. You wouldn’t happen to know if she had a roommate? It appears that two women are living there.”

“I really don't know anything about her home life. Detective, I was calling about another matter.”

“What is it?”

“It’s about the Bianca Villa murder.”

“What about it?”

“I heard this morning that the autopsy shows that she was poisoned.”

“How did you hear that?”

“Her husband told me,” I said.

“Her husband? You know Mr. Villa?”

“Yes. We go back a long way. I know that he didn’t kill her, Detective Anderson.”

“How do you know that?”

“I just do. He couldn’t! Can you tell me about the poison?”

“I guess so. We’re about to release it to the news media anyway. Bianca Villa died of Belladonna poisoning. It comes from a plant called *Nightshade*. Not used too often, but very lethal. Whoever killed her, knows their poisons" Anderson said.

I nearly dropped my phone! *Belladonna* …the poison that killed my mother! I caught my breath, unable to form any words. What were the chances?

"Ms. Snow? Ms. Snow, are you there?"

"Yes…yes." I had to pull myself together. "Has the time of death been established?"

"The corner estimates between 9:30 and 10:30 am," Anderson said.

"Thank you, Detective. I'll be in touch if I can think of anything regarding Dr. Forrest."

"Ms. Snow, I'd be careful if I were you. Messing around with murder. Things aren't always what they look."

If he only knew! I hung up the phone. "Okay, here's what we've got… Belladonna poisoning. I just can't believe it! It's the same poison that killed my mother!

"You're kidding?" said Crystal. "Coincidence? When was the time of death?""

"Between 9:30 and 10:30 am."

"That would be right after the committee meeting," said Sloane.

Crystal nodded. “Yes” I think we adjourned around 9:00 or 9:15, didn’t we? I know that we were out of there before 9:30. I checked the time on the way to my hair appointment, hoping I wouldn’t be late. So, if we all left before 9:30, the only occupants of the house would be Vincente, Marisol the maid, the butler, and Bianca herself.”

“You know, we’ve all been giving that maid, Marisol, a pass. What do we know about her? Where is she from? What’s her background? How long has she been working for Bianca? Maybe there’s more there than meets the eye” I said.

“I’m sure the police are doing a thorough background check on her,” said Crystal.

I nodded. “Of course, they are, but that doesn't mean that there are things about her past, and present that they might not uncover.”

“Ivy, why don't I look into that?” said Sloane. “With my connections there’s not much that I can’t find out about anyone.”

“Right. And, what about the butler, we don't know anything about him either.”

Crystal rolled her eyes. “Oh Ivy, *the butler did it*...come on!”

"You know, if you're a butler, you can probably get away with murder. That cliche is the perfect cover!"

"Touché."

"One of our biggest obstacles now is that we don't have access to the crime scene. We might be able to learn a lot in the room where Bianca died. I wonder how the poison was administered? Did she ingest it, like my mother? Or was it injected into her bloodstream? We need to know more about Belladonna poisoning."

"Why don't you let us help with that?" said Jaycee, as she and Trina came in from the balcony.

"Perfect. You girls can do some research," I smiled.

Robert lit the tip of his Montecristo No. 2, taking in the ocean view from their terrace. It was amazing what these landscape architects could do with a high-rise rooftop now. He could swear that he was in a Japanese garden. Bamboo grew tall to frame the folding glass doors. Bonsai lined the path of smooth round ivory stones that meandered throughout the space. Wicker chairs and couches covered in luxurious pure white cushions were positioned to optimize viewing the stunning vista. Teak tables shaded by sapphire umbrellas paid homage to the sky above, and the sea below. He smiled to himself. His life had been transformed since meeting and marrying Crystal. She was the breath of fresh air he needed to revive his life, in these, his later years. Why not go along with her idea to open a real estate office down here? It was a career she loved. She was always so willing to indulge his passions. It was time he did what he could to make her dreams come true. She was too young to settle for a life of social obligations, charity events, and afternoon bridge games. She's a vibrant woman who thrives on making things happen. Isn't that what attracted him to her in the first place. Although he had some ideas of his own, he would put them on the back burner to help Crystal get started.

Things were very different here than they were up north. He thought about the discussions he'd had with Ross Spencer about building Palais Palm Beach. It really was a very good idea. It would be extremely profitable, and a valuable addition to the equestrian industry here, but Spencer's way of going about things was all wrong. Yes, the land owned by the Villa would be the perfect spot for the arena, near the existing festival grounds, and polo fields. But surely there were other options? Spencer seemed almost obsessed with getting his hands on that land.

Robert wheeled over to the bar cart and fixed himself a Bloody Mary. He positioned his chair under one of the umbrellas to capture shade from the increasingly intense morning sun. He thought back to his last meeting with Ross Spencer. It was at IL Bellagio; the night Crystal had her first meeting with Bianca's committee. The night that ended with Bianca throwing her drink in Vincent's face. It was clear that Spencer relished that scene. He saw cracks in the veneer of the Villa marriage, which to him translated to an opportunity to get his hands on that land. A messy divorce, split assets, resource consolidation. The fallout could be monumental.

Robert observed Ross and Lena very carefully that evening. Her eagerness to infiltrate Bianca's inner circle, and his obvious reluctance...at first. And then a change of heart? Ross Spencer was the type to ferret out any opportunity that would further his interests. So Lena finally did get an invitation to attend the committee meeting at Casa Verde that fateful morning. An intriguing turn of events for Ross Spencer.

CHAPTER THIRTY-TWO

It didn't take long for the news media to jump on the story of the shooting at Villa Stables. It served to add fuel to the flame created by Bianca's murder. Detective Anderson was put in charge of investigating both crimes, which was a positive development for me, since I was intertwined in both. In the possible chance that they were somehow related, it made it easier for me to stay in the loop. Vincente hired a shark of a defense lawyer, who promptly escorted him out of police custody. No charges...no questions...no answers.

Unfortunately, Casa Verde was still a crime scene under investigation, so Vincente opted to take a suite at the Chesterfield Hotel. The media circus was speculating that Vincente was responsible for both crimes, but somehow hard pressed to tie the two together. The idea that Vincente poisoned his wife, and then shot his vet ...whom he believed *may* have poisoned his horses...it just didn't gel. True, poison played a part in both scenarios, Belladonna for Bianca, and Black Walnut for the horses, but the timeline didn't work. Vincente couldn't be in two places at once. The police had not released any additional information about the Forrest shooting, so my account of hearing women arguing was not revealed. If it was, and the press gets wind of my association with Vincente...well, I hate to think how that might look.

I heard the door to our suite open and close, and I assumed correctly that it was Jaycee and Trina coming up from the pool.

"Hey Mom!"

"Hi girls. I didn't expect to see you back so soon."

"We thought we'd come up and eat lunch here with you," Jaycee said.

I suspected that they'd seen the scrumptious salmon salads that Sloane brought home from Publix yesterday and didn't want to miss out.

"That's very nice of you."

"Not only that, but we've also got a lot of great info on Belladonna. That Bianca lady died a pretty sick death."

I thought of my poor mother. Her life cut short…the pain…the betrayal. I had to stay calm and focused, when all I really wanted to do was cry.

"Bianca had to have had the lethal dose sometime that morning. Thanks for your hard work on this girls, I really appreciate it."

"No problem, Mom. Is there anything else we can do?"

"No, not right now. Oh wait...if you could both think back to anything you might have seen or heard concerning Dr. Forrest, it could be important. No matter how small a thought."

"Sure Mom."

The girls retreated to the kitchen in search of the salmon salads. I heard the house phone ring, and I answered it to learn that we had a visitor. Detective John Garrett! John? What on earth was he doing here? I was so startled; I could hardly speak. I took a deep breath and tried to gather my wits.

"Send him up please."

I opened the door to see John standing there with a sheepish look on his face.

"Hello Ivy."

"Hello John. I must say, I'm surprised to see you. What are you doing here?"

"I have to talk to you, and it can't be over the phone."

"We're not alone here John. The girls are in the kitchen."

"Why don't we go down to the restaurant. I'll buy you lunch" he smiled.

"Okay. Give me a minute." I went to the kitchen and told the girls that I had to go out for a while. They looked at me with question marks in their eyes. I didn't want to explain. I just turned and joined John at the elevator door.

We nabbed a table at The Beach Club. The waiter was prompt, and John ordered a bottle of Esprit Gassier. He knew I loved a rose in the warm weather.

"So to what do I owe the honor?"

"Listen Ivy, I don't blame you for being angry."

"I'm not angry. As a matter of fact, I thought you were angry with me."

"I was. At first. Then, I thought that you must have a good reason for not being upfront with me about Vincente Villa."

"I'm as confused about that as you are. Everything that has happened since we came down here has been insane. You don't know the half of it."

"Ah...I think maybe I do know *the half of it*, and maybe more," John said.

"What do you mean?"

"I've been on top of this all along. As a matter of fact, I just got back from London."

"London? You're kidding me?"

"You asked me about my contact at Scotland Yard. I went to see Fiona Wescott."

"Yes. I was hoping that you could find out what was going on with my mother's case, but I never thought you'd go all the way to London to find out!"

"Ivy, I had a good reason for going over there. It's complicated."

"Please uncomplicate it for me, John."

"Fiona Wescott and I had an affair."

"What?!"

The waiter arrived with the wine. I hadn't even glanced at the menu. John pointed to the Salad Niçoise, and I shook my head in agreement.

"It was a long time ago, when I was with the NYPD. I was sent to Scotland Yard to do a training seminar for their rookies. That's when I met Fiona."

"I see. So, you went back to rekindle an old flame?"

"No. Not at all. I just thought that If I saw Fiona and met with her in person, I might be able to persuade her to drop the idea of reopening your mother's case."

"And how did that go?"

"Not very well. As a matter of fact, the whole thing backfired. It seems that time didn't heal all wounds. At least not in Fiona's case. She's held a grudge all these years about how things ended with us. Emotionally, she's never moved on."

"Why? What happened, John?"

'When I went over there, I was already engaged to Angelique. Fiona found out when Angelique called my hotel room. I was in the shower, so Fiona answered the phone."

"Oh wow! Well, you can't blame her for being upset."

"No. I should have been honest with her from the beginning. I should never have gotten involved with her at all."

"What about Angelique? I guess she forgave you."

"Yes. She said she forgave me, but she certainly never forgot. We should never have gotten married."

"I'm sorry John."

"Me too. And now it looks like I did more harm than good by going over there. Fiona is digging her heels in. She's more determined than ever to solve the case, and I hate to say it, but it looks like you are her number one suspect. To make matters worse, I told her about our relationship."

"Ah, that probably wasn't the best idea under the circumstances," I said.

"I can see that now, but at the time I was determined not to deceive Fiona in any way, even unintentionally."

"On second thought, it was probably the right thing to do. If she proceeds with reopening the case, chances are she would find out about us, and it would damage your credibility even more."

"Not to mention igniting a flame to see you behind bars."

"I was afraid of that. Lloyd told Jaycee that I might be extradited. At first, I thought he was saying that just to scare her. But now…"

The waiter arrived with our lunch.

"Speaking of Lloyd, has he been badgering you?"

"Not lately. He rattled Jaycee, but he's been low profile since then."

John shook his head. "I don't like that. I'd rather that he was in plain sight where we could keep track of him."

"I know. He's probably out there digging up, or making up, something he can do to implicate me. The fact that he contacted Jaycee…"

"I know. Listen Ivy, I was pretty upset when I found out that you weren't completely upfront with me about Vincente Villa, but I realize that you were in a tough spot."

"That's no excuse. I should have told you everything, but I have to admit that my head was spinning. First Lloyd showing up, and then Vincente, and that vile Bianca. We came down here to show horses, and now all this."

"Ivy, I must know. Have you been seeing Vincente?"

I took a deep breath. "Yes John. But we've only been talking. Nothing more."

"Do you know what you want?"

"Don't ask me that right now. I have too much on my plate. The fact that I came here in the first place created a mare's nest. I've got to protect myself against Lloyd, and his mission to get me convicted of killing my mother. I've also got to protect Jaycee from him, and now I'm mixed up as a 'witness' in Dr. Forrest's shooting."

John lowered his eyes. "I see."

"Bianca's murder, the horses being poisoned, Dr. Forrest's shooting, they all seem to be tied together...tied to Vincente. He's the one that helped me when I was the prime suspect in my mother's death. He got Bianca to write that suicide note, and the price he paid was enormous. A life of hell married to her, all to buy my freedom. I can't abandon him now."

"Of course not. I want to help, but I need time to think. I'm booking a room at the Chesterfield Hotel."

CHAPTER THIRTY-THREE

Lloyd Snow once more removed the smooth vellum sheet from its envelope. The sheet that bestowed upon him the power to control the outcome of the Lacy Snow murder investigation...well, almost. There was still the matter of influencing Inspector Fiona Wescott. He re-read the words that "Lacy" wrote so many years ago and vowed that this time things would jolly well turn out differently.

It had been much easier to obtain this document than he originally thought it would be. The fact that a palatial house such as Casa Verde didn't have a security patrol, or even guard dogs, was daft. He'd waltzed right in like he owned the place. That ridiculous maid was scurrying about like a peahen, preparing pastries for *Her Majesty's* committee meeting. The butler was snoozing in the foyer, waiting for the demanding task of answering the doorbell when it rang. A right comedy, it was.

Having practically free run of the place, there was no difficulty in obtaining entrance to Bianca's boudoir. There he would wait until he could have a little "meeting" of his own with

Bianca Villa. It wasn't long before those silly women departed, and Bianca made her way up the marble staircase to her rooms. He hid in the closet and watched from behind the door as Bianca went to her dressing room. He could see her rummaging through things, and then she removed the Chagall from the wall, revealing the door to a safe. She turned the dial. He wished that he could see the numbers as she moved it one way, and then another. She removed a manila envelope and took it into her sitting room. He heard something. Marisol, the maid, entered the room carrying a large silver coffee service. A gold, foil wrapped box sat on the tray. He recognized the packaging. Godiva Chocolates. She entered the dressing room in search of Bianca. He heard voices, but he couldn't make out what they were saying. A few minutes passed. It was like an eternity. Finally, the maid came out of the dressing room, and left the suite. A few more minutes passed, and Bianca came out, and went into the bath.

Lloyd saw his chance. He quietly slipped into the sitting room where the coffee service and box of chocolates sat on a cocktail table. He glanced around and saw the manila envelope that Bianca removed from the wall safe. It was sitting on a chinoiserie table under the bay window. He quickly opened it to reveal the contents, a satisfied smile crossing his face.

I was pulling into the parking lot at the festival grounds when my cell phone rang. It was Detective Anderson.

“Sorry to bother you, Ms. Snow, but we have a rather serious problem at the hospital, concerning Dr. Forrest.”

“Oh! What kind of problem? Is she having a relapse?”

“No. No, her wound is healing quite nicely. It's another matter. I’m calling to ask you to meet me at the hospital this afternoon. Maybe you can help.”

“I don't understand Detective. What’s this all about?”

“I don't want to discuss it over the phone. Can you be here by two?”

I looked at my watch. I had to coach Trina in some practice rounds and help Jaycee with

Pirate's mane. If I ate lunch on the run, I could be there by two. "Alright Detective, I'll meet you there."

I walked over to the practice ring where Trina was warming up. Dynamo's rich bay coat gleamed in the morning sun. I waved as she passed by on the rail. Trina was a beautiful rider. She and Dynamo defined elegance and grace as they sailed over each jump in the arena. Jaycee and Pirate painted a more vigorous picture, charging each challenge with gusto. Different styles, but successful in their own way.

Trina stopped Dynamo at the gate, and I gave her instructions for improving her next rounds. We worked throughout the morning, as the sun got increasingly hotter. Sloane was schooling Jaycee and Pirate in the ring on the other side of the stables, so I texted her and suggested that we meet back at the stalls. She agreed, so the girls walked their horses back to give them a chance to cool off before hitting the wash rack. I brought a refill of ShowSheen with me, so that we could give a little extra attention to grooming manes and tails today. I began spraying, and Jaycee reached for the wide toothed comb that worked best on Pirate.

"Mom, you know when you asked me to think about Dr. Forrest...about anything strange, or any details that might have to do with the shooting?"

"Yes, is there something?"

"Yeah, I was thinking about it, and I remembered that morning when Dr. Forrest came out here and was acting weird."

"What do you mean *weird?"*

"She came out here for no apparent reason. She didn't look in on any of the horses, and she hardly spoke to me, like she didn't even know who I was. She just walked straight through the barn and out the other end. I followed and saw her heading toward the polo grounds. She dropped a piece of paper, and I ran to pick it up. It was a receipt from a cab driver. I called after her, but she just kept walking, like she didn't even hear me. Then, you came to pick me up. I showed the receipt to you. Don't you remember?"

I thought back. I did remember the incident. Jaycee looked up at me over Pirates' haunches. "I didn't see Dr. Forrest's truck in the parking lot. But I thought I saw it later the road, heading in the opposite direction," Jaycee said.

"Yes, I do remember something like that. What do you make of it?"

Jaycee stared into space, concentrating hard. Maybe she was having one of her psychic visions. I kept silent.

Jaycee whispered, "It wasn't really Dr. Forrest."

I caught my breath.

"It was, but it wasn't. She was different. Her hair was different, long and scraggly. Her clothes were different, baggy and frayed. She walks differently...heavy steps. She *smelled different.*"

At that, Jaycee blinked. The vision was over. The trance was broken. Moist beads of perspiration covered her delicate skin.

"Jaycee, honey, are you okay?"

"Yeah Mom."

"You saw something."

"I saw a woman that I thought was Dr. Forrest. It was her, I know it!" But it was like her ghost or something."

I could see that Jaycee was very confused about the vision. I didn't want to push her. "I think we should just tuck this away. Let's see what happens. Detective Anderson asked me to meet him at the hospital this afternoon. Something to do with Dr. Forrest."

"Can I come with you?"

"I don't know if that's such a good idea."

"I need answers Mom. I need to figure this out."

The plea in her voice got me to agree. Sloane and Trina decided to head for Robert and Crystal's box for lunch. Jaycee and I opted for the drive-thru at McDonalds on our way to the hospital. We parked the Range Rover and went through the front entrance. Detective Anderson was waiting for us in the lobby. He was wearing a navy blazer and khaki pants. Kind of preppy for a cop. He looked at Jaycee and me in our riding clothes.

"Hello Detective. This is my daughter, Jaycee."

"Thank you for coming, Ms. Snow."

"Could you please tell us what this is all about?"

The patient in room 412... the one you registered as Dr. Julia Forrest, insists that she is not Dr. Julia Forrest."

"What? She most certainly is. She's been our vet for the entire time we've been here in Florida. I know Dr. Forrest when I see her, Detective."

"I'm not doubting that you believe that Ms. Snow, but the woman insists that she's Sharon Zelinsky, and that she's never heard of Dr. Julia Forrest."

“That’s absurd. She must have amnesia.”
“The doctors don't think so.”
“Well then how do you explain it?”
“I don't, but the fact is that she had no ID on her, and the trailer she lives in... it's as though it's been wiped clean of any personal effects. Like a motel room.”
“Let’s go see her now. Jaycee will tell you.”

We stepped into the elevator, and Detective Anderson pushed the button for the fourth floor. When the door opened, the floor nurse on duty grabbed Detective Anderson’s sleeve.
“I was just about to call you. The patient in 412...she’s disappeared!”

CHAPTER THIRTY-FOUR

The coroner's office refused to release Bianca's body for burial. Her will stated that she wanted to be cremated, since she couldn't stand the idea of maggots eating her flesh after she was put in the ground. She was convinced that it happened that way. Cremation was definitely out of the question until the circumstances of her death were determined. Suicide wasn't being considered. Belladonna poisoning was a horrible death that someone like Bianca would not subject herself to. Besides, there was no note, and that too was out of character, since Bianca wouldn't miss the opportunity to lay the blame on someone else for her death, sending them on an eternal guilt trip.

No, they were looking at murder, and they were looking at more than just the obvious candidate, husband Vincente Villa. The cops already questioned him, twice. And Marisol, the maid. Those interviews brought up the names of other possible perps, especially one Enrico Alvero. It was his turn.

Mr. Alvero was seated at the table in the white box of the interview room with the two-way mirror. He was dressed in dark jeans, and a white T-shirt with the Ariat logo. He was joined by Detective Anderson in his requisite navy and khaki, and Sargent Drew Jackson, a strapping African American cop in uniform.

"Mr. Alvero. Thank you for coming in. We have a few questions to ask you about the death of Bianca Villa," said Anderson.

Enrico swallowed hard. His leg was shaking involuntarily under the table. He was afraid that they would try to pin Bianca's murder on him. At the very least, he was afraid that they would find out that his work visa had expired and send him back to Argentina.

"Mr. Alvero, we understand that you were acquainted with Mrs. Bianca Villa, is that correct?" asked Anderson.

"Yes Sir." Enrico knew he must answer in as few words as possible. Giving too many details could backfire.

"How did you know her?"

"She was my boss's wife."

Anderson looked at Jackson conveying a look that said this interview was going to be like pulling teeth.

"Did you ever have occasion to be in the company of Mrs. Villa?"

Enrico’s eyes shifted. He cleared his throat.
“Yes, she sometimes came to Mr. Villa’s stables, where I work.”
“And did you have occasion to speak with her?”
“Yes. I said ‘hello.’ I was polite.”
“Were there ever any occasions where you and Mrs. Villa were alone?”
“I... I don't understand,” said Enrico.
“It’s a straightforward question. Were you and Mrs. Villa ever alone? Just the two of you, together?”
Enrico sat very still, staring at his hands. He did not know how he should answer this question. Of course, he and Bianca had been alone together, many times. They made love in his apartment, had clandestine dinners in little out of the way places. Took long drives along the ocean in his convertible Miata, her hair blowing in the wind. His mind wandered.
Anderson raised his voice. “Mr. Alvero! Will you please answer the question?”
“Yes, probably. Maybe in the tack room at the stables, or maybe in her husband’s office. She sometimes waited for him there, while I checked the invoices. I don't remember.” Enrico was speaking faster and louder than he wanted to.

He heard the panic in his voice with his own ears.
"Think harder Mr. Alvero. Do you recognize this man?" Anderson showed him a picture of the doorman at his high rise. The doorman was fairly new. He's only worked at Enrico's building part time for the last few months. Enrico didn't even remember his name, although they'd exchanged pleasantries.
"I recognize him. He's one of the doormen that works at my building" Enrico said. He knew where this was going, and it wasn't good.
"Would you be surprised to learn that this man has seen you with Bianca Villa?"
Enrico stuttered, "I... I don't know?"

Anderson placed the photo on the table directly under Enrico's face. He stared at it, and began to feel dizzy. Going back to Argentina didn't seem like such a bad idea now.
"Mr. Alvero, this man's name is Diego Perez, and yes, he is employed as a doorman at the building where you reside. We spoke with Mr. Perez and showed him photographs of both you and Bianca Villa. Mr. Perez is certain that he has seen you enter the building in the company of Bianca Villa on several occasions."

Enrico breathed a heavy sigh. "Okay, yes, it is true. Bianca and I had an affair. But it's *over.* It's been over for *quite a while."*

"How long is *quite a while?*" asked Anderson.

Enrico considered how to answer this question. He thought back, trying to remember when Bianca had last been to his place. If he could remember that, then there was no way that Perez could swear that he saw them recently.

"Mr. Alvero. Mr. Alvero! I'm waiting."

"Ah, yes. Halloween. It was late October."

"You're sure?"

"Yes, I remember because of the decorations."

"Decorations?"

"Yes. Halloween decorations. Ghosts and goblins...you know?"

Anderson rolled his eyes. That's how this guy marked the end of the affair. Halloween decorations!

"So, you're saying that Halloween was the last time you saw Bianca Villa?'

"No. I saw her at the polo matches, of course."

"Did you speak to her?"

"NO!"

"So, Mr. Alvero, are you saying that you've never spoken with Bianca Villa since Halloween?"

"Yes."
"You are positive, Mr. Alvero? You did not speak to Bianca Villa after October 31st?"
"Yes, that's right." A bead of sweat began to form on Enrico's forehead.
"What about phone calls? Were there any phone calls, Mr. Alvero?"
Enrico closed his eyes. *Shit!* He'd forgotten about the dozens of phone calls with Bianca. They'd talked as recently as last week. Of course, the police had Bianca's phone records. He was sunk.

The Chesterfield Hotel turned out to be much more luxurious than John Garrett realized. He was standing at the reception desk talking to the beautiful young brunette in charge. It seemed that the only accommodation to be had was a deluxe suite at a deluxe price. Pretty hefty for a policeman's salary, but John had his reasons for being there. He took his American Express card out of his wallet and slid it across the desk. The young woman, whose name tag said *Celeste*, asked how long he would be staying. He said that he wasn't quite sure, he didn't know how long his business transactions would take. The young woman, Celeste, assured him that accommodations would be available for as long as he needed. Or as long as it took to max out his card, he thought. The bellhop put John's luggage on the trolley and assured him that it would appear at his room momentarily.

John accepted the room card and started for the elevator. A tall dark man, exquisitely dressed in a lavender linen sports jacket passed him in the hallway. A gut feeling told John to turn around and follow him. The man walked into the lounge and took a seat at the bar. John approached the bar and sat two seats down. The man ordered a Gimlet. John ordered a gin and tonic. The man seemed oblivious to the fact that he wasn't the only patron. He stared down at the glass in front of him, deep in thought. It was Vincente Villa alright. He recognized him from his picture in the papers. John considered how to break the ice.

He finally decided that the direct approach would be best. He caught Vincente's eye and mouthed "hello." He moved down to the barstool next to Vincente and handed him his card, glad that they were the only two in the place. Lou, the bartender, caught the action out of the corner of his eye, but pretended he saw nothing as he continued to wipe cocktail glasses till they glistened. Vincente read the card and met John's eyes.

"Police Detective from Pennsylvania...hmm."

"Yes. John Garrett."

"What can I do for you?"

"It's not what you can do for me. More the opposite, or maybe *mutually* beneficial."

"I don't get it."

"It concerns Ivy Snow."

"Ivy? What about her? Oh, wait, I get it. John Garrett. John from Pennsylvania. You're her, how shall we say, *significant other?"*

"I hope that's still the case."

"Just to let you know Garrett, there's nothing going on between Ivy and me now, except a few cocktails and conversation."

"That's what she told me," John said.

"Don't get me wrong. It's not that I wouldn't want more, but the timing is just not right, if you know what I mean."

"Yeah. You're in some pretty hot water right now, aren't you Villa?"

"You could say that. I guess it makes things easier for you."

"I don't see it that way. I have some rather interesting choices to make, but my decisions depend a lot on you."

"Me? I don't understand."

"Well, you see, Ivy has it in her head that it's up to her to help you beat the rap for your wife's murder."

"I don't want Ivy getting involved in this mess," Vincente said.

"It's too late for that. She's already involved. The guy in charge of your wife's murder case is also in charge of investigating that vet's shooting over at your stables. Ivy was there at the time. She called the ambulance. She's considered a "witness."

"I still don't get it," Vincente said.

"You see, what Ivy doesn't know is that Anderson and I were once classmates. We were at the Police Academy together in upstate New York."

Vincente rubbed his chin. "So, what you are saying is that you have some inside track on these investigations?"

"What I'm saying is that I *could* have some influence on how these investigations are being played out. I know that old Anderson would be happy to have me *consult,* in an unofficial capacity, that is."

"So, cut to the chase Garrett. What are you trying to tell me?"

"I'm suggesting that we could help each other. Ivy is convinced that you're innocent of your wife's murder."

"I am."

"I don't know if you are, or not," said John.

Vincente breathed a heavy sigh.

"So, here's what I'm thinking. I could assist Ivy in pointing Anderson in a different direction in your case. But there's something that you need to do to help me as well."

"What's that?"

"Years ago, in the Lacy Snow murder case, you had Bianca write a fake suicide note to get Ivy off the hook. You even had to marry her in the bargain, but you did it anyway. Now, a cold case investigation is being stirred up at Scotland Yard by a cop named Fiona Wescott. That suicide note is missing, but I have a strange feeling that you know where it is, Villa."

Vincente locked his eyes on Garrett's.

"It would be helpful, no, *imperative*, for you to destroy that note so that it never surfaces in Wescott's investigation. Lloyd Snow's presence in Palm Beach tells me that he's trying to get his hands on that note. That can't happen. The DNA evidence would now prove it was a fake, and if that happens, Ivy is back on the hot seat. Without the note, Wescott's investigation will never get off the ground."

"I would be happy to make such a bargain, Garrett. There's only one problem. As of a week ago, that note went missing."

CHAPTER THIRTY-FIVE

Ross Spencer stood in his dressing room staring at a wall full of tropical hued hand tailored sports coats. He was trying to decide which one to wear for the imminent inquisition he was facing. He was incensed, and he had a right to be! The police must be crazy to think that he had anything to do with Bianca Villa's death. Sure, he hated the bitch, but he was just one in a long line. He desperately wanted her land for his Palais Palm Beach. It was foolhardy for him to let that be known in this tongue wagging town, but too late now. The cops are looking hard at that as a motive, and now he must make an appearance at police headquarters. The Hibiscus pink jacket would do nicely. There was something so innocent about the color pink.

He called down for his Tesla and headed for the police station. As he was pulling into the parking lot, he caught a glimpse of Enrico Alvero's red Miata leaving. Hum, so they've already interrogated Alvero. They must be questioning everyone who ever crossed paths with Bianca Villa. Who would they call in next?

Lena and the Bimbo Brigade? He chuckled to himself. No wonder everyone looked down on the cops...idiots!

Ross climbed the stairs to the interrogation room and was frisked. He took his seat behind the table and stared at the two-way mirror. Was there anyone left on earth that didn't know it was a *two-way* mirror? Detective Anderson entered the room, accompanied by Sargent Jackson, the "Uniform" that brought him here left. Ross looked at them with contempt.

"Good afternoon Mr. Spencer," Anderson said. Ross just nodded. The less breath he wasted, the better.

"You're here to answer questions about the murder of Bianca Villa."

"Yeah. That's what I was told, but I don't know anything about the murder of Bianca Villa."

"You did know Mrs. Villa though, did you not?"

"I knew her," said Ross.

"In what capacity Mr. Spencer?"

"I don't know. Like everyone else in Palm Beach. Bianca was a mover and shaker around here. You know, she was high society, the queen bee."

"That doesn't answer my question."

"Okay. I saw her at the polo matches, the Everglades Club, Mar a Lago, every charity event in town."

"Are you acquainted with her husband, Vincente Villa?"

"Yes. I know Vincente."

"You two do business together?"

"That was a long time ago."

"Word has it on the street that you're now competitors, rivals even," said Anderson.

"I don't care about what the word on the street is. I have no business dealing with the Villas."

"Isn't it true that you wanted to buy land owned by the Villas?"

Here it comes, thought Ross. "I speculate on property all the time."

"But there's one piece of property that you're particularly interested in. Isn't that true, Mr. Spencer?"

Ross said nothing.

"The piece of property positioned near your show jumping venue, and the polo fields."

"Sure, I'm interested. Everybody in Palm Beach County is interested in that land."

"But you, in particular, were hot to get your hands on it. Isn't that right Mr. Spencer?"

“I don't know what you’re talking about,” Ross said.

I’m talking about plans for an indoor arena. Palais Palm Beach.”

Spencer’s jaw dropped. How did this cop know about Palais Palm Beach? “I was looking at something like that.”

“More than looking. You had the blueprints drawn up. You were out shopping for investors, but you needed that particular piece of land to make your plans work. Bianca Villa was ruining that for you. Isn’t it true that at one time Vincente Villa was considering working with you to finance the deal?”

Ross remained silent.

“With Bianca Villa out of the way, Vincente Villa might reconsider. He might sell the land to you.”

“I don't think that’s probable,” Ross said.

“But if Villa is convicted of killing his wife, and gets the chair, the land might come up for grabs.”

“Might? May? Whatever? Listen Anderson, I did not kill Bianca Villa.” Ross’s patience was wearing thin.

“Where were you on the morning of her death?”

"I was at home in my penthouse on Ocean Drive."

"Can you prove that?"

"Yeah. My girlfriend, Lena, was there with me."

"She'll swear to that?"

"Sure."

She'll swear to anything I tell her to, he thought.

Crystal settled into the Daffodil yellow cushion on my chaise lounge. "So, he went all the way to London?"

I shook my head *yes.*

"And you had no idea?"

"Of course not. I simply suggested that if John had any contacts at Scotland Yard, it would be helpful to know if my mother's case had been reopened, or if it was just a possibility. I never dreamed that he would fly over there."

"He must really have it for you really bad."

"Ah, well there's more to the story than meets the eye!"

"What do you mean?"

I filled Crystal in on the whole Fiona Wescott fiasco. "So, you see, John may have had another reason for going to London besides my mother's case."

"To see Fiona again?"

"What do you think?"

"Oh Ivy, I don't know."

"Seriously, why would he spend all the time and money to go over there if not to see her? He could have accomplished the same thing with a few phone calls."

"I suppose, but…"

"And he's made matters worse. This Fiona knows that he wants her to cease reopening my mother's case. Now she knows about John and me and is probably more determined than ever to see me take the rap."

"That's kind of farfetched, don't you think? I mean what kind of cop would want to nail someone just because she's with her ex-boyfriend?"

"A woman cop, that's who! Fiona Wescott may be a police officer, but she's a woman first. Embers of jealousy burn long and hard. Revenge ignites a firestorm," I said.

Crystal starred at her Pina Colada. The sun was slowly setting into the infinity of the sea.

The sky was that spectacular sky-blue-pink color that promised a fabulous tomorrow.
"I don't know what to tell you Ivy. There are so many moving parts."
"I know, and I'm getting more nervous by the day about Lloyd."
"Why?"
"He hasn't surfaced in a while. I don't know what he's up to. I'm keeping a close eye on Jaycee. I don't want him around her."
"I don't blame you."

I stared at the foamy white waves lapping up on the shoreline, my thoughts drifting. I realized that I really know very little about Lloyd Snow before he married my mother. True, he worked for the BBC, but what about before that? Had he spent his entire career there? Where *exactly* in the UK was he born? London? I don't even know for a fact how old Lloyd is. Was he ever been married before? Did he have children? Of course, those are questions that he might not want me to have the answers to, but I wonder if even my mother knew all the details of his past life. I suppose she must have, but I think it's strange that Lloyd never talked about his past. It's about time we found out.

"Ivy? Hello in there!"

"Sorry Crystal. I've got Lloyd Snow on the brain. I called the Brazilian Hotel this morning, and he's still registered there. He's up to something...I know it!"

"So, what are you going to do?"

"I may suggest that Detective Anderson have a few words with him."

"Oh?"

"Yes. He knew Bianca. He's been in her company more than once. Maybe if Anderson shakes the tree, something will fall out."

"Genius!" said Crystal.

My cell phone rang. I saw on the caller ID that it was Sloane. I hit "answer."

"Ivy, thank God!"

"What's the matter?"

"It's Villa Stables. They're on fire!"

"Oh no! No!"

Crystal came rushing towards me. "What's wrong?"

Sloane was trying to catch her breath. "I was with the girls at the practice ring, and I saw billowing smoke coming from the direction of the polo fields. We got over here as fast as we could. The fire department is here, thank heaven, and they're putting it out. There's not much left to save."

"Is Vincente there?"
"No. Not yet. They're trying to reach him, but he's not answering his phone. You don't happen to know where he is, do you?"
"No, I don't."
"Listen Ivy, there's something else. On our way over here, I saw Julia Forrest's truck barreling down the highway going in the opposite direction."
"You don't think...?"
"I can't say for sure. I saw the truck, but not who was driving it."

Ever since Julia left the hospital she hasn't been seen or heard from. We don't even know if she's still alive. Those gunshot wounds are serious. At least she has medical training. Maybe she's nursing herself. If it wasn't her in the truck, who could it be? Poor Vincente. First his wife's murder, then his vet is shot in his tack room, and now his stables are burning down. It's just all too much! They say trouble comes in threes.

I hung up the phone and considered. Wait! Vincente is staying at The Chesterfield. Maybe he turned off his phone to take a nap. Or he could be at the pool swimming laps. Who knew? The only way to find out was to go over there. Sloane has the Range Rover… "Crystal, can you get George to take me over to The Chesterfield?"

"I drove myself," said Crystal.

"Well, what are we waiting for?"

Crystal called down for her Maybach, and they were off!

CHAPTER THIRTY-SIX

The air was thick with the stench of acrid smoke. Steam rose from the smoldering embers and ashes soaked with gallons of water, gratis the Wellington Volunteer Fire Department. The only positive was that there were no horses in the stable. They'd all died earlier from the Black Walnut poisoning. Tears filled Jaycee's eyes, and it wasn't from the smoke.

"How could this have happened?" she sobbed.

"I don't know honey," Sloane said.

Trina put her arm around Jaycee's shoulder. The fire department was finished with their work. Besides reports, there wasn't much more to be done. Sloane helped to fill in a few details about the stable and its owner, but Vincente Villa still wasn't answering his phone. She didn't mention anything about seeing Julia Forrest's truck. There would be an official investigation of the fire, and she could mention it then if deemed necessary. The person who really needed to know, besides Ivy and Vincente, was Detective Anderson. Ivy could tell him about it, but Anderson would still want to talk to her and the girls since they were the ones that saw Dr.

Forrest's truck. It was true. They did see Dr. Forrest's truck, which was unmistakable, but she hadn't actually seen who was driving. Did they?

"Girls, on our way over here I saw Dr. Forrest's truck heading in the opposite direction. Did either of you see it?"

"Yes," said Trina. "She was going awfully fast."

Jaycee blew her nose. "I saw the truck too, but I didn't see Dr. Forrest. I mean it *was* her truck, but I didn't see who was driving. My mom said that Dr. Forrest left the hospital before being discharged. No one knows where she is."

"I didn't really see Dr. Forrest either," Trina said.

Well, that makes three of us, thought Sloane. It would be easy to assume that Julia Forrest would be driving her own truck, but none of us saw her. If it wasn't Julia Forrest...then who?

"Aunt Sloane!" Jaycee was poking around in the dying embers with a stick. She dragged a small object onto the grass and stared down at it.

"What is it honey?"

Jaycee bent down and gingerly touched the small round object. She picked it up and examined it. She looked at Trina, and then Sloane. It was exactly the same as the one Lloyd

Snow, *her grandfather*, lost at the stable when they met earlier that week.

Crystal parked the Maybach in a lot near The Chesterfield. They didn't want their arrival announced by the valet parking attendant.

"If he's here, we'll find him," I said. "He's in room 306. Let's check there first.

Crystal gave me a sideways glance, as in *how did you know that?* We slipped through the butter hued lobby, and around the corner to the elevator. The amusing door was painted with a leopard in the jungle scene, providing some entertainment as we waited for the painfully slow elevator to arrive. I'd never been in The Chesterfield Hotel before...pretty swank!

Crystal was tapping her Manolo clad toes on the plush wall-to-wall, conveying her impatience. I pushed the elevator call button again, and the door finally slid open. Good, no one is coming out. Crystal and I alighted, and I pushed number three. As we stepped off, it occurred to me that we could have taken the stairs.

Obeying the directional sign, we turned left, and headed to 306. After knocking several times, with no answer, we decided to give up. Even if Vincente was sleeping, he surely would have heard the racket we were making.

"Okay, so he's not in there. Let's try the pool."

"What makes you think he'd be there?" Crystal asked.

"Vincente is an avid swimmer. It's how he keeps in such great shape."

"Obviously it works," Crystal smiled.

This time we wisely took the stairs and headed for the pool. We found tranquility itself. Aside from two elderly women on lounge chairs, their wrinkled bronze skin shimmering with oil, the pool area was deserted.

"Well, it's a little late for lunch, and a little early for Happy Hour, but let's check the Leopard Lounge anyway" I said.

We snaked around the tables in the alfresco dining area and peered through the panes of the French doors leading to the splendor of the Leopard Lounge. Black lacquered walls glistening, frescoed ceiling mesmerizing. My eyes were struggling to adjust from the bright sunshine at the pool, and the dim atmospheric lighting in this ultra-chic watering hole. Not much action here, as expected. I did spot two male patrons most likely drowning their sorrows in gin. As my eyes adjusted, I realized that the two gentlemen at the bar were no strangers. Vincente Villa and John Garrett! What the hell were they doing together? I nudged Crystal on the elbow and gestured toward the bar. She squinted, trying to make out the figures. I saw the *ah ha* moment in her eyes.

We shuffled backward, out of sight in case one of them turned around.

"Oh my God, Ivy! John and Vincente together! What should we do?"

I tried to keep my mind from racing. If ever I had to act in a calm and rational manner, it was now. But calm and rational was not my forte. I rushed over and burst through the French doors into the Leopard Lounge. Both men immediately spun around, shocked looks on their faces. The bartender was standing behind them with a sly grin, and twinkle in his eye.

I took a deep breath, folded my arms, and sauntered over to the unsuspecting duo.

"What are you doing here?" they said in unison.

"I was just about to ask you the same question. Perhaps comparing notes?" I was incredulous.

The two men in my life kibitzing over cocktails, unbeknownst to me.

"It's not what you think," said John.

Vincente shifted his weight and took a sip of his drink. "We met by accident. As you know, I've taken up residence here, since Casa Verde is off limits."

"I'm aware of that."

John followed suit with his drink. "It turns out that I'm staying here too. I thought it might be a little crowded at The Breakers.

"Perfectly understandable, since there are only two hotels on this island."

Crystal, who had been unusually quiet through this discourse, nudged me and whispered, "Ivy, have you forgotten why we came here in the first place?"

"Oh yes" I said. "Vincente, your stables are on fire."

Crystal drove me back to The Breakers after Vincente bounded from the Leopard Lounge as if *he* were on fire. John sat on his barstool, stupefied, which was very unusual for him. I think he was just at a loss as to what to say or do. When we reached the suite, Crystal mixed a pitcher of Martinis for us, which we both needed badly at that point. I took hold of the cold stemmed cocktail glass that Crystal offered.

"What is John up to, Crystal?"

"What makes you think he's up to anything?"

"Oh, he just *happens* to check into the same hotel as Vincente's staying at. Really?"

"Well, maybe it's just a coincidence."

"Coincidence, my ass! John is nothing if not deliberate. He's there for a reason. He's gotten himself stuck in the middle of my mother's murder case, thanks to his visit to Inspector Fiona over at Scotland Yard. Now, he's "accidently" snooping around Vincente Villa, a key player in that case. Coincidence? I don't think so!"

"Maybe you're right, Ivy."

"Of course, I am. John's ego won't let him be used as a patsy by Fiona Wescott, or anyone else."

Anyone but you, thought Crystal.

"He probably has it in his head that he can solve the case and exonerate me."

"Let's hope so, Ivy."

Detective Anderson slammed the door of his squad car and surveyed the desolate scene surrounding him. Smoke and steam sped up from the earth into the sky. Only one firetruck remained in case of any errant flare-ups. He considered the last two weeks, and how his usually calm and serene little part of the world was turned on its ear.

First, it was the death of all those horses, apparently brought on by bad shavings, according to Dr. Forrest's report. Then, there was Dr. Forrest herself. Shot right here on the premises, hospitalized, then disappears. The murder of Bianca Villa, and now a fire at the Villa stables. What was the one thing that tied it all together? Vincente Villa, of course.

Anderson had to admit it. He didn't like Vincente Villa. Never did. There was something about that guy...he was just too good to be true. Wealthy, but philanthropic, powerful but self-effacing, handsome, yet humble. Anderson wasn't comfortable with too many contrasts.

"Detective Anderson?"

He turned around to face Sloane Parker and her charges, Jaycee and Trina. It hadn't escaped him that trouble also started brewing when Ivy Snow and her crew showed up here.

"Hello ladies. Shame about this, huh?"

"Yes. Perfectly wonderful facility destroyed," said Sloane.

"You don't happen to know how any of this got started, do you?"

"No. We saw the smoke and came right away. We hoped that maybe we could help, but it was too late."

"That's a shame. You didn't see anyone strange hanging around here? Anyone who didn't belong?"

"No…" Sloane thought that maybe she should say something about seeing Dr. Forrest's truck.

"Well, actually Detective Anderson, we did see something unusual," said Jaycee.

"What was that?"

"When we were on our way over here, we saw Dr. Forrest's truck heading in the opposite direction."

Well, thought Sloane, no more deliberating that question!

"Really, are you sure?" said Anderson.

"Yeah. It was her truck alright. The thing is, I didn't see who was driving it. Neither did Trina or Aunt Sloane."

Anderson looked at Sloane for confirmation.

"That's right, Detective. We all saw the truck, but not the driver. Is there any news about Dr. Forrest?"

"No, we have an APB out, but no one's spotted her. It's like she vanished into thin air."

"Ivy said that she was acting strange at the hospital. She insisted that she wasn't Julia Forrest. Amnesia, maybe?"

"Possibly. But she didn't stay long enough for the necessary tests. We can't know for sure."

"I just hope she's alright. There's been enough tragedy around here lately. So now what?"

"Now we'll have a forensic team investigate, and hopefully find out what caused this fire."

They heard tires on gravel and turned to see Villa's Rolls pull up. Vincente jumped out of the driver's seat and ran to where they stood.

"What happened?" he asked.

Anderson shook his head. "Looks like your stable burned down, Villa."

Vincente just stood there. Sloane detected signs of shock. There was only so much one human being could take. She pulled a bottle of water from her tote bag and offered it to him.

He just stared at her. No, more like *through* her.

"Here Vincente. Please have some water."

He didn't move. "How? Why?" he asked.

“Villa, we don't know anything yet. I assume that you’re properly insured?” asked Anderson. Sloane shot him an angry glance. How dare he be so callous at a time like this! Vincente shook his head *yes*. He turned, and slowly walked back to his car.

John paid Lou the bartender, making sure to give him a generous tip. After all, he was probably going broke Palm Beach style anyway, so what difference did a few bucks make? He walked out to the pool area to catch the sun just ready to set. It was tranquil here. A good place to think while listening to the dulcet sound of water pouring from the fountain at the head of the pool. The golden rays created a surreal effect on the horizon. He didn’t know if he should dare entertain the thoughts that were gnawing at the edges of his brain. To deny them would be honorable, to allow them would be deplorable. John was in no mood to be honorable.

After all, who was Vincente Villa to him? An uber wealthy guy who had his own jet and tooled around in a Rolls Royce. Vincente Villa didn't have to worry about mortgage payments or maxing out his credit card. Villa wanted Ivy and would get her if he could. After all, they were engaged once. The only reason that he married Bianca was to save Ivy.

Now that Bianca was dead, he was free to go back to Ivy. She's convinced that Vincente didn't kill Bianca to gain his freedom. He had the perfect opportunity to get rid of a wife he detested and re-unite with the woman he loved. He'd be a fool not to. But was Villa capable of premeditated murder? That was a question to which John had no answer.

CHAPTER THIRTY-SEVEN

Detective Anderson sat at his desk drumming his fingers against the hard metal surface. He was perplexed. His gut told him that Vincente Villa was guilty of killing his wife, but he didn't have enough evidence to build a case. The D.A. wouldn't even consider trying Villa with the scant amount of evidence he had. No jury would convict, and they weren't anxious to spend the taxpayer's money and come out looking like fools in the process.

His phone rang, and the desk sergeant informed him that he had an Ivy Snow on the line. Ivy Snow! What did she want now? Anderson hated it when civilians went sticking their noses where they didn't belong. Ivy Snow was one of those people. Oh well, he was at a stalemate anyway, so he may as well see what she wanted.

"Put her through."

"Hello. Hello Detective Anderson. It's Ivy. Ivy Snow" I said.

"Yeah. I know. What can I do for you?"

"It's about the Villa case."

Of course, it is, he thought.

"I was wondering...have you talked to Lloyd Snow?"
"Lloyd Snow? What would he know about it?"
"He's known the Villas for a very long time. He knew Vincente in London years ago, when my mother died. He knew Bianca too. I don't know for how long, but they were both at a dinner party hosted by my friend Crystal Montrose a few weeks ago."
"So?"
"So, he may have seen or heard something that might have bearing on the case."
Hmm. Anderson considered. "Isn't he a relative of yours?"
I took a deep breath and let it out slowly. "He married my mother after my father died. Then he adopted me."
"Oh, so he's your father."
I cringed. "Only on paper. We haven't been in touch since my mother died. Meeting here in Florida is the first time I've seen him in years."
"I'll think about it Ms. Snow."

Anderson hung up the phone. It was getting to the point where he would have to call every Tom, Dick, and Harry in Palm Beach who ever said *howdy* to a Villa. He was grasping at straws, but the media had their teeth into this nonstop. He had to move forward. He put on his holster and sport coat and headed for his car. Maybe it was time for a visit to the Brazilian Court Hotel after all.

He turned onto Australian Avenue and parked across the street. The desk clerk knew he was a cop, so he pretended to look elsewhere as Anderson breezed by. Ivy Snow texted him Lloyd Snow's room number. So, he hit the elevator button to arrive on the third floor. He located Snow's room and banged on the door. A moment passed. He banged again. He heard footsteps approaching, and Snow opened the door.

"Yes?"

"Lloyd Snow?"

"Yes. what can I do for you?" Lloyd said tentatively.

"I'm Detective Anderson with the Wellington Police."

Lloyd just stood there staring at him.

"I'd like to ask you a few questions about a murder case I'm investigating."

"Murder? What murder?"

"A Mrs. Bianca Villa."

"Bianca Villa? Shouldn't the Palm Beach Police be investigating that?

"They are. We're cooperating on this one."

"Oh, well, I know nothing about it anyway" Lloyd said in his curt British accent.

"That's not what I hear."

"What do you mean? Who said so?" Lloyd's mind was racing. What the bloody hell?

"Listen, we can talk here, or we can go downtown."

Lloyd did *not* want to go downtown. "Alright, come in."

Anderson entered the suite and sat down on the pink brocade sofa. Lloyd sat down in the chair opposite.

"Mr. Snow, what was your relationship with Bianca Villa?"

"I hardly knew the woman. I met her recently, here in Palm Beach at a dinner party."

"What dinner party?"

"Robert and Crystal Montrose. Over on Ocean Drive."

"When was that?"

"I don't remember exactly. A few weeks ago."

Anderson jotted down a note on his pad. "Have you seen her since then?"

Lloyd paused. How should he answer this? He thought back to his lunch with Bianca at Eau Palm Beach. Did someone recognize them?

He'd carefully chosen that spot because the likelihood that anyone there would know him was remote. But someone knows something. *Someone* put Anderson on his tail. "I don't recall seeing her," he lied.

Anderson raised his eyebrow. "So, you had no contact with Bianca Villa after the Montrose dinner party?"

"No."

"Not even by phone?"

Bloody hell! The phone conversations! First to set up the luncheon, and then about that damn note. He'd have to backtrack. "Ah, now that you mention it, I did speak with Mrs. Villa. (Calling her *Mrs. Villa* would add a remote nuance, he hoped.) I contacted her about a story I'm doing on equestrian sporting life here in Palm Beach."

"Really? Her husband is the one involved in polo."

"Yes, but Mrs. Villa is instrumental in the Palm Beach Masters. I was hoping to interview her for my story."

"What about her husband, Vincente Villa?"

Lloyd felt beads of sweat forming at his hairline. It wasn't going to be easy to dodge this one.

"Ah, yes. I know Vincente Villa."

"In what capacity, Mr. Snow?"

Lloyd figured that he'd better be more forthcoming about Vincente Villa. There were too many threads tying them together going back to England.

"I've known Vincente Villa for quite some time. We met in London many years ago. He was engaged to my daughter, Ivy."

"Really?"

"Yes. It was a long time ago. We lost touch. I hadn't seen him in years. Not until the Montrose party."

"Have you ever been to the Villa home? Casa Verde?"

Lloyd snapped back an emphatic "No."

"Are you sure Mr. Snow?"

The color drained from Lloyd's already pasty white face. Fingerprints...had he left any fingerprints at Bianca's house when he went to retrieve the suicide note? Maybe that was it. They found fingerprints. That's what brought Anderson to his door. He had to think up a lie, and fast!

"Oh, well now that you mention it, I did have cause to visit the Villa home." Lloyd went on gathering bravado in his story. "The evening of the Montrose dinner party I dropped off a compact that Mrs. Villa left behind in their loo."

"Compact?"

"Yes. You know, Detective, ladies face powder. She had a rather valuable solid gold one. I volunteered to return it to her."

"Did you see Mrs. Villa when you went to the house?"

"Yes, of course. She thanked me personally for bringing the compact."

What a Boy Scout. Anderson jotted in his notebook. Ok, so Lloyd Snow only saw Bianca Villa once, at the Montrose party. But then, no. He saw her again at her house when he returned her compact. He first said that he hadn't had any phone conversations with her. But yes he had, when he called her about his story on equestrian sports. A lot of lobbing back and forth, like a game of British lawn tennis.

"Okay Mr. Snow. That's all for now. Don't leave town without telling me."

"Oh no officer...Right Oh!"

Anderson left the Brazilian and headed straight for the Montrose penthouse on Ocean Drive. He was stopped at the security gate, but his badge bought entrance to the stunning high-rise on the sea. The uniformed doorman also became more obliging after seeing Anderson's badge.

"I'll call up to the Montrose penthouse," he said. Robert answered the phone. "There is a Detective Anderson here to see you and Mrs. Montrose."

Anderson was escorted to the elevator and whisked up to the top floor. As the door opened, Robert wheeled into the foyer to meet him.

"Good afternoon detective. What can I do for you?"

"I'm investigating the murder of Mrs. Bianca Villa. I'd like to ask you, and Mrs. Montrose a few questions."

"Mrs. Montrose isn't in at the moment" Robert said.

"Sorry to hear that. May I come in?"

"Of course," Robert turned his chair around and led the way into the expansive living room.

Detective Anderson's eyes swept throughout the space, noting the obviously pricy contemporary art pieces, and the overstuffed furniture upholstered in luxurious fabrics. An entire wall made of glass invited the vista of the sea into the room. He'd never seen anything quite like it. Robert gestured to a deep white sofa facing the fireplace and wheeled his chair into a position directly across.

Anderson removed his notebook and pen. "Dr. Montrose, how well did you know Bianca Villa?"

"Not very well, I'm afraid. I met her for the first time right here. She was a guest, along with her husband Vincente, at a dinner party hosted by my wife and me."

"How did the Villa's get on the invitation list?"

Robert considered the wording of the question quite crude. "I met Vincente Villa at the Everglades Club a few weeks ago. We had a pleasant conversation, and I wished to get to know him better. We're relatively new here in Palm Beach, Detective, so widening our social circle...making friends, is important to me and my wife, Crystal.

At the mention of her name, the elevator door opened, and Crystal sauntered in swinging her black Prada bag by the shoulder strap. She was obviously *feeling good.* Robert wheeled over to meet her.

"Give me a kiss, darling," he said.

Crystal bent down to kiss him, and he whispered, "Detective Anderson is in the living room."

"I know," Crystal replied, a little too loudly. "Randell warned me!"

Robert could see that she was quite tipsy. He shuddered at what might happen next. As she breezed into the living room, Anderson turned around to see her drop her purse on the table and head for the bar cart.

"Good afternoon detective. Can I get you a drink?"

"Hello Mrs. Montrose. No thanks, I'm on duty."

"That's a pity," she said.

Robert wheeled over. "Do you really think that's a good idea?"

Crystal ignored him. After a few martinis with Ivy, inhibitions lowered, she fell back into the persona of devil-may-care Crystal Pritchard of Wellington Pennsylvania, instead of the more refined Mrs. Robert Montrose of Palm Beach.

"So detective, what brings you here?"

"I'm investigating the death of Bianca Villa," Anderson said.

"Humph. That certainly has caused a stir around here."

"How well did you know Mrs. Villa?"

"We just moved here. We don't really know anyone very well."

"I understand that Mr. and Mrs. Villa were guests of yours for a dinner party recently."

"Yes. That is c o r r e c t, detective!"

"Is that the first time you met Mrs. Villa?"

"It is. She sashayed in dripping with diamonds and drama."

"Crystal!" Robert gave her *that look.*

"Well, it's true!"

"What do you mean?" Anderson asked.

"It was like she was suspicious of every other woman in the room, especially my friends Ivy and Sloane."

Robert rolled his eyes and let out a deep sigh. There was no stopping her now.

Crystal took another gulp of her martini. "She was darting dagger eyes everywhere."

Anderson stayed quiet, letting Crystal go on.

"In a way you couldn't blame her. After all, there was Ivy, her husband's ex-fiancé looking fabulous. Vincente couldn't take his eyes off her. And Sloane...Sloane Parker that is. She's another friend of mine, she absolutely *captivated* that handsome Latin stud, Enrico Alvero. The jealousy in Bianca's eyes when she saw them communing in the corner! Definitely something going on there!"

"What about the other guests?" Anderson asked.

"Well, let's see. There was Ross Spencer, who if you ask me, has a chip on his shoulder over the Villas. He was with his girlfriend, Lena.

"Who is this, Lena?"

"Don't know much about her. Anna Nicole Smith wannabe. Awestruck by Bianca."

Crystal poured another measure from the martini pitcher. "Then, of course, the surprise guest, Lloyd Snow. He came all the way across the pond to worm his way back into Ivy's life and cause trouble. You know, come to think of it, Bianca didn't seem all that surprised to see Lloyd Snow. It was like they were familiar; you know?"

"Yes. I see. Did you have any occasion to see Mrs. Villa again? After the party?"

"She asked me to be on her committee to build an equine wellness center. We had a couple of meetings. Oh...the first one was a doozy! We met at a restaurant where Bianca saw Vincente having a drink with Ivy. She threw a margarita right in his face! She showed everybody who wore the pants in that family."

Robert cringed.

"Was that your last encounter with Bianca Villa?"

"No. We met again. I mean the committee met again at her house. Gee, I guess that was the morning of the murder!"
"Who was present at that meeting, Mrs. Montrose?"
"Ah, hmm...there was me, of course, and Bianca. Sloane was there too, and let's see, Lena, and the vet, Dr. Julia Forrest. That's the whole committee."
"Do you recall when the meeting ended?"
Crystal took a long moment gazing up at the ceiling, as if to consult the chandelier for an answer. "I remember now. It was around nine. I had a hair appointment and didn't want to be late. You know, I think Bianca held that meeting at her house just so she could show it off. She was like that, you know?"
"Crystal!"
"Oh Robert! I feel so sleepy."
She put her glass on the bar cart and stumbled off to her bedroom.
"I'm sorry Detective Anderson. My wife usually doesn't behave like this. I'm afraid she's had too much Happy Hour."
"No problem, Dr. Montrose." I'm finally starting to get somewhere, he thought.

CHAPTER THIRTY-EIGHT

Sharon pulled into the parking lot. She climbed the three rickety steps to the stoop and felt around the bottom of the black metal mailbox attached to the siding. Humph, no key. She always kept a spare key in the mailbox in case she lost hers. Her eyes scanned the trailer park as she wondered what she should do. Maybe she'd decided to hide the key somewhere else and forgot. She looked under the doormat...not there. She climbed back down the stairs and looked underneath. No key. Her eye caught a glimpse of the green plastic flowerpot on the other side of the steps. The mums that she bought last fall for half price at Walmart were long dead. She stepped closer to the pot and lifted it to see the brass key hiding beneath. There it was. She didn't remember putting it there. But, oh well, what did it matter? The important thing was that she could now get into her trailer.

She opened the dented aluminum door and stepped onto the green olefin wall-to-wall carpet. She immediately felt a strange vibe. She could sense that someone else had recently been there. She looked around the room. Nothing seemed to be missing. As a matter of fact, it was the tidiness of the place that felt out of sync. Magazines were stacked neatly on the coffee table. The large ceramic ashtray that she picked up at Goodwill was devoid of butts. No crumpled fast-food wrappers or empty beer cans to be seen. Sharon was confused.

She stepped into the kitchen to see sparkling plates that dried in the dish rack next to the empty sink. She didn't remember tidying up the trailer. Her examination of the other rooms found the same. Beds were neatly made, clothes hung uniformly in the closet. The bathroom was scrubbed clean with fresh towels hanging on the bars. Was she going insane? A "neatnik" she wasn't, and she couldn't fathom that the "cleaning fairy" paid an altruistic visit. Something was very wrong.

She went back into the living room and crossed over to the coat closet to deposit her jacket. She opened the door and caught sight of a white sleeve peering out from between the other coats. She spread open the clothes hanging there and pulled the long white garment off its hanger. It was some sort of lab coat. A lab coat? What was that doing here? She laid it over the back of the sofa, revealing an embroidered logo on the pocket. Treasure Coast Veterinary Center. She recognized that logo. It was the same one printed on the doors of the truck she'd been driving. It occurred to her that she didn't remember when she'd got behind the wheel of that truck. Where did it come from? Why was she driving it? None of it made sense.

She slipped into the coat. There was something familiar about it. The smell? She went to the refrigerator, pulled out a Bud and cracked it open. Damn, it was hot in here. She adjusted the thermostat to sixty degrees, sat on the sofa and lit a cigarette, as she started at the blank TV screen. She felt a terrible headache coming on and stubbed out her cigarette in the oversized ashtray. She laid her head back onto the rough fabric of the sofa cushions and fell into a deep sleep. Soon, the terrifying dream that haunted her almost nightly seeped into her brain.

There she was, standing at the kitchen window in their small house on the outskirts of Akron Ohio. She was watching her husband Steve light the bar-b-que grill. Their tiny daughter, Sally, circled the perimeter of their patio on her trike. She walked over to the fridge and took out the hamburgers and hotdogs that would soon be sizzling on the grill. There was mustard, ketchup and onions...but where were the buns? She searched the pantry, the cupboards and drawers. Damn! She forgot to buy the buns! Another trip to the 7-11! She called out to Steve, telling him that she would be right back. She ran a comb through her hair and put on a fresh coat of lipstick. Grabbing her straw tote and car keys, she headed to their Chrysler minivan parked in its usual place in the driveway. She put the keys in the ignition and turned it over smoothly, stirring the engine into a soft hum. The radio was perpetually tuned to her favorite country station and greeted her with Keith Urban's smooth sexy voice. "Take your records...take your freedom..." She grabbed the gear shift and slid the indicator to "R" putting the van into reverse. She stepped on the gas pedal. A horrible thud reverberated in her ears. What was that? She slammed on the brakes, and screamed "NO!" She threw the van into park and jumped out, catching a glimpse of her husband rounding the corner of the house. His eyes were filled with terror. There she lay, her little body twisted under the bumper of the van, blood seeping into her soft blond curls. They both fell to their knees, pulling her by the arms to free her from the undercarriage. The sound of neighboring doors slamming...a voice screaming "call 911!"

She was suddenly jarred awake by a thunderous pounding on the trailer door. She rubbed her eyes, trying to shake off sleep...to shake off the dream. She stumbled to the door, opening it a crack.

I stood on the stoop with Jaycee behind me and found myself face to face with Dr. Julia Forrest. "Dr. Forrest, are you alright? Everyone's been looking for you."

"Ivy, Jaycee? What are you doing here?"

"Jaycee had a vision. She saw you here."

"Oh!"

It was apparent that she was utterly confused.

"Come Dr. Forrest...Julia...we're going to get you back to the hospital."

CHAPTER THIRTY-NINE

Detective Anderson was dumbfounded when I called to tell him that Jaycee and I took Dr. Forrest back to Wellington Regional Medical Center. The police had an APB out on her for days with no success.

"How did you find her?" he asked.

"It might be hard to believe at first, but my daughter, Jaycee, has well, a sort of psychic gift."

"Psychic gift?" Anderson was skeptical about all that kind of stuff. It was too hocus-pocus for his way of thinking. Larger police departments did call in so-called *psychics* from time to time, but that was primarily a West Coast kind of tactic. Regardless, Dr. Forrest was back in the hospital where she belonged.

"Dr. Forrest seems to have regained her memory. She responded to us calling her Dr. Forrest...Julia. She made no mention of a *Sharon*, or anyone else for that matter. I'm afraid that Dr. Forrest might have bigger problems than a bullet wound," I said.

"I see what you mean." He hadn't actually heard the woman claim to be someone other than Dr.

Forrest, but Ivy Snow and her daughter swear to it. He'd better check with the hospital staff to make sure, he thought.

Somehow, I didn't think that I was getting through to Detective Anderson. He's so skeptical, and stubborn. "Detective, a crime has been committed here. A woman's been shot! It's your job to either find the person that shot her or determine that it was self-inflicted."

"Self-inflicted?"

"Yes. As I said before, Dr. Forrest has bigger problems than a bullet wound. She may have had a psychotic break, which led her to believe that she's someone else. It's also possible that she had amnesia or DID."

"What is DID?" he asked.

"Dissociative Identity Disorder. It's what they used to call Multiple Personality Disorder."

"Oh. You mean like a *split personality?"*

"Yes. It's been known as that too."

"Hum. Well, we'll have to have the doctor look into that. Do you think that Dr. Forrest had anything to do with the fire at Villa Stables?"

"I don't know. Sloane and the girls did see her truck in the vicinity when the stables were burning. However, they didn't see who was driving the truck, so there's no proof that Dr.

Forrest was near the stable. Anyway, she's always out there...it's her job."

"The whole thing is crazy. We've got no leads on the *other* woman that you heard her arguing with on the day she was shot. Even if you didn't see her. It's like she vanished into thin air. Dr. Forrest claims that she's *not* Dr. Forrest and leaves the hospital with a bullet wound in her side." He shook his head. "I don't know what to make of it. I'm going to go and see her myself as soon as the doctor clears it."

Detective Anderson was just about to hang up… "Ah, Ms. Snow, have you seen or heard from Vincente Villa recently?"

Oh shit! Why did he have to ask me that? I don't want him to know about my encounter with Vincente and John at the Leopard Lounge. I disconnected my phone. Hopefully he'll think the call dropped. I had the distinct feeling that Anderson was trying to build a case against Vincente, and I didn't want to inadvertently give him any ammunition. I needed to act fast. Anderson was going to come up with something in the next few days...I feel it in my bones. But he's got to have more than theory and conjecture. He needs more than circumstantial evidence to pin this on Vincente. He needs either physical evidence, or an eyewitness. Of course, he wouldn't tell me about anything he's discovered. The only place I can think of finding physical evidence is the scene of the crime. Casa Verde. But how do I get in?

John Garrett's American Express was about to max out. He'd been staying at The Chesterfield, where the rooms are five-hundred bucks a night. That, plus pricey meals...you couldn't get eggs for under twenty dollars. Then, there was the rental car, not to mention the trip to London and back. He still had to book a flight back to Pennsylvania, and his work there was piling up. Something had to give. He picked up the phone and dialed Ivy's number.

"Hey" he said.

"Hey" I said.

"So, how are you? He asked."

"I'm fine. How are you?" We are talking like we're two strangers, I thought.

"I'm fine."

"Listen John, I'm sorry about yesterday. I had to track Vincente down. His stables were burning, and the fire department couldn't reach him."

"Yeah, I understand. How did you know where to find him?"

"I knew he was at The Chesterfield since Casa Verde is still under investigation.

"Oh." He didn't take it any further.

Suddenly, an idea struck me. John was a police officer. He could get me into Casa Verde! They didn't have to know that he wasn't on the case. All he would have to do is flash his badge, and we'd be in!

"John, I need your help. I want to get into Casa Verde, but it's still a crime scene under investigation."

He knew better than to ask why. He still hadn't come to terms with the moral issue of helping his rival. But, if he refused Ivy, it might be the final nail in his coffin.

"Alright. I'll pick you up in half an hour."

"Thanks, John."

I adjusted the setting on my smartphone to be sure that I could get recordings of anything I might need. This is a fishing expedition for sure, but I can't help Vincente if I don't know what evidence the police might have against him.

I fixed my hair and make-up. I slipped into a pair of fresh white jeans, a lime green polo and MK athletic shoes. I had no idea what would come of this venture, but I needed to see that crime scene. The house phone rang to alert me that John arrived. I grabbed my backpack and headed down to meet him. As I came out of the front entrance to The Breakers, I saw John in the Toyota rental car waiting for me. I know that he wasn't happy about this, but I didn't know who else to turn to.

"Hi John!" I said a little too brightly.

"Hi Ivy."

"Thank you for helping me."

"Don't thank me yet. This whole thing might be futile."

"I know. But it's something I have to do."

John started up the car and pulled into the street, heading in the direction of Casa Verde. He was overwhelmed when they pulled up to the massive iron gate manned by two police officers. John pulled out his badge. The young cop nodded to the older one, and he just nodded back. The gates were opened.

"Wow John! That was a lot easier than I expected."

“They didn't look too closely at my badge. They could just tell that I was one of them. Ivy, you’ve got to be careful. We don't want anyone to know that we don't exactly have a one hundred percent right to be here.”

I smiled at John. “No worries.”

We walked up the few stairs to the massive front door. The uniformed police officer let us in. Apparently he didn't feel that he needed to check our credentials. He must have a great deal of faith in the boys down at the gate. I walked around the massive front foyer, with its black and white checkered marble floor. A large round mahogany table stood in the center, holding a massive vase of fresh tropical flowers. Just because Bianca was no longer running the show, it didn't mean that the whole place could go to rack and ruin. Someone was keeping things up, and that someone just emerged from the recesses of the hallway beyond. Of course, it was Marisol, Bianca’s maid.

“May I help you?” she said, skeptically.

John flashed his badge at her. “I’m Detective John Garrett.”

Marisol nodded and then turned her attention to me. She looked me up and down for a long moment. I said nothing. I wasn’t about to give out any information unless directly asked. John broke the silence.

"I need to survey the crime scene. The room where Mrs. Villa was killed."

Marisol tilted her head. "The police have already been through the room. Several times."

"I'm handling a different aspect of the case," John said with a policeman's confidence.

"Okay. Follow me then."

Marisol led John and me up the wide marble staircase. I glanced at my surroundings from the higher altitude and had to admit that Bianca created a very impressive residence. She did have a bottomless bank account, and the social standing to command the services of the most sought-after architects and interior designers. I sensed the nuances of Carlton Varney in the elegant tropical color palette.

We continued down the lushly carpeted hallway to a set of substantial French doors lacquered in shiny black and accented with heavy gold hardware. Marisol turned the knob and gestured for us to enter. The room was magnificent. The original Renoir and Monet set the tone for ethereal romance. The canopy bed was generously draped in a vibrant floral Scalamandre silk. The window treatments, fashioned in the same fabric, puddled down onto the room sized oriental rug. I was awe-struck. This was the room where Vincente made love to Bianca. I felt sour bile churn up from my stomach. It was because of the predicament with Scotland Yard that drove him into her arms. If none of that happened...how different life would be today!

John was poking around the room, not really knowing what he was looking for. Anything that might prove to be important evidence would have already been confiscated by the police. He surveyed the bathroom where Bianca's body was found. The marking tape on the floor indicated that she had been at the sink when she took her final breath. It must have been a horrible death.

"Well John, what do you think?" I asked.

"I don't see anything here that could help."

I took a deep breath and looked around the room. There were full length mirrors on every wall, and crystal chandeliers hanging from the ceiling. I tried to picture Bianca on that last day of her life.

"John, I wonder what Bianca was wearing when she died?"

"I don't know, but I'm sure the police have photographs of the body."

I pulled out my cell and hit the number for Sloane. She picked up on the third ring.

"Hi Ivy. What's up?"

"Sloane, do you remember what Bianca was wearing on the morning of your last committee meeting? The day she was murdered?"

"What was she wearing? Hmm...let me think. Yes. She was wearing a yellow linen sheath. It was sleeveless, knee length. Very understated."

I tried to picture Bianca in the yellow linen dress. It would be a good choice with her raven hair. "Shoes?" I asked.

"Nude Christian Louboutin pumps."

That wouldn't be hard to miss with the signature red soles.

"What about jewelry?"

"Ha! That was kind of incongruous," said Sloane.

"What do you mean?"

"Believe it or not, she wore that huge diamond necklace that she had on at Crystal's dinner party."

"You're kidding! Seems kind of inappropriate for a breakfast meeting, don't you think?"

"Yes, I did, and I do. But Ivy, I think that the whole meeting was about *putting on the dog*, so to speak."

"Really?"

"Yes. First the *invitations* to the meeting were last minute, and very insistent. More like a command performance."

"Bianca's style, for sure," I said.

"The fact that she held it at her house was like a power move. Who wouldn't be impressed with that place? Then, the way she had everything laid out. Each committee member was given precise instructions. We had absolutely no input into the plans for the fundraiser. We were given our assignments and our marching orders. Come to think of it, I'll bet wearing that necklace was just part of the show. The show of superiority and power."

"Absolutely! I know that you and Crystal wouldn't be impressed with her dog and pony stunt, but it certainly set the stage to intimidate Lena and Dr. Forrest into doing her bidding."

"You've got that right!"

"Okay Sloane. Thanks, I've got to run."

John was staring at me. "What are you up to?"

"I have a hunch. Let's head over to police headquarters. Maybe you can persuade your old buddy Anderson into letting us see what evidence the police have."

John rolled his eyes and ushered me out through the gleaming French doors.

CHAPTER FORTY

It was raining by the time John pulled the Toyota into the parking lot at police headquarters.

"I think you should wait for me," I said.

"Why?"

"Because if Anderson suspects that I was snooping around Casa Verde, he'll want to know how I gained entrance. I don't want you to get in trouble down here."

"He's liable to find out anyway if those cops blab, or if Marisol says something."

"That's true, but if he isn't given a reason to be suspicious, it might not come out."

"Okay. You're probably right. It'll be easier for you to get around him if I'm not there."

"I wouldn't be too sure about that. I don't think Anderson likes me."

"Not like *you?*" John smiled.

I rolled my eyes and headed for the building.

The desk sergeant called Anderson's office and announced my arrival. I was told to wait. Fifteen minutes later, Anderson appeared. He might have assumed that I was here because of Julia Forrest, so he seemed surprised to hear that

I wanted to talk to him about Bianca Villa. He probably thought that I would want to avoid talking about the murder because of my association with Vincente. He was right...up to a point. Now, if my hunch is right, all that is about to change.

"What can I do for you, Ms. Snow?" Anderson asked.

"I'm here about the Bianca Villa case," I said. He had a quizzical look on his face, which confirmed my suspicion.

"What about it?"

"I would like to see the photos of the body."

"Why?"

"Because I have an idea that might help establish a motive for the murder."

"Really? And what might that be?"

"Please let me see the photos, Detective. It's the only way I can be sure."

The police were desperate to solve this case, and the evidence they were seeking to arrest Vincente, or anyone else for that matter, was just not materializing.

"Okay, follow me," he said reluctantly. He led me to a room where evidence in open cases were cataloged and stored. He went to a tall black file cabinet and retrieved a manila envelope. It wasn't very thick. He rifled through and pulled out a packet marked *CRIME SCENE PHOTOS/VILLA*. He spread them out on a table in the middle of the room. There were about twenty or thirty of them. There were photos of Casa Verde both inside and out. I was only interested in the ones of Bianca's body lying on the bathroom floor.

In the first few pictures she was face down, on her side. That's how her body was found. I couldn't see what I was looking for from that angle. It was in the later photos, the ones taken when they were removing the body that interested me. There she was, the yellow linen sheath… nude Christian Louboutins still on her feet. And just as I'd suspected *no* diamond necklace!

I looked up at Anderson. "Detective, I think that I just discovered your motive."

I rewarded John's patience in the parking lot with a full account of my meeting with Anderson. Of course, he had no idea about the missing necklace, how could he? When the police arrived, the necklace had already been removed from Bianca's body. There was no way for him to know that it was ever there. Supposedly, the only people that could have known that she was wearing the necklace that day were the ladies at the committee meeting, Bianca's maid, Marisol, and the butler. If theft was the motive for her murder, the necklace would have been gone by the time that Vincente discovered her body.

John quietly contemplated this turn of events. "Very interesting, but you know that this doesn't exonerate Vincente."

"What do you mean?"

"He could very well have removed the necklace himself before Marisol arrived."

I thought about that for a moment. "Why would he do that?"

"Several reasons. Maybe he wanted to make it look like a robbery gone bad. Maybe he wanted to keep it for himself. It's worth a lot of money. Or maybe he just didn't want it to fall into the hands of the police. After all, evidence goes missing all the time."

"Obviously he would be insured, John. And, if his intention was to make it look like a robbery, why didn't he say anything about the necklace being missing. You'd think he'd be all too anxious to establish that as the motive. I need to find out if he knew that Bianca was wearing the necklace that morning."

"Yeah, and sooner rather than later, when the police question him about it."

He pulled out of the parking lot and headed for The Chesterfield.

"Something else puzzles me, John. Why wouldn't Marisol have said something to the police about the missing necklace? She knew Bianca was wearing it that morning. She knew it was missing when the police arrived."

"Maybe she thought Vincente confiscated it, or maybe she thought Bianca took it off after the meeting."

"Well, if she did, surely she would have put it in the safe."

"If she had time. Maybe old Marisol thought it would look mighty fine around her own neck."

"I'd say that's a possibility worth considering. Vincente told me that Bianca brought Marisol with her from Argentina. He felt that Marisol's loyalty belonged to Bianca, and not him. With Bianca gone, Marisol's job, and her future in the United States might be in jeopardy."

"That would be a motive for Marisol to protect her mistress's wellbeing," said John.

"True, but what if Marisol found Bianca's body *before* Vincente did, removed the necklace, and laid low until Vincente made the discovery?"

"If that were the case, the robbery theory would go right out the window, unless Marisol herself was the murderer."

"Not necessarily. Bianca could have already been dead when Marisol found her. At least the necklace would provide a decent lifestyle back in Argentina...if it came to that."

"In any case, I need to get to Vincente ASAP." I looked at my watch as we pulled up to the entrance of the Chesterfield. It was five o'clock.

"I know where to find him" I winked at John.

Of course, I was spot on. I found Vincente at the bar in the Leopard Lounge. He was sitting alone, nursing a Manhattan, and watching Walter the bartender polishing Martini glasses to a fine luster. I slid onto the stool next to his.

"Ivy! What are you doing here?"

"Tracking you down, Vincente. There's something I need to ask you."
He raised his left brow. "What's that?"
"Do you know what happened to Bianca's Harry Winston necklace?"
"Which Harry Winston necklace? She had many."
"The huge one with the multi-colored diamonds set in platinum"
"I suppose it's in the safe with the rest of her baubles."
"I guess the police will want to look into that."
"They already went through the safe."
"Yes, I know. Detective Anderson told me. The thing is, they wouldn't know if something is missing if they didn't know it was supposed to be there in the first place."
"What would you like to drink, Ivy?"
"I'll join you in a Manhattan."
Vincente gave the order to Walter. "Ivy, tell me, what's this all about?"

I told Vincente about Bianca's ensemble for the committee meeting on the day she died. Her outfit included the Harry Winston necklace. He was visibly confused.

"So, you see, Bianca was wearing the necklace at the meeting. When her body was removed from Casa Verde, she was not. The only people present at the house that morning...that we know of, were the committee members, Crystal, Sloane, Lena, and Dr. Forrest. Then of course the staff, and you. Detective Anderson showed me the inventory list of the items in Bianca's safe. The Harry Winston necklace in question was not listed."

"So, what did Anderson say?"

"He had several theories. But the one he seemed to favor, was that *you* removed the necklace when you found Bianca's body. That you hid it away until you could remove it from Casa Verde."

"That's preposterous! Why would I do such a thing?"

"To establish robbery as a motive. He figures that sooner or later the whereabouts of that necklace would come into question...just as it has. Honestly, Vincente, I was hoping that he would run with the robbery theory, but sorry to say, he's still stuck on you as the guilty party."

Vincente took a sip of his Manhattan, as Walter set mine on the bar.

"What should we do, Ivy?"

"Find out who stole that necklace. That's what

CHAPTER FORTY-ONE

I called Sloane and Crystal, and we arranged to meet for lunch at the Palm Beach Grill. When I arrived, Sloane was already seated at a corner table sipping iced tea.

"What's up Ivy? You sounded stressed out on the phone."

"I am. After you told me about Bianca's wardrobe choice for the committee meeting, I had a hunch...and it turned out I was right."

"What kind of hunch?"

I turned to see Crystal breeze through the door, headed for our table.

"Sorry I'm late, ladies. Robert couldn't find his glasses, and as you know, that's an all-out crisis."

I smiled. "No problem. I was just telling Sloane about my latest discovery."

"And what might that be?" Crystal asked.

"I'm quite sure that I now know the motive for Bianca's murder."

They both looked at me, wide eyed.

"Robbery. Plain and simple. Well, maybe not so simple."

"What robbery?" Sloane asked.

"You told me that Bianca was wearing that outrageous Harry Winston diamond necklace at the committee meeting."

"Right."

Crystal sighed. "I should have such an outrageous necklace."

I smiled. "Robert would get you one if you really wanted it. The fact is that when Bianca's body was removed from Casa Verde, that piece of jewelry was not around her neck. Anderson let me see the inventory of evidence. No necklace."

"Maybe she put it away in her safe," Sloane said.

"Nope. Not there either."

"Wow! That sheds a whole new light on the situation. Robbery? Who do you think did it?" asked Crystal.

"I don't know. But I do know that Anderson thinks Vincente removed it when he found Bianca's body...before Marisol came into the bathroom."

"You don't think that? Do you, Ivy?"

"Of course not. I've already talked to Vincente about it. He didn't do that."

Sloane breathed a deep sigh. "Hmm. So, when Bianca was wearing the necklace, we know that

Marisol was present, as was the butler, and the Equine Wellness Center committee. Oh, and Vincente, I suppose. But he didn't make an appearance...as far as I know. So, unless some random thief was lying in wait, I'd say we've got our suspects."

Crystal was staring into her Niçoise salad.

"What?" I asked.

"It's probably just a coincidence, but my diamond earrings are missing."

"Really, when did you discover that?"

It was the morning of Bianca's murder. I was going to wear them to the meeting, but when I looked in my jewelry box, they weren't there."

"Maybe you took them off somewhere else in the apartment," Sloane said.

"I don't remember."

"Think back. When was the last time you wore them?"

Crystal furrowed her brow. "Hmm...I don't...wait a minute! The last time I wore them was at the dinner party. That first dinner party that Robert and I gave."

Lloyd Snow was sequestered in his hotel room, pacing the floor. Even though Detective Anderson had already questioned him about Bianca's murder, he couldn't help but think that the other shoe was about to drop. Maybe it was his guilty conscience, although he never let that bother him before. No, it was more than that. His intuition told him that there was something going on behind his back. He hadn't been able to get in touch with her for days, and alarms were going off in his head. He held onto that fake note that Bianca wrote before she died. He needed it as insurance in case things went backward at Scotland Yard, and they suspected him. If he was to succeed in seeing that Ivy was convicted for Lacy's death, it would have to be soon, or the case might go back to the "cold" file, or worse... if they suspected *him.* What to do?

He picked up his cell phone again and punched in the number. Direct to voicemail. He didn't dare leave a message. That phone could end up in anyone's hands. Worst case scenario...the police. He had to figure out his next move. He was running out of money fast, and he loathed the idea of leaving the Brazilian. Maybe it was time to turn in his leased Jaguar.

No! He would not be defeated. He had to sort this out straight away! He picked up the phone and dialed her number once again.

Jaycee finished mucking out Pirate's stall and looked around the tack room at all the stuff she would have to pack for the trip home. She hadn't realized how much she'd bought here in Florida, but the tack shops here were so amazing, and after all, she and Pirate had to look the part. She thought about home. About her brother, her school, and Ryan...the guy she liked in her geometry class. She'd ask him to help her get up to speed, since she'd been away so long, and doing her classes virtually. It's the perfect excuse to get him to notice her. The fact is, Jaycee was homesick.

"Penny for your thoughts" Trina said.

Jaycee turned to see her best friend standing behind her. "Really, Trina, that's something old people say."

Trina smiled. "I know. It's one of my mom's favorites."

"Sure."

"Speaking of coins, do you still have the ones you found here, and at Villa Stables? You know, the British Pounds, or whatever they are?"

"Yeah. I put them in my tack trunk."

The girls went over and dug them out. There were two. They looked interesting...foreign. They were heavier than American coins. Jaycee closed her hand tightly over them and shut her eyes. She was getting a vibe. A mental picture formed. It was that guy who said he was her grandfather. That made sense. She knew that he dropped one when he came to see her. But there was another image in her mind. Someone else. Someone she didn't know...a woman.

"Jaycee, did you notice that these coins have little holes in them?" asked Trina.

"I see. How weird. Why would anyone drill holes into coins?"

Trina smiled. "I think I know. These coins were worn as earrings. See, the ear wire can slip right through, and they would dangle. My mom has a pair."

"I think you're right," said Jaycee.

CHAPTER FORTY-TWO

Inspector Fiona Wescott pulled up the Lacy Snow file for the hundredth time. She felt a knot in her stomach. She was getting nowhere fast with this one. She was kind of amazed that she was put in charge of the Cold Case Division at Scotland Yard. Yes, she was a good cop. Thorough with her due diligence. Relentless in her pursuit of the truth, tracking down every lead with the persistence of a predator. But this one had her flummoxed. Every line followed got her no closer to the answer. It didn't help that all the suspects were in the United States.

Fiona was frustrated, and a little bit scared. She had to prove herself capable...show that she was competent. She didn't want them thinking that they'd made a mistake putting her in the job. Maybe she'd bit off more than she could chew delving into the Lacy Snow case straight away, but she couldn't deny it, it was personal. John Garrett was in love with Ivy Snow. *Her* John. He should have belonged to her all along. Why he ever went back to Angelique was beyond reason. He only married her out of a sense of duty. He'd proposed, she'd said yes. She had a ring, and the date was set. He thought he had to do the *right* thing. He had to marry Angelique. But that was all over now. Now he would be free. They could start over. Things would be as they should have been, so many years ago. Thank heaven she'd waited. Waited for John. Angelique was no longer in the way, but Ivy Snow was.

Fiona scrolled through the pages on her computer screen. The archives displayed photos of the crime scene. Lacy's body crumpled on the kitchen floor. Fragments of the shattered teacup precariously close to her lips. If Lacy did commit suicide, why would she do it in the kitchen? It didn't make sense. Why wouldn't she carry the teacup to her bedroom? Soft peaceful surroundings would have made a much more dignified setting. It just didn't seem to fit with Lacy Snow's persona. She was a celebrated interior designer. A woman of refinement and taste. Her signature style exuded a luxurious ambiance. Why would she choose to drink that poison tea in the basement kitchen where she would take her last breath on a cold, hard tile floor?

She continued to scroll through the pages, forcing herself to go back to a place and time when Lacy died. Mayfair, in the fall. Probably getting a bit chilly just about then, especially in the mornings. She Googled the articles on the Newmarket Horse Sales that gave Lloyd Snow his alibi. Hmm, October 1999. What else was going on that day? Fiona researched the archives of The London Times for that date. Yes, the weather had been chilly. Rain was in the forecast. Nothing unusual there. The Queen had her knickers in a twist over another gaff made by Prince Andrew. The sporting news did mention the Newmarket sales, and ah, interesting...a blurb on the latest Mayfair burglary. Mayfair burglaries. Yes, Fiona remembered them. She had some minor assignments having to do with those cases. They were never solved.

She sat back and lit a cigarette. It was her office...she'd smoke if she wanted to. Her thoughts drifted back to her first rookie days at Scotland Yard. It was where she first met John Garrett. He came to lecture the new recruits. She'd made an ass of herself in the lecture, unable to answer the simplest questions. John was so kind. Took her for a pint to soothe her wounded ego. He was interested in her career. He told her that he thought she'd be "brilliant!" They discussed the Mayfair burglary cases, and her small part working on them. Now, they were in the cold case files, just as the Lacy Snow case had been. Maybe it was time to revive them as well. It all happened in Mayfair. Could there be a connection?

There'd been eight break-ins total. They began in January 1999, and abruptly ended in October. The wealthy neighborhood had been terrorized. Fortunately, none of the residents were home when their townhouses were broken into. Approximately nine hundred thousand pounds worth of jewelry was stolen. Fiona checked on the dates that each burglary had taken place. A pattern began to take form. Every burglary occurred on the same day as a bloodstock sale at Newmarket, ending on the day that Lacy Snow died.

CHAPTER FORTY-THREE

My cell phone rang at seven AM. I didn't recognize the number, so I let it go to voicemail. The spam calls were getting worse and worse. The little bell told me that they left a message, so I bit. It wasn't a sales pitch. It was Vincent's attorney informing me that Vincente had been arrested for Bianca's murder. I couldn't breathe. No! Anderson could not have done this! What evidence did he have? I hit the re-dial to connect, but this time I got voicemail. WTF! I couldn't believe it. I rapped on Sloane's door.
"Come in," she said.
I burst into the room to see her lying in bed checking her messages.
"You won't believe this!"
"What?"
"Vincente has been arrested for Bianca's murder!"
Sloane shook her head. "We saw that coming...didn't we?"
I figured that Anderson was moving in that direction, but I never expected him to act so soon. "What information could he possibly have unearthed that would lead to this?"

“I don't know Ivy, but I think we’d better get dressed.”

Sloane ordered room service for a quick continental breakfast, while I rallied the girls to get ready. We’d drop them off at the showgrounds on the way to the police station. When we arrived, we were informed that Vincente had been transferred to the Palm Beach County Jail. I asked to speak to Anderson but was told that he wasn’t in his office.

“What do we do now?” asked Sloane.

“We go to the jail, maybe we can see Vincente, or his lawyer.”

When we arrived, we were informed that Vincente was in a “holding tank” waiting to be arraigned. We were ushered into a waiting room, where countless bored and listless people sat waiting for visiting hours to resume. The place couldn’t be more dismal than some set designer’s creation on the Hollywood backlot. It was almost cliche. Walls painted a sickly green, a linoleum floor that hadn’t seen a good cleaning in who knows how long. The seating was hard plastic, likely chosen for their discomfort. The county didn't want anyone lingering in their precious air conditioning. Get in, visit with your incarcerated friends and family, and get the hell out.

We settled in and waited as agonizing seconds ticked by until visiting hours got underway after the lunch break. I looked up and saw an impeccably dressed man standing in the doorway. He was scanning the room, obviously looking for someone. Although I never met Vincente's attorney, Joseph Appel, I had a feeling that I was looking at him now. I took a chance and walked right up to him.

"Are you, by any chance, Attorney Joseph Appel?"

"Yes, I am."

"Representing Vincente Villa?"

"Yes."

"I'm Ivy Snow. You called me earlier today."

"Vincente wants to see you."

"I know. I got your message. That's why I'm here. What is this all about, Mr. Appel?"

"Please, call me Joe. As you know, Vincente is under arrest. He's waiting to be arraigned, and then I can petition the court to set bail."

"Do you think they'll go along with that?"

"I don't know. The charge being murder, it's unlikely. Although, Vincente, being who he is, might be an exception. It could go either way.

The judge might look at him as a flight risk given his financial situation, not to mention the fact that he has his own private jet."

"So, if they deny bond, then what?"

"In that case we'll go to an Arthur Hearing. The state will have to establish that the proof is evident, and presumption great that he's guilty of the charge. It will be hard for them to prove that, but in the meantime, Vincente will have to remain in jail."

"Oh God! I can't imagine! What evidence do they have against him?"

"I don't have all the facts yet Ivy, but unfortunately it appears to involve you."

"Me? What do I have to do with it?"

"Motive, I'm afraid."

"Motive?"

Sloane elbowed me. I didn't even realize that she was standing next to me. She gave me *that look.* Suddenly, it dawned on me. Appel gestured to the door.

"Come on. We can go to another room, and talk" he said.

He led us to a small interview room. We sat across from the gray metal desk.

"The DA is saying that Vincente killed his wife because he's in love with you, and she absolutely refused to give him a divorce. He hated her, and wanted her out of his life, but she wasn't about to let that happen. They were still living together, so he had the opportunity." Motive, means, and opportunity. There you have it.

"That's absurd. Vincente and I never discussed divorce, or us being together."

"Isn't it true that Mrs. Villa found the two of you together at IL Bellagio and threw a drink in his face?"

"Well, yes, that did happen, but it was a misunderstanding."

"Is it true that you were engaged to Vincente at one time?"

"Yes, but that was years ago. Another lifetime. Where is all this coming from?"

"Anderson's been a busy guy. He's interviewed everyone that's remotely connected to the Villas, and to you. I'll know more after I meet with the DA tomorrow."

"And what about the robbery? The missing necklace?"

"They figured Vincente got rid of it to make it look like a robbery," Appel said.

"I knew it! I want to know where Anderson's getting his information."

Appel pushed back his chair and stood. "I'll be in touch. Try and take it easy."

Sloane and I walked back to the waiting room.

"I'll bet Lloyd had something to do with this."

"Possibly" said Sloane. But he wasn't at IL Bellagio that night."

"I know, but word travels fast. Besides, not that many people know about our past."

"Are you kidding? Everybody's been buzzing about it since you two met up again."

"Maybe what we should be looking at now is not so much who wanted Bianca out of the way, but who wants Vincente out of the way."

"Good point!"

Visiting hours resumed. We got in line and shuffled up to the gatekeeper. When asked who we were here to see, we were told *no go.* He was still in the holding tank.

CHAPTER FORTY-FOUR

"It was me." Crystal dabbed her tear-filled eyes.

"What was *you?"*

"I was the one that blabbed to Anderson about Bianca zinging Vincente with that margarita."

"What!" I put her on speaker phone as I came in from the balcony.

"Robert just told me. We were having a cocktail before dinner. I was about to pour my second martini when Robert warned me about what happens when I have too many. He told me about my rant to detective Anderson. Honestly Ivy, I don't remember a thing about it. But if Robert said I did it, well then I guess I did. Can you ever forgive me?"

I was surprised by Crystal's behavior, but we all get a little sloshed sometimes and don't know what's coming out of our mouths. Lord knows I've been guilty.

"Don't worry about it Crystal. I'm sure that Anderson heard enough from everyone else to put the pieces together. You can make it up to me by hosting us again."

"What do you mean?" asked Crystal.

"I think it's time for another dinner party at Chez Montrose."

"You're kidding, right? After the last disaster?"

"No, I'm not. We've got to break this wide-open Crystal. Now that Vincente's been charged with Bianca's murder the police will stop looking for anyone else."

"You're right. What do we do?"

"How about next Saturday night? Robert can invite the guests. They won't be as suspicious. Ross Spencer will think that Robert is reconsidering his business proposition. Lloyd's curiosity will get the best of him."

"What about Enrico Alvero?"

"Robert could drop a hint that he's thinking about pulling together a polo team and needs advice."

"Sloane's not going to like that," Crystal said.

"No. I think she'll be fine with it. She has no interest in working with Alvero, but they're still on cordial terms."

"Okay, so that's Lloyd, Ross Spencer. He'll probably bring Lena, and Enrico Alvero."

"Yes, then there's Sloane, me, you and Robert. I think John should be invited as well."

"I agree. You know Ivy, it's going to be weird. Getting that group together without Vincente and Bianca there like they were last time. Kind of creepy."

"Yes, I know. Just the situation I'm looking for."

Enrico Alvero was folding the last bits of his wardrobe, intent on getting everything into one suitcase. His presence in the Palm Beach area was no longer required...at least for the time being. He liked the US, and wanted to stay, but South America was always an option. At least his financial picture was starting to look up, if his latest scheme succeeded, that is. His phone rang, and he answered it to hear Robert Montrose's voice on the other end.

"Hello Mr. Montrose. How are you, sir?"

"I'm fine, Enrico. And you?"

"Very well sir. Thank you." He could hear the pandering in his own voice, and it sickened him. Soon enough, he'd be pandering to no one. Well, almost no one.

"Enrico, I'm calling to invite you to dinner next Saturday evening. A group of us are getting together to talk about polo."

"Really? That sounds intriguing."
"Yes, I've been thinking, now that Villa Stables are gone, maybe it's time for a new team to debut. Interested?"
"Of course, Dr. Montrose."
"Enrico, please call me Robert."
"Ah, yes Robert, I'd be delighted to come."

Enrico puffed up his chest. He was dying to know who the other guests would be, but to ask would be gauche. Whoever they were, they'd have to have deep pockets. He bid Robert Montrose goodbye and considered whether he should keep packing.

Lloyd Snow was popping the collar on his periwinkle polo fresh from the hotel laundry. It would be a shame if his dwindling cash flow got to the point where he'd have to leave the Brazilian for lesser accommodations. He heard his phone buzz to see a text message from Robert Montrose. It was an invitation to dinner at his place next Saturday night. What was that all about? His mind raced to every scenario he could think of, but none made any sense. He hadn't seen Montrose since the last dinner party...the one where he re-connected with Ivy. *That* had certainly been satisfactory. He could still see the look of shock on her face when he walked into the room. Should he accept the invitation? Who else would be there? Perhaps it might be more dangerous not to go. He hit the return button and accepted.

Ross Spencer opened his email and saw the message from Robert Montrose. He hadn't been thinking very kindly of Montrose after he blew off the Palais Palm Beach proposal. Was he changing his mind? Well, well, well! An invitation to dinner. Maybe he did change his mind. Now that Villa's been arrested for his wife's murder, the possibilities were opening up. Montrose wouldn't want to miss out on the deal now. The question is, would he really need Montrose anymore? If he could pull this deal off himself, then the profits would be all his. On the other hand, there was nothing quite like other people's money. He hit *Yes, thank you* in reply.

"Lena! Lena, where are you?"

She came out of the adjacent exercise room dabbing at the mist of perspiration on her brow. She spent an inordinate amount of time working out. It must not be easy to maintain that voluptuous figure, especially with her penchant for chocolate.

"Yes Ross?"

"I've just accepted an invitation to the Montrose dinner party Saturday night."

Lena hesitated. "What Montrose dinner party?"

"Just a dinner party. He showed her the email.

"What do you think he wants?" she asked.

"I'm not sure, but he might be rethinking my offer to let him in on the Palais Palm Beach deal."

Lena's eyes shifted as she tried to assess this abrupt change. "Who else will be there Ross?"

"I don't know. You saw the email. He didn't exactly pass along the guest list. Maybe we're the only guests. Why so many questions? I thought you'd be happy to hobnob with high society again."

"Oh Ross" Lena said, forcing a smile.

I called John to let him in on my plan to "round up the suspects" at Crystal and Robert's place.

"You know Ivy, you're playing with fire here. If one of these people is the killer, they're likely to come after you."

"Don't think that I don't realize that. But I can't continue to let Vincente rot in that jail until the courts get around to letting him out. Besides, I'm taking you along as my plus one, so you can protect me."

"Great, I'm reduced to being a bodyguard at dinner parties," said John.

"Not all dinner parties. Just this one."

"Ivy, I've got to be heading back up north soon."

"Yes, I know, so do I. That's why I need to act fast. The girls have their last virtual classes this week, then they've got to get back to school."

"Okay, I'll go to the dinner."

"Thank you, John."

"Have you talked to the lawyer?"

"Not since I saw him at the jail. He's supposed to get in touch after he meets with the DA.

"Ivy, Joe Appel is one of the best lawyers money can buy. Villa's lucky to have him in his corner."

"I know. I'll keep you posted. By the way, have you heard anything from Scotland Yard?"

"No. Been pretty quiet. I'm hoping Fiona will just drop the whole thing."

"Dream on. Now, more than ever she'll want to solve the case. Especially if it means putting me away for good!"

CHAPTER FORTY-FIVE

I was pacing around the hotel room, waiting for Joe Appel to call. Whoever coined that "wheels of justice" axiom got it right. I decided to go to the hospital and check on Julia Forrest. As far as I knew, she had no one. No friends or family to watch over her. She did have one intimate...the one who shot her.

I parked the Range Rover in the underground parking lot and checked with the geriatric volunteer at the help desk. I was told that Dr. Forrest had been relocated to the sixth floor. I was just about to push the elevator button, when I turned to see Detective Anderson heading my way.

"What brings you here, Detective?"

"I'm here to see Dr. Forrest."

"So am I. Do you have any news about her assailant?"

No, but there's something strange going on. I got a call from the woman who owns the trailer park up in Delray. The one where you found Dr. Forrest. She said that one of her tenants is missing."

"Really? Who?"

"She said the woman's name is Sharon Zelinsky."

"Sharon Zelinsky?" *Sharon? I wonder...?*

"She lives at the same trailer number as Dr. Forrest."

"I didn't know Julia had a roommate."

"According to Mrs. Pritz, there is only one name on the lease. As far as she knows, only one woman lives there."

"Maybe Julia's subletting."

"I don't know, but I'm going to find out," Anderson said.

We arrived at Julia's door together. Anderson wrapped a few times, and we walked in. It was a private room. The curtains were drawn, blocking out the bright Florida sun. There were no flowers or cards on the bedside table, and the TV was on, but mute. Julia sat silently in the semi-darkness. We approached her bed.

"Dr. Forrest, It's Detective Anderson."

"I'm here too. It's Ivy Snow."

She sat staring straight ahead, as if catatonic.

"I'd better get the nurse," Anderson said.

I took Julia's hand. It was clammy. Even in the dim light, I could see that her face was pale. The dull green hospital gown worsened the effect. Anderson came back in with the nurse.

She checked the chart. Surgery was performed two days ago. The wound was healing nicely. That was good news. But there was also bad news. After Julia awoke from the anesthesia, she refused to eat. She was pretty much shut down emotionally, and made no effort to communicate verbally, or otherwise. The doctors consider it a mental breakdown. A disassociation with reality. Disassociate...that word. It was what I thought the last time I visited her in the hospital, when she insisted that she was not Julia Forrest.

Attorney Appel's call finally came. The Arthur Hearing was scheduled for Vincente's bond.

"I'm pretty optimistic, Ivy. The state will have to show that proof is evident, and presumption great. That's even harder than *beyond a shadow of a doubt."* I don't think they have enough solid evidence, but they'll have thirty days to come up with it. I'll have thirty days to build a case that will refute them."

"I wish I could feel relieved, Joe, but I know how fickle the courts can be."

"In light of what Vincente told me about your past, I can see why you'd feel that way."

"When can I see him?"

"They just got him settled into his cell block, so you can visit him next session."

"When will that be?"

"Friday morning, ten AM."

"I'll be there. By the way, Joe, I'm working on an angle myself."

"What's that?"

I told him about the dinner party that Crystal was planning for Saturday night.

"What do you hope to accomplish? Appel asked.

"I'm not sure, but if I get everyone closely associated with Vincent and Bianca in one room, chances are that *something* will come out to shed light on all this. I can't help but feel that something deeper is going on. Something we know nothing about."

"Alright. It can't hurt, I guess."

"I have an idea, Joe. Why don't you come to the dinner too? John Garrett will be there. He's our police friend from Pennsylvania. (boy was I glossing over that one.) He'll be another set of eyes to observe the goings on. Your viewpoint as a criminal defense lawyer would be really valuable. Can I count you in?"

Appel sighed. "I suppose so. You never know, I might see or hear something to help build my case."

I gave him the details. "See you Saturday night."

I picked up the phone and called Crystal. "Set another place. Sloane has a *Plus One.*"

Crystal was in a tizzy. Another dinner party! After that last disastrous one, she swore never again. But she was calling the caterers once more. It was her own fault. If she hadn't gone overboard with the martinis and started blabbing to that detective about Ivy and the Villas, she wouldn't be in this mess. Oh, who was she kidding? She'd do anything to help Ivy, no matter what. Okay? Maybe lamb chops? Did she have lamb chops the last time? She couldn't remember. The caterers would know. It would be best to just leave everything up to them. They could take care of the linens and the flowers too. Since they'd been in her apartment before, they knew the decor and color schemes. They'd have to stay away from any kind of lilies though...Robert's allergic.

There was so much to think about! What would she wear? Oh, what did it really matter? The whole point of this dinner was to get the goods on whoever killed Bianca. Crystal's money was on that polo playing Argentinian, Alvero. She saw how jealous Bianca was when he was kissing up to Sloane at the last party. Her eyes were blazing with fury. And, as they say, if looks could kill, Sloane would be the one pushing up daisies. Yes, Alvero did it. Bianca was going to dump his ass, and his machismo wouldn't stand for that!

Jaycee and Trina decided to take a break from riding and spend some time at the pool. They'd be going back up north soon, and the weather report for Pennsylvania was pretty dismal. Freezing cold temperatures, and heavy snowfall.

They wanted to bask in the warm Florida sun as long as possible. Trina was wearing her Maui blush and black lace bikini, while Jaycee sported her La Perla gold polka dot.

"Those earrings look really cool with your suit," Trina said.

"Yeah. Just like two more polka dots," laughed Jaycee. "I probably shouldn't be wearing them at the pool, I'll bet they're valuable. After you said that these coins were really earrings, I just had to get ear wires and try them on. You know what, Trina?"

"What?"

"Ever since I put these on, I've been getting my, you know, *visions.*"

"Oh no. Not the visions. Every time that starts, trouble follows," Trina said.

"I know, but I can't help it."

"What are you seeing?"

"I see a racetrack. I see a woman. A blonde like that movie star from a long time ago. The one that has that picture with her skirt blowing up."

"Oh, you mean Marilyn Monroe."

"Yeah."

Suddenly, Jaycee felt a chill, as though the sun went behind a cloud. She turned over in her lounge chair, and there was that awful man. The

one that said he was her grandfather. Trina saw the look on Jaycee's face, and looked up, shielding her face against the brightness. Lloyd stared at their bikini clad bodies lasciviously.
"Hello, Jaycee," Lloyd said.
"What do you want?"
"I thought I'd visit my granddaughter."
"I'm *not* your granddaughter. I told you that!"
"So, you did. But, Jaycee, my dear, you cannot change the facts."
"I can change anything I want, and I'll disown you."

Lloyd caught the glint of light shining from the gold earrings.
"Jaycee, where did you get those earrings?"
"None of your business."
"Now, young lady, I will not have you speaking to me in that manner. Where did you get those earrings?"
"I found them."

Trina touched Jaycee's arm. Her eyes were hidden behind sunglasses, but Trina knew they were filled with fear.
"Mr. Lloyd...Mr. Snow, whatever your name is, please leave. You are making us feel uncomfortable."

"I'll leave, Trina dear, right after Jaycee gives me those earrings."

"What? I'm not going to give you anything. You're crazy."

"No, my dear, I'm not crazy. Those earrings belong to me."

"What do you mean?"

"I lost them a few weeks ago. Now that you've found them, you must give them to me."

Jaycee began stuffing her things into her beach bag. Trina followed suit. The girls stood up and stomped away from Lloyd Snow.

CHAPTER FORTY-SIX

Fiona Westcott felt a breakthrough coming on. The "coincidence" she discovered while researching the Mayfair burglaries might just lead her in the right direction. The fact that each break-in occurred during a sale at Newmarket was uncanny. Her next step was to look at the victims to see what they might have in common other than the fact that they all lived in Mayfair. It was a big job. She'd assign it to her rookie assistant. She had another line to follow...that of Lloyd Snow. The cold case files contained very little of Snow's background. Reports showed that detectives working on the case began researching his background since the *husband* is usually the number one suspect in the wife's murder. Unfortunately, that line of investigation waned once the suicide note appeared. It was up to her to dig in where they left off.

She studied the file and learned that Lloyd Snow had been with the BBC for about thirty years. His focus was on equestrian sports. Prior to that, he was with The London Times, where he started in obituaries, and ended up with the society pages. It was during his time there that he met and married his first wife, Lucille Benedict. Fiona wasn't aware that Lloyd had been married previously. She searched the case files for anything on Lucille Benedict and found nothing.

Fiona turned to Google and entered the name. First ranking item was Lucille Benedict Snow's obituary. The article revealed that "Lucy," as she was more commonly known, died at a young age. She was just thirty-five years old. Cause of death was a tragic horseback riding accident. She'd been riding alone over the moors, when apparently, her horse spooked. She was thrown and suffered a broken neck. When her horse returned to the stable riderless, her husband set out to find her. The coroner said that death was instantaneous. She was survived by her husband and a young daughter, Lydia.

So, Lloyd Snow was married once before he met Lacy. Maybe more than once? Were there other marriages? He and Lucy had a daughter...whatever became of her? The deeper Fiona dug, the more unanswered questions she unearthed.

Friday morning finally rolled around. I dressed quickly and simply in a tan linen sheath...no hat, scarf or jewelry. I noticed that the guards at the jail made everyone remove accessories and leave them at the door during visitation. They weren't going to let anyone smuggle in drugs, or devices for escape to the prisoners. I chose a small clutch bag that would easily fit in the locker where you had to store your personal items. I was both nervous and excited to see Vincente. What that poor man must be going through. Well, it won't be much longer if things go my way.

I called down to the valet to have the Range Rover brought around and headed straight for the jail. The parking lot was jammed. I entered the waiting room and had to squeeze past a rotund couple to claim my hard plastic chair. The TV monitor on the wall above was tuned to Dr. Phil. I looked around at the other visitors. Most of them had their noses buried in their cell phones. An ancient dark-skinned man was staring into space. A woman with a t-shirt proclaiming love for her dachshund fiddled with her rosary. The fluorescent lights cast a dim pallor over the room. The air was tinged with the scent of disinfectant and despair.

The guard called those with names beginning with letters A through G to line up. This first group would be ushered to the elevator, which would take them to the visitation stations. So, that's how it's done. I would be called when they got to the letter S. It was going to be a long morning.

Finally, my turn came and I joined the others in the elevator. It opened up to a hallway, which led to a bank of chairs facing clear plastic panels. There was a phone receiver mounted on the wall. Vincente was led to a chair opposite mine on the other side of the panel. He slumped into it, ran his fingers through his hair, and propped his head up with his fist. I picked up my receiver. He picked up his.

"Hello Ivy."

"Hello Vincente." Now that we were face to face, I couldn't think of anything to say. His eyes were dull, and his mouth downturned. He didn't look like the Vincente I knew.

"Vincente, how are you?"

"I didn't do it, Ivy. I didn't kill Bianca."

"Of course, you didn't. I'm so sorry this happened to you."

"They don't believe me. They think I killed her so that I could be with you."

"That's what Joe Appel told me."

"Honestly, Ivy, if I had killed Bianca, that would have been the reason."

"Don't say that!"

"It's true!"

I shook my head *NO and* mouthed the words "they might be recording our conversation." The color drained from his face. "God, Ivy, you know I didn't kill her. What's going to happen?"

"I'm going to find out who *did* kill her."

"How?"

"I have a plan."

I returned to The Breakers to find Sloane sipping an iced tea on the balcony.

"Hey there. How'd it go with Vincente?" she asked.

"As well as could be expected, I guess. He's depressed, and scared."

"Can you blame him? He's lost so much already, and he stands to lose everything, even his life. Who wouldn't be depressed? Who wouldn't be scared?" Sloane said.

"Of course, you're right. It's just that I've never seen him like that before. He was always so cool in a crisis. It's one of the things I admire about him most."

"So, what's next?"

"Tomorrow night at Crystal's should be interesting. More than interesting...informative, I hope. By the way, you have a date."

"A date? What are you talking about?"

"I invited Vincent's attorney, Joe Appel, as your *plus one.*"

"You're kidding? Why?"

"He'll be another set of eyes observing the actions and interactions of the other guests. Or should I say suspects? I think it'll be very beneficial to have both Joe and John in the dynamic. They both have a *fresh set of eyes,* so to speak."

"I get it. We have experience with these characters, they don't. It'll give them more objectivity. When does this shindig get under way?"

"Seven o'clock cocktails. Dinner around eight. We can go together and meet our *dates* in the lobby.

CHAPTER FORTY-SEVEN

Ross Spencer quickly rummaged through the rack of sports coats in his dressing room. He was looking for his vintage white dinner jacket. It was classic, and a little unexpected, just like he was. Of course, he wouldn't wear a white shirt, or a bow tie. No, his hibiscus pink shirt, open at the neck, would perfectly accentuate the jacket's slender shawl collar.

"Ross! Where are you?" Lena called.

"I'm in here getting dressed."

Lena walked out of the bathroom wrapped in her Turkish terry robe fresh from a shower. She stopped abruptly when she saw Ross holding the jacket against his body as he admired himself in the full-length mirror.

"You're wearing *that?"* She said.

He spun around. "Yes, I am. Do you have a problem with it?"

"It's just so *old!"*

"Old? It's vintage. Great style is great style. You wouldn't know anything about that...now would you Lena?"

She bristled. "I guess not, Ross."

He fixed himself a pre-dinner drink while he waited for Lena to finish dressing. He wanted to arrive at the Montrose penthouse relaxed and ready to finesse Robert into backing his Palais Palm Beach project. He looked at his watch. What was taking her so long? He thought about fixing himself another drink, but then he thought better of it.

Lena walked into the room. Ross did a double take. She was wearing a white halter dress, with a full pleated skirt. Her feet were clad in dainty spike heeled sandals. White jade earrings glistened beneath her platinum waves. She looked stunning.

"Wow Lena, you're really pulling out all the stops tonight" Ross said.

"Since you look so handsome in your vintage dinner jacket, I thought I'd channel a vintage look myself."

Ross noticed that she was wearing that cameo ring. The only shot of color in her ensemble. He held the door for her, and they headed for the parking garage. They'd take the Aston Martin DB5 tonight. It fit in with the theme.

Crystal breathed a sigh of relief when she smelled the heavenly aroma wafting out from the kitchen. Palm Beach Catering had done it again. Their miso glazed sea bass was nothing short of fabulous. No matter what happens tonight, at least their guests will eat well. She walked around the living room fluffing pillows and setting out coasters. The portobello bon bons would make a nice appetizer to compliment Stoli martinis. It was all very elegant, except for maybe the cartoon cocktail napkins. She especially liked the one that said "If you can't say something nice, say it to your husband. He's not listening anyway!" Ha! Her stab at comic relief.

"Crystal?"

"Yes Robert?"

"Don't you think it's time to get dressed? Our guests will be here in an hour!"

"Yes, I was just getting ready to hop in the shower."

"Honey, why don't you wear your diamond bracelet tonight? It looks so lovely on you."

Oh no! That bracelet, Crystal thought. She'd almost forgotten about it. It was because she was avoiding telling Robert that she'd lost it. Maybe it wasn't really lost, just misplaced.

She'll do a thorough search of the apartment tomorrow. In the meantime, she'd have to come up with an excuse. She'd choose an outfit that called for another jewelry choice. Damn, diamonds go with everything. Maybe he wouldn't notice if she wore his mother's vintage diamond brooch. He'd love that. It really was a statement piece. As Chanel said, "Before you leave the house, take a look in the mirror and take one thing off." If Robert noticed that she wasn't wearing the earrings, she had a Coco quote at the ready.

My plan was coming together. If ever I were able to help Vincente, it would have to be tonight. One of those characters that killed Bianca would be at the dinner tonight. I felt it with every fiber in my body. I'm so glad that John will be there. It's more than generous of him to help, especially knowing of the past that I'd shared with Vincente. Was he doing it out of some sense of moral high ground that he felt obligated to uphold as a police officer? Or was it about his feelings for me? I suppose it really doesn't matter, at least for now. What matters is that he'll be there to help me.

I thought about what to wear. I had to look *no nonsense,* but, after all, it was a dinner party. A simple little black dress was always the right answer. A quick rap on the bedroom door, and Jaycee bounded in.

"You look great Mom!

"A gold shoe...what do you think?"

"Yeah, sure!"

Ralph Lauren came up with an elegant gold pump for spring, the perfect accent. I slipped them on.

"Now, I have the perfect jewelry," said Jaycee. She held out the gold coin earrings.

"Where did you get those?"

"Remember the coin that I found at the stable?"

"Yes."

"Well, I found another one at the fire. When Mr. Villa's stable burned down."

"Why didn't you tell me Jaycee?"

"I don't know. I guess I just forgot."

"Forgot?"

"Sorry Mom. Trina and I noticed that there were little holes in the coins. She said that they were just like her mom's earrings. The ones made from Greek coins. We bought some ear wires, and now these are earrings too!"

"So, Jaycee, you found one gold coin at the stable?"

"Yeah. Remember Mom? I told you about it. It was the day that the guy saying he's my grandfather came to see me."

"Yes honey. Of course, I remember."

"I found the other one on the ground by the Villa Stables. I was so freaked out by the fire, that I just stuck it in my jacket pocket and kind of forgot about it."

"That's okay."

"Mom, there's something else."

"What?"

"When I wear these earrings, I see visions."

"Visions of what?"

"A blonde woman. At first, I didn't know who she was, but I told Trina about it, and she said that she thinks it's that old time movie star, Marilyn Monroe."

"Marilyn Monroe? I don't get it?"

"Me either Mom, but we Googled it, and saw a picture of her. It's the lady I keep seeing in my visions."

I wondered what that meant? What was the connection? Did Marilyn Monroe wear coin earrings? What did it have to do with Jaycee? With us?

"Let's just keep that in mind. Sometimes your visions are symbolic. But you are right about one thing honey. These earrings do work with this dress." I had a feeling that wearing them could be advantageous. As I slipped the earrings on, Sloane popped her head through the door.

"Are you almost ready?" she asked.

"Yes. Come in. I'm just putting on the finishing touches."

Sloane looked elegant in her blush pink dress. A single strand of pearls glowed against her sun tanned decolletage.

"So, what does this Joe Appel, my *date*, look like?"

"A Jewish George Clooney" I winked.

"Yeah...sure!"

"Well, maybe not so much, but he's not bad."

"I'll be the judge of that," Sloane said with a smile.

"We'd better get going...it's showtime!"

CHAPTER FORTY-EIGHT

Fiona Wescott gently blew on the tendril of steam wafting up from her cup of Darjeeling. She was waiting to meet with her rooky assistant to review his findings on the Mayfair burglaries. Her research on Lloyd Snow further revealed that his first wife, Lucille Benedict, was from a very old and prominent British family. She'd attended the Malvern St. James Girls School, came out at Queen Charlotte's Ball, and matriculated at Hartpury College where she captained the dressage team. After graduating, she authored several books on horsemanship.

Not too much was written about Lucille after that. Only the announcement of her marriage to Lloyd Snow, the birth of their daughter, and her obituary. Further reading unearthed an article detailing the fall of the Benedict family after World War II. They suffered great casualties on the battlefield, and subsequent generations failed to sustain the family wealth. Unfortunately, Lucille's father died destitute. That must have been devastating for her, and certainly unlucky for Lloyd Snow.

Fiona's assistant, Officer Adam White, entered her office carrying a thick file containing his research on the Mayfair burglary victims. Of the eight residences robbed, six were owned by married couples, one by an older, single gentleman, and one by a widowed lady. Also included was an inventory of the items stolen, and their assessed value. Various rings, pearl necklaces, gold bracelets...all pretty standard. Hmm… a Victorian cameo poison ring? What's that she wondered?

Fiona felt especially sorry for the widow. The thieves stole her deceased husband's wedding band. Irreplaceable! Oh, and another irreplaceable item. The older gentleman's Duke of Cornwall trophy won at the Guards Polo Club in 1962. It must have broken his heart to lose that.

As Fiona read through the files, her anger mounted. It was bad enough to steal valuable jewelry, but to take items with such sentimental value as a wedding ring, and a hard-won sporting trophy...that was bloody low! Each report contained a detailed background on the unfortunate individuals that suffered losses. Age, occupation, extended family, time living in the home, other occupants, etc. Very thorough.

Even religious affiliations. Well, here's something interesting. Every single burglary victim was a member of Blacks Club. The same club as Lloyd and Lucille Snow.

John Garrett pulled navy blazer and khaki slacks from the closet. He couldn't afford to dress in the swanky way that these other guys did in Palm Beach. Not on a cop's salary. The ten-year-old blazer would have to do. He wasn't going there as a fashion plate; he was going there to catch a criminal. He had to admit that the fluid pattern on his tie was sharp. Light hues of pink, green, and lavender reminded him of an impressionist painting. Ivy had given it to him for his birthday. He hoped that it would please her to see him wear it.

What would happen if Vincente Villa did beat the murder rap? Would Ivy go back to him and pick up where they left off so many years ago? Where would that leave *him?* He thought about Fiona Wescott. Fiona was still a very attractive woman, but there was something so different about her now. The years had hardened her. But, was it just the passage of time in a stressful job, or had deep disappointment caused her to become so bitter? It was obvious that she still had feelings for him, but he hoped that wouldn't cloud her judgment investigating the Lacy Snow case.

John made his way to the ultra-luxurious high rise on Ocean Blvd. that Crystal and Robert Montrose called home. He parked underneath in one of the visitor's spaces and stepped into the elevator that would transport him to the lobby. When the doors opened, he spotted a guy sitting in a wing chair. It just had to be Joe Appel. He had *lawyer* written all over him. John approached and introduced himself.

"Pleased to meet you Garrett," Appel said.

"I guess we're to wait here for Ivy and Sloane." John put his hands in his pockets and surveyed the lobby. He was trained to be hyper aware of his surroundings. Joe Appel kept looking at his watch as if staring at the hands would make them move faster.

"What do you think Ivy Snow hopes to accomplish here?" Joe asked.

"To expose Bianca Villa's killer."

"That's a long shot."

“Maybe, but Ivy adopts the axiom, give 'em *enough rope and they'll hang themselves.* It's really about the arrogance of most criminals. They generally think that they're smarter than everybody else, and they won't get caught.”

“I've seen enough of that. The fact that they're wrong is what keeps me in business” Joe said.

John grinned, and shook his head...yeah, in business and in the big bucks!

Sloane and I hit some traffic on the way over to Ocean Drive. There was a big golf tournament going on at Mar-A-Lago, and the spectators were out in droves.

“I hope we're not going to be late. We've got to meet up with John and Joe and get to Crystal's before the others arrive. The element of surprise is so important. I want to observe their reactions when they see us there, and when they learn that a police detective and Vincent Villa's lawyer will be joining them for dinner.”

"Ivy let's take the side streets. There are more stop signs, but we'll get there faster" Sloane said.

Miraculously, we arrived at the lobby in time. I introduced Sloane to Joe Appel. I could tell that she was thinking that I wasn't that far off with the Clooney comparison. I pushed the button for the private elevator that would take us to the penthouse.

CHAPTER FORTY-NINE

Detective Anderson sent a memo to the DA as soon as he learned that Vincente Villa's lawyer was petitioning for an Arthur Hearing. He was convinced that Villa killed his wife, and if he were granted bail he would waste no time in heading for Mozambique or some other country with no extradition treaty. Villa had deep pockets. So even if bail was set for a million dollars, it wouldn't pose a problem for him. Even if the court was to ground his private plane, Villa has a lot of contacts that would be willing to help. Anderson wanted to make sure that the DA had the big picture.

He got behind the wheel of his Crown Victoria and started for Delray. He was meeting with Mrs. Pritz, the woman who owned the Sparkling Sands Trailer Park where Julia Forrest lived. He'd taken a photo of Julia during his last hospital visit. He'd show it to Pritz and get this whole thing cleared up.

He headed down 95 in light traffic, so he should be there in about half an hour. He turned on the radio to catch up on local news. What he heard was an Ashanti Alert issued for a Missing

Vulnerable Adult from Wellington Hospital. The woman's name...*Dr. Julia Forrest.* Shit! Could this get any worse? He could tell that there was something wrong with the woman the last time he saw her. He should have assigned a patrolman to guard her room, especially since she'd left the hospital once before.

They had no leads on her assailant. What if there's a second attempt on her life? Anderson berated himself for being so careless. At the very least he should have insisted that she be moved to a secure floor. He stepped on the gas and moved into the passing lane. The pressure to solve this case was greater than ever. The chance of finding a missing person alive after twenty-four hours is very slim.

He arrived at the trailer marked "Office" at the Sparkling Sands Trailer Park. He was met by a woman who appeared to be in her late sixties or early seventies.

"Mrs. Pritz?" he asked.

"Yes. You must be Detective Anderson."

She led him to a folding chair opposite her desk. The office was bare bones. Brownish gray carpet, faux walnut paneling on the walls. A calendar with a beach scene photo that served as art. What did he expect? It wasn't like she was renting a pied-a-terre on Park Avenue. He wondered why Julia Forrest would want to live in such a place. She was a veterinarian with a well-established practice. Surely, she could afford better.

"Mrs. Pritz, you said that one of your tenants is missing? A woman?"

"Yes. I haven't seen her for a couple of weeks. Rent was due last Thursday, and she didn't drop off a check. She always pays on time, so that got me worried."

"What do you know about this woman? How long has she lived here?"

"Almost a year. She's the quiet type. Maybe I shouldn't say *quiet.* More like anti-social. She didn't mix with any of the other tenants. It was even hard to get a 'hello' out of her. But Sharon didn't cause any trouble. Like I said, she paid her rent on time."

Anderson took out the photo of Julia Forrest and showed it to Mrs. Pritz.

"Yes, that's her! Sharon Zelinsky."

Fiona Westcott felt her Cold Case warming up a little. Her next step was to contact the burglary victims to see if they might be able to shed some light on her growing theory. The first try was for Edgar Hughes, the older gentleman who was robbed of his Polo trophy. Unfortunately, Mr. Hughes died two years ago. Next was Dr. and Mrs Henry Morgan. Mrs. Morgan claimed loss of an Opera length strand of pearls, an emerald ring, and a Harry Winston Diamond brooch. Fiona discovered that the Morgans had retired to the Amalfi Coast 6 years ago. She would try to contact them if need be.

It was with the next burglary victim that her luck changed. Mrs. Cecilia Cartwright. The widow who was robbed of her husband's wedding band, among other items. The phone number listed on the report was defunct. Not surprising since cell phones have taken the place of landlines for so many. She jotted down Mrs. Cartwright's Mayfair address and had officer White drive her. The door to the elegant townhouse was answered by an equally elegant lady.

"Mrs. Cecilia Cartwright? I'm inspector Fiona Westcott from Scotland Yard."

“Yes, I'm Mrs. Cartwright. What's the matter inspector?”
“Nothing. I heard about the burglary. Would you have a few minutes?”
“Yes, of course. But I can't even imagine! It happened so long ago. Please come in.”

Fiona entered the charming foyer. It was painted a lovely shade of yellow, which was the perfect backdrop for the gilt-framed portrait of Cecilia and the man who was most supposedly her husband. Cecilia ushered Fiona into the sitting room. The soft blue and white colors reflected the owner's fine taste. Fiona removed a file from her briefcase, containing the report on the Cartwright burglary.
“Mrs. Cartwright, we may have a new lead in the case.” Fiona was exaggerating a bit, but she needed to have a probable reason for these inquiries.
“Really! I'm amazed. Have there been more robberies?”
“Not In this area. I don't want to frighten you, but maybe there's something seemingly unrelated that could lead us in the right direction. I would like to just review a few facts.”
“Alright, I’ll try to help in any way I can.”

“This report says that your deceased husband's wedding ring was among the stolen items.”
“Yes, it's what devastated me most. Of course, I wasn't happy about losing my diamond bracelets, or my Phillipe Patek watch, but all those things could be replaced. My husband's wedding ring could not. Nor, for that matter, could my Victorian Cameo ring. It was a family heirloom…from my great grandmother.”
Fiona frowned. “Yes, about that ring? It was listed as a ‘poison’ ring. What’s that?”
“Well, it's really kind of a novelty, I suppose. It opened…like a locket. Victorians liked their little secret compartments. I think my grandmother hid her lover’s picture!” Mrs. Cartwright blushed.
Fiona nodded as she made a note. “How long had your husband been deceased when the burglary took place?”
“Charles passed away about a year prior.” Mrs. Cartwright said.
“I’m so sorry, oh, it must have been very difficult for you. Are you aware that seven other households in Mayfair were burglarized in the same time frame as yours?”
“Yes, that was very frightening for the entire neighborhood.”

“Did you know any of the other victims?”
“Why yes, but not all that well.”
“It says in the report, that besides being Mayfair neighbors, you were all members of Blacks Club.”
“That’s right. I believe that the police suspected that someone from the club might have been involved. I know that the staff was questioned, but nothing ever came of it.”
“Mrs. Cartwright, did you and your husband socialize with any of the others that were robbed? Outside of the club, I mean?”
“Not really. We had dinner with Doctor Morgan and his wife Susan at Claridge's a few times, and of course we did see the others at the club, but we didn't have that much in common. After Charles died, I didn't feel much like going out. Not that I wasn't asked.” Cecilia said with a slight smile.
“I understand.” Fiona said.
“Well, there was this one fellow I dated some. A man from the club, as a matter of fact.”
Cecilia's eyes reflected the memory surfacing.
“He was a widower. He'd lost his wife a few years ago. I knew her of course. A wonderful horsewoman and a gifted writer. Lucy Snow.”
Fiona snapped to attention, “Lucy Snow?”

"Yes, I did go out with her husband Lloyd a few times. It might have worked out if not for that repulsive daughter of his. She was a cheap little tart, nothing like her mother. Lucy would have been so disappointed. But Lloyd doted on her. You know, I don't even remember her name. Must have deliberately put it out of my mind. Lisa? Linda? Something like that."

"Thank you, Mrs. Cartwright. If you remember anything else about the robbery, please contact me," Fiona said. She left her card.

CHAPTER FIFTY

I introduced Joe Appel to Robert and Crystal. "So, Joe, are you going to get Vincente out of this mess?" Crystal was never one to mince words.

"That's the plan. But first I'm petitioning the court for bail."

"How soon do you think he'll be out?"

"I'm waiting to hear when I can go before the judge."

"That shouldn't be too hard. Vincente is an upstanding citizen, and he's got plenty of money for bail."

"That's all in his favor, but the court will look at him as a Flight Risk. He can live anywhere in the world. Now that Bianca's dead, and his stable is gone, there's nothing to tie him here."

John looked over at me. I knew what he was thinking. As Robert began pouring the drinks the buzzer rang. It was Ross and Lena. They arrived in the foyer seconds later and couldn't hide their surprise at seeing us. Robert hadn't mentioned that there would be other guests. He introduced John and Joe by name only, no titles.

As far as Ross and Lena knew we were all just on one big date.

Next, Lloyd and Enrico came up in the elevator together. Lloyd was wearing a hearty smile, which quickly disappeared the moment he saw me. It took him a moment to adjust his countenance, his eyes fixed on my golden coin earrings. But his smarmy smile was back in no time. That is until Lena returned from the powder room. His eyes narrowed when they met hers. She stopped in her tracks and scanned the room as if she were looking for an escape hatch. Enrico quickly moved in and took her hand. "Lena. It is so nice to see you again. You look lovely as always. Lena quickly composed herself and smiled. I noticed Enrico's *as always.* Had they seen each other after Crystal's last dinner party? Perhaps on the polo field? Palm Beach was a small town. Ross stepped in and handed Lena her drink. As she reached for the glass, I noticed a large ring on her right hand. It reminded me of one my mother often wore. I hadn't thought about that ring in years. Wonder whatever happened to it? I noticed Lloyd was already on his second martini. He was fidgeting with his Rolex. The air was rife with tension, despite the infusion of Stoli. Finally, Robert raised his glass to make a toast.

"Welcome everyone. Thank you for joining Crystal and me for what I'm sure will be a delicious dinner, especially since neither of us prepared it!"

We all chuckled, except Crystal, who rolled her eyes.

"Since we're all involved or would like to be involved in the horse business, I thought it would be beneficial to have a conversation about the landscape here in Palm Beach County now that Villa Stables is gone, and the prospect of Bianca Villa's Equine Wellness Center are no more. A deafening silence fell over the room. Enrico looked at Sloane. She looked at Ross, and he couldn't take his eyes off Robert.

A voice from the dining room shattered the silence. "Dinner is served." We all looked at each other, and then slowly moved to take our places at the table. There in the doorway stood Dr. Julia Forrest, dressed in a server's uniform, brandishing a Glock 26.

"Are you sure Mrs. Printz?" Detective Anderson asked.

"Of course, I am. Sharon Zelinsky has been my tenant for, oh, I guess eight months now."

"Is there anyone else living with her? Another roommate... a woman?"

"We don't allow subletting here. Everybody living at Silver Sands has to have their name on the lease."

"May I see a copy of her lease?"

Mrs. Pritz pushed her chair away from her desk and spun around to face the tall black filing cabinet behind. She bent down and opened the bottom drawer pulling out a folder marked Zelinsky. She handed the lease document to the detective. Just one signature, and the handwriting matched that of Dr. Julia Forrest... exactly.

Anderson climbed back into his Crown Victoria. It all began to make sense. There was no perpetrator of the assault on Dr. Forrest. The argument that Ivy Snow heard in Villa's tack room was an argument between two women in the same body. The wound was self-inflicted. What was Ivy saying at the hospital? Multiple Personality Disorder? Where was Dr. Forrest... or Sharon Zelinsky now?

CHAPTER FIFTY-ONE

We all froze. I was mesmerized as I stared down the barrel of the Glock, but more so as I stared into the eyes of Julia Forrest.

"Put down that gun," John said.

Her hand moved slowly, pointing the barrel at each one of us in turn. I could see that she had no intention of putting it down.

"Julia please" I said.

"Julia? You know very well I'm Sharon. I told you that in the hospital. Remember? I couldn't possibly be Julia. Julia is the smart one, the golden girl. She's a doctor, a renowned veterinarian. Oh yes, those precious horses! Too bad for the ones in Kentucky. Too bad for the ones in Villa Stables. Too bad they had to die. But they were just animals. They weren't humans. Not like my little girl. My little girl that Julia killed.

I caught my breath. What was this woman talking about? What little girl? It was obvious that she was mad.

She stared into my eyes. "And you. You and your meddling daughter, Jaycee. Following me around, spying on me. I should have done away

with that Pirate when I had the chance. That would have sent you packing back to Pennsylvania."
"Listen Julia... Sharon. You need help. We'll help you, but you've got to put down that gun."

My cell rang, I glanced down to see that it was Detective Anderson. Julia glanced down too. John grabbed her arm pointing the gun to the ceiling. It went off into the chandelier sending a shower of Baccarat crystal onto the exquisitely set table below. We all gazed on it in horror, all except Lena and Enrico who silently backed out of the room. I didn't notice their departure until I saw the elevator door close behind them. I rushed over and hit the button. It was too late. They were gone.

It was as though everyone snapped to at once. Lloyd, and Ross darted for the elevator.
"Stop," shouted John.
It was no use. The elevator was gone. John had Julia in handcuffs. I called Detective Anderson and told him where to find us. Sloane suggested that we all adjourn to the living room and wait for him there.

Lena fished the car keys out of her tiger shaped Midori as she and Enrico hurried toward the Aston Martin. They sped down Ocean Boulevard toward Ross's penthouse. As soon as they were able to breathe, they laughed.

"How lucky could we get Enrico?"

"No luckier la mujer. I can't believe how Dr. Forrest freaked out!"

"This makes it all so much easier," Lena said as she pulled in front of the condo. Leave the Aston here. We're going to need the Escalade."

They took the express elevator to the top. Lena headed to the bedroom where she had a suitcase filled with the designer clothes Ross bought, and millions of dollars' worth of stolen jewels.

"We may as well take the paintings too," Enrico said.

"We can take all but the painting of the Texas range."

"Why not that one?" he asked.

"It's attached to the wall. See?"

Lena pulled at the painting to reveal a wall safe. She smiled as she moved the dial one way, then the other. Open Sesame! She grabbed Ross's jewels, and piles of neatly wrapped cash, and headed for the door.

There was a ship leaving from the Port of Miami at midnight, and they would be on it. They dropped off the paintings with a friend of Enrico's who would fence them for a generous commission. Enrico and Lena, now Mrs. Enrico Alvero actually... Lena Snow Alvero... would soon be enjoying a martini at the dock, waiting to board. Lloyd's daughter had never been happier. She just killed two birds with one stone.

Detective Anderson was met with shouts of protest.

"They have no right to keep us here! That crazy bitch tried to kill us," said Ross.

"Bloody well right," said Lloyd.

"Calm down, we'll need your statements." Anderson wasn't having any of it.

Ross was shaking. "That bitch Lena and Enrico Alvero took off! You've got to find them!"

"First things first," Anderson said.

I explained everything that happened, and Anderson thanked John for getting the situation in hand. Julia sat silently in the corner, staring into space. I was afraid she might be having a total psychotic break.

"Another successful dinner party," said Crystal.

I put my arm around her shoulder. "Listen, we may not have accomplished our mission... exonerating Vincente, but we did flush out Julia Forrest. Now maybe she'll get the help she needs."

"That poor woman. She couldn't cope with losing her daughter. Sometimes I think it's easier if you don't have kids."

I stroked Crystal's hair, knowing that she didn't mean a word of it.

Sloan pointed to her watch. We'd better go. The girls would be wondering where we were. I shot a glance at Lloyd... this wasn't over, not by a long shot.

Detective Anderson placed Julia in the care of a policewoman, placed an APB out on Lena and Enrico, and went to his office to start the mound of paperwork that this case would require. He hung up his jacket and poured a cup of coffee.

As he sat down at his desk, he saw a large blue envelope sitting on top of his keyboard. The handwriting was loopy and feminine. He read Lena's letter…

Dear Detective Anderson,

By the time you read this, I will be far far away. Don't even think of trying to find me. I'm writing to you because I believe in a certain kind of Justice. Maybe it's not your kind of Justice, but it'll be useful all the same. First, let me assure you that Vicente Villa did not kill his wife. How do I know? Well, I'll tell you more about that later. But for now, I want you to know that you can't blame yourself for not being able to solve this crime. You see, it all started a long time ago in a place far away... London, England. That's where I was born. My mother was a horsewoman, and my father was a writer. One day my father told me that my mother fell off her horse and died. He said that we lost all our money and wouldn't be able to live in Mayfair unless we got a lot more. I loved Mayfair. I was only 14. I didn't understand. My father said that we would form our own secret society. We would call ourselves "The Snow Storm." Our mission was to get jewelry from the rich people in the neighborhood, who had a lot more than we did. Daddy would choose the people, mostly from his club, and he would tell me when they wouldn't be home. I learned how to sneak into their houses and get their diamonds and pearls... everything beautiful and valuable. Dad was very proud of me. We wouldn't always stay in Mayfair, sometimes we went to other places in London. Sometimes we even went out to the country.

Then one day, he told me that he met a lady that he wanted to marry. Her name was Lacy. She had a daughter, younger than me. He didn't want me to live with them. He said that I was 18, and I could live on my own. My dad had another family, but he didn't really abandon me. We were still "The Snow Storm." Although I didn't live with them, I would visit once in a while. Lacey was a decorator. They had a beautiful home, they had beautiful clothes, they had a beautiful life.

I learned that my father adopted the girl, Ivy. I hated that. She became a horsewoman, just like my mother had been. One day, my father told me that Lacy was getting suspicious about "The Snowstorm." She said that she knew he was "up to no good." She asked him if he was having an affair. He said "no," but she was watching his every move. If we didn't do something, we could no longer be "The Snowstorm." So, I made a plan. One cold morning I went to visit Lacey. Dad went to New Market. I made her a cup of my special Belladonna tea. When she died, I got scared that they'd find out it was me! So, I went to Texas where there were more rich people, leaving Mayfair forever.

That's when I met Ross Spencer. He was rich, but he was an asshole. The saving grace was his penthouse in Palm Beach. Ross always thought I was stupid, but he was the stupid one. Then things got complicated when my father showed up out of the blue. He said I owed him money from the haul we made in England. I said that money was long gone. He told me about his ideas for reviving "The Snow Storm." I told him that I work alone now. He wasn't happy about that.

Things were coming to an end in Palm Beach. Ross was getting angrier and meaner every day. His grand plans for the Palais Palm Beach weren't working out, mostly because of Bianca Villa owning the land he needed so badly. I decided to help him out there, (not to mention myself!) You know, kill two birds with one stone. That Harry Winston necklace Bianca had was worth at least a million. It could set Enrico and me up in style. So, you see, Detective, Vincente Villa didn't kill his wife, Bianca. I did.

Regards,

Lena Snow Alvero
P. S. I sent a copy of this letter to Scotland Yard.

Shit, shit, shit! Anderson pounded his fists on the desktop. He hit the computer keys with a vengeance. How could he have been so stupid? Was he losing his grip? His instincts? How could he not have seen through that Lena? She was a caricature. A cardboard character acting the part of the "dumb blonde." So typical...so easy to overlook. Just Ross Spencer's arm candy. And here she was...pulling the strings all along.

Well, he wasn't the only one she fooled. What about Garrett? Always the "Golden Boy."

Always the prime example of exemplary police work. What about *him*...he didn't see it! He didn't see that "nobody" Lena was a master jewel thief, and Lloyd Snow's daughter to boot! And what about *oh so clever* amateur sleuth Ivy Snow. Lena got right past her too. Hmm...wait a minute. Think about that! What an uncanny turn of events! Lena and Ivy are actually stepsisters! Anderson laughed out loud as he wiped beads of sweat from his forehead. He really blew it this time. There would be consequences. His career was about to implode.

Julia Forrest/Sharon Zelinsky was back in the hospital psych ward. Who was she really? The dedicated and caring vet that took such good care of our horses? Or the former nurse practitioner whose grief over her dead child drove her to madness? I closed my eyes and tried to imagine the two women living their separate lives, but in the same body. I took a deep breath, filling my lungs with the sweet aroma of tropical air that I almost started taking for granted here in paradise.

The girls were done with their classes. They'd done very well, and could certainly be proud of their performance, especially for the first time in such a competitive arena. It would be time to head back home soon to cold, snowy Pennsylvania. To be honest, I wasn't looking forward to it. I missed Jayson, of course, and my lovely Little Paddocks. But there was something here that was compelling me to stay. What would Dr. Frick say? *Perhaps unfinished business, Ivy?*

CHAPTER FIFTY-TWO

Jaycee awoke with a start, wondering if what she just saw was a dream, or a premonition. It was so hard to tell sometimes. In her vision she saw that blonde woman and a man. He looked familiar, but she couldn't place him. They were sitting in a bar near the ocean, drinking fancy drinks. There were giant ships everywhere. She groped for her cell on the nightstand and hit the speed dial to reach her mom. Voicemail. She'd have to leave a message. "Mom! Where are you? I saw that woman. I mean I dreamed about that woman...I think? You know, the one that looks like that movie star...Marilyn something. Mom, she's the one! The one who killed grandma! She's getting away. We've got to stop her! Call me!"

Jaycee hit the "end call" button and scrambled out of bed. Where was her mom? She shimmied into her jeans and pulled a gray t-shirt over her head. Where were her Chucks? A frantic search located them under the bed. What to do now? Get Trina? No. No use waking her up. Besides, she was unsure of what would happen, and she couldn't put her friend in danger. Not again.

Those ships...where were they? Where were they going? She grabbed her phone and Googled “ships traveling from Florida.” A bunch of ads for cruise lines came up. Of course! That was it! They were getting away on a cruise ship. Where do you get on a cruise ship? She ran through posts and saw that the best bets were from the Port of Miami. It was the biggest port, so it made sense. She hit the UBER app and grabbed her jacket from the back of the desk chair.

The car that responded was a white KIA. The driver was a young, dark-skinned guy, blasting a Rap station. As she opened the rear passenger door and slid in, he turned the radio off. “Port of Miami? " he asked.

“Yes, said Jaycee.

“Where in the Port of Miami? It's a big place.”

“I’ll let you know when we get there,” she said. She really had no idea.

Her mom’s phone went to voicemail again. She could feel her heart racing in her chest. Her cheeks burned, even in the cool night air. She took a deep breath to get grounded, just like she did when Pirate got panicky. She had to get a grip and make a plan. According to Google Maps, it would take a little over an hour to reach

Miami. Not much time. The ping, pong sound of her ringtone signaled a call from Trina.

"Hey...hi!"

"Where are you? I woke up and you're gone!" Trina said.

"I'm in an UBER, headed for Miami."

"What the hell for?"

"I don't even know how to explain it. I got one of my visions…"

"Oh, no Jaycee…"

"Listen Trina, I need your help. Remember when we were talking about that blonde movie star?"

"Yaa. Marilyn Monroe. I remember."

"Well, it's *HER*."

"Who's *HER?"*

"The one that *looks* like the movie star! She's the one who killed my grandmother back in England when my mom was accused."

"How do you know that?" Trina asked.

"I had a vision."

"Oh God, Jaycee."

"Comeon, you gotta help me here."

"Sure, sure." Sometimes it was really weird being Jaycee's friend. "So, why are you going to Miami?"

"Because I think she's at the seaport there, waiting to board a ship. She's with a guy. He looks familiar. That's all I know."

"Jaycee, this is crazy. You'll never find them. That place is huge. There must be dozens of ships leaving there tonight."

"You're right Trina. You're right! There are only so many ships sailing tonight. They're waiting for one of them...one that will be boarding soon!"

"Okay, Jaycee. That does narrow it down...but still."

"It's a start. See if you can find out which ships are leaving there tonight. You've got to hurry Trina. I'm only about forty-five minutes away."

"Okay. I'm on it."

"Oh, and Trina, try and call my mom. She's not picking up."

"No need. Your mom and Aunt Sloane just walked through the door."

CHAPTER FIFTY-THREE

Trina filled us in on what Jaycee was up to. I could skin that kid alive! I pulled out my cell to call her, and tell her to get her ass back here, but soon realized that the damn battery was dead.

"Sloane, can I use your phone?"

"Wait!" said Trina. "I'm onto something! Here's the website with the departure schedules."

I scanned the itineraries for each terminal. There were quite a few. It would take forever to check the manifests...even if we could get that information. Hmm...what would that bubble head be doing? That's just it. Lena wasn't a bubble head. It's an act...an act we all bought into. It was like she was hiding in plain sight. No, Lena was clever, she had to be. After all, she was getting away with murder.

I studied the list of cruise lines and their impending destinations. They were embarking ships worldwide...so many destinations! Where would Lena and Enrico be going? South America? Back to Argentina? Probably not, it would be too easy for Vincente to find them. Wait...the smart thing to do would be to go where they couldn't be found or arrested. Somewhere without an extradition treaty to the United States.

"Sloane, Google countries without extradition treaties to the U.S."

She smiled broadly. "Yes, that narrows the list somewhat. Only fifty -six countries Ivy!"

I picked up the phone and called Detective Anderson. We needed intelligence and back-up, and we needed it now. He set a rookie on the task of investigating cruise ships sailing tonight to countries without extradition treaties. He and Wilson would head for Miami. I called John and he agreed to pick me up here. Sloane got the Range Rover and headed for Crystal's.

With search parties assembled, we stood a better chance of finding Lena and Enrico before Jaycee did. I couldn't imagine what that girl was thinking! Even if she found those two, what would she do? Citizen's arrest? Kids! She's only putting herself in danger and scaring the hell out of me.

Jaycee tried stretching out her long lanky legs. The Kia afforded little room in the backseat, and she was feeling cramped. They were only about half an hour from the port, and she still had no idea what she would do when she got there. Where were they? Where were they going? She had to find out. That woman killed her grandmother. She was sure of it. Her premonitions were never wrong. But why? Why would she do it? That was the question turning over in her mind. Everything that happened since they arrived in Florida was so strange. First, all those polo ponies died. Then her "grandfather" showed up. Finding out that her mother had been arrested for murder. And then, Mrs. Villa's death. They came down for a horse show, and all hell broke loose.

Her phone pinged again.... Trina. "What's up? Whaddya find?"

"Okay Jaycee, I'd say your best bets are The Royal Caribbean to Montenegro, or The Norwegian Princess to the Maldives. Neither country has extradition to the US " Trina said.

"Okay good!"

"And, both countries have English as a second language."

"Hmm, so what do you think?" asked Jaycee.

“I don't know. One advantage is that Montenegro uses the Euro. It would be easy to convert money.”

“That’s true. What about the Maldives?”

“It’s the Rufiyaa...don't ask!”

“That might pose a bit more of a problem,” said Jaycee.

“There’s something else to be considered,” said Trina.

“What’s that?”

“Montenegro is 1093 miles from London. The Maldives is 5,330 miles. I’ll bet that they want to get as far away from London as possible.”

“Maldives it is then! Joe...Joe…”

The Uber driver snapped out of his Hip Hop haze. “Yeah, what?”

“Take me to The Norwegian Princess terminal. And hurry!”

Lloyd slammed the door of his rented silver Jaguar and mounted his cell phone on the dash. He revved up the engine and threw the car into reverse. The tracking app that he'd installed on Lena's phone told Google Maps where to go. It was so easy. The moment Lena headed to the Montrose's bar for her martini dividend, Lloyd slipped her phone out of her purse. He excused himself to the powder room and downloaded the tracking software onto her cell. He returned to the living room and waited for an opportunity to place the phone back in her purse. He didn't have to wait for long. That little bitch had her back turned and was whispering something in Alvero's ear. Perfect. He slipped the phone back into her tiger shaped Midori without detection, smiling like the Cheshire Cat. Now we'll see who has the brains in the family! If Lena thinks she'll abscond with Bianca's outrageous necklace...and whatever else from chez Spencer...she's got another thought coming! Hmm, looks like they're heading south.

CHAPTER FIFTY-FOUR

"I suppose you can't go any faster?"
"I'm already doing eighty, Ivy" John said.
"Sorry, I'm on my last nerve!"
"I know. Try and stay calm. We'll find her."
"We've got to get to her before she finds Lena and Enrico. I have no idea what she thinks she's doing, but those two are ruthless."

My cell rang and I hit the answer button to hear Anderson's voice. I put him on speaker phone.

"Where are you?"
"I'm halfway to Miami. Listen Ivy, there's something I've got to tell you, and you're not going to like it" Anderson said.
"What?"
"Lena left a note for me at the station. Turns out Lloyd Snow is her father, and that's not all. She confessed to killing your mother...and Bianca Villa."
"What?" I gasped.

My whole body froze. What was Detective Anderson saying? John shot me a look, then quickly averted his eyes back to the road. I tried to compose myself. Lena killed my mother?" It was the only thing I homed in on. Why? “That’s insane, Detective.”

“It could be the ramblings of a mad woman, but I don't think so. We’ll check it out, of course, but for right now I’m going on the assumption that it's true.”

I sat quietly for a moment, staring at the oncoming headlights, trying to comprehend everything Anderson said. Lena killed my mother. Lena is Lloyd’s daughter. Oh my God! If that’s true, does that mean that I’m her *stepsister?* Woah! No way! That can’t be!

“Ivy! Ivy!”

“What? What John?”

“We've got to focus here.”

“Of course. Of course.” I whispered. I hadn’t realized it, but Anderson was still on the line. “Detective, what’s your plan?”

“We’re headed to the port. I’m waiting to hear from the Harbor Police. We sent them a description of Lena and Alvero. And Jaycee.”

Lloyd Snow walked into the cocktail lounge, scanning the room for Lena and Enrico. His gaze stopped at the bar, where he saw Lena sitting alone. He slid onto the barstool next to her and slipped the barrel of the Glock 42 gently into her ribcage. She froze.

"Where's Alvero?" Lloyd whispered under his breath.

"Men's room."

"Okay, not much time," he said.

"Time for what?" Lena hissed.

"To get out of here."

"I'm not going anywhere with you, *Daddy*."

"You most certainly are," Lloyd said, as if ordering a child to her room.

Lena's eyes blazed with fury.

"Where's the rest of the stuff? Lloyd demanded.

"Enrico has it." Lena looked down at her carry on, her gaze betraying her.

"Ah! Let's go!" Lloyd said.

Lena slid off her bar stool. They turned to leave, only to see Jaycee standing right in front of them.

"What are you doing here, my dear?" Lloyd said, trying to hide his shock at seeing her.

"I'm here looking for *her,*" Jaycee said, pointing at Lena.

"You should be at home, young lady!" Lloyd said, trying to muster authority.

Jaycee started at Lena. "You killed my grandmother!"

"Who are you?" asked Lena.

Jaycee was silent for a moment. "Well, I guess I'm your niece."

Lena shot a look at Lloyd.

"She's Ivy's daughter. So, she's right" he said.

The wheels in Lloyd's brain were spinning. He made a snap decision. *The Snowstorm* could use some psychic intuition. He moved toward Jaycee, nudging Lena along with him. He gently put his hand on Jaycee's arm, and subtly revealed the barrel of the gun in Lena's ribs.

"You're coming with us," he whispered.

"No I'm not" Jaycee hissed.

He tightened his grip on her arm, ever so slightly, not wanting to call attention to this little scene.

"Just walk with me and no one will get hurt" he whispered in Jaycee's ear.

They moved quickly and quietly across the room before Enrico returned. Lloyd led them to the elevator and ordered Lena to hit the button for the tenth floor. The Jaguar was parked at the far end. He instructed Lena to get in behind the wheel, while he slid into the backseat with Jaycee.

"Alright, we're going with you. You can put that gun away." Lena said.

"Oh no Daughter. Not until we're far from here! Far from anyone who might try and stop us."

As instructed, Lena backed the car out of the parking space, and started the slow descent down the circular ramp. She could see Lloyd's gun now pointing at Jaycee. He'd stop at nothing now, she thought.

CHAPTER FIFTY-FIVE

Enrico returned from the men's room to find Lena's bar stool empty. His head spun like a swivel searching the room for her. His blood ran cold. She was gone. That double crossing little bitch! How could she do this to him? He trusted her. He trusted her with the jewels. He even trusted her enough to *marry* her! What a fool he'd been. He wasn't gone that long. She couldn't have gotten too far. She had the key to Spencer's Escalade. She must have planned this all along. She never had any intention of getting on that ship for the Maldives. He bolted out of the cocktail lounge, almost knocking down an elderly lady and her Chihuahua, and headed straight for the parking garage.

Lena reached the ground floor, and Lloyd handed her his credit card to pay the toll. She pulled out into the open air to see Enrico charging right at them, screaming obscenities. She had no choice. She pressed the accelerator pedal to the floor and headed straight for him. He was blinded by the headlights and froze. Lena slammed the car into his body full force. He flew through the air and smashed down hard onto the pavement. Jaycee screamed in terror. Lena threw the Jaguar into reverse, and spun around, heading for the open road.

"What the bloody hell do you think you're doing?" shouted Lloyd.

"Kicking up a *Snow Storm* Daddy!" Lena laughed. As she reached the exit, she caught sight of a car coming in the opposite direction. As they passed, her eyes locked with those of the passenger, Ivy Snow. Lena squinted in determination. With a death grip on the wheel, she slammed her foot on the gas.

"John! It's them! Turn around!" I screamed. He twisted the wheel hard and took off after the speeding car in front of him. He gained on them quickly, his skills homed in by more than one high speed chase.

"Oh my God John! Jaycee is in that car!" I could see her thrashing about in the backseat, fighting with someone. Who? We were gaining ground. It was Lloyd! No!

Lena kicked the F-Pace into full gear, leaving John's Toyota in the dust. "We've got to get rid of this kid" she shouted at Lloyd.

He knew that. Ivy would follow them to the ends of the earth. He didn't want to hurt Jaycee. She *was* his granddaughter. "Pullover!"

She pulled the car to the side of the road. Lloyd opened the door, and shoved Jaycee out, sending her rolling down into a trench. He slammed the door shut, and Lena hit the gas, tires spinning.

John was pushing the Toyota as fast as it would go, but it was no match for the Jaguar as we watched its turbo engine jettison the car out of our reach. I sat next to him terrified and helpless. If Lloyd did anything to harm Jaycee, I'd kill him with my bare hands. Woah! What's that?

"John! Slow down!" I screeched.

"What?"

"Oh my God! John! He pushed her out!"

Jaycee slid down the ravine, landing inches from the drainage ditch. John pulled the car to the side of the road. I jumped out of the passenger side and ran to the boulder-strewn edge, squinting into the dusky light in search of my daughter. I spotted her lying still, *so close* to the water. Oh no! What's that? I could barely make it out. The water was moving, rippling quickly, steadily toward Jaycee. What was it? I realized then that John was standing next to me. Even in the semi-darkness, I could see that his face was chalk white.

"Ivy!"
"What is that John?"
"Alligator."
I choked a scream! I lunged forward, trying to find my footing as I half-ran, half-slid down the embankment. I could see the gator's snout moving closer and closer to the water's edge. Closer to Jaycee. He was too fast...I'd never make it in time! I could see his hooded eye sockets as he emerged to the surface. I sensed something rushing past me. A large boulder tumbled down the hillside, barely missing me, but landing squarely on the gator's head. He stopped...just floated there...deadly still in the water.

I scrambled toward Jaycee, grabbing her by the ankles, dragging her away from the water. I felt John's arm around my waist, hoisting us upward toward the road.
Tears were running down both of our faces.
"Come honey. Get in the car. Are you alright?"
"I'm okay," she said as she brushed the dirt from her jeans. She was shaking.
I put my arms around her and held her tight.
"What on earth did you think you were doing, coming down here?"

"I don't know Mom, but I had a vision. I knew it was that blond woman that killed your mom and Mrs. Villa. I couldn't reach you, so I had to do something to stop them from getting away."

I shook my head. I must never allow my cell phone battery to die again. We could have avoided all of this.

"Mom, we have to stop them."

"I know honey, but how?"

"I heard her say that they could circle back and still make the ship to the Maldives."

John turned the car around and sped back to the Port of Miami.

After Lloyd and Lena ditched the Jaguar in South Beach, they took an UBER back to the port. They headed to the terminal to board the ship to the Maldives, only to find that they were too late. The ship had already sailed.

"Bloody Hell" Lloyd said. "Now what?"

Lena smiled. "I always have plan B, Daddy."

"What's Plan B?"

"Montenegro."

"What? Why on earth would we go there?"
"Because of extradition laws. Enrico and I debated whether we should go to the Maldives, or to Montenegro. Neither country has an extradition treaty with the United States. We picked the Maldives because it's on the other side of the world...and it's a tropical paradise! So, Montenegro will do just fine for now. The money exchange is easier anyway, and we can fence these jewels without any problem."
"I've forgotten how smart you are, Lena."
Cunning is more like it, he thought.
She smiled. We've got to get our tickets. May as well be upper deck suites. It's a good thing Ross had plenty of cash in his safe."

The suites were luxurious, as they should have been for the price. Private balconies, butler service, champagne greeting. Perfect. It would be smooth sailing all the way.

CHAPTER FIFTY-SIX

We arrived back at the port to find that the Maldives ship had sailed. The Harbor Police cooperated with John and provided the passenger list. It included Lena and Enrico but showed that neither boarded. Where were they? The APB resulted in finding the abandoned Jaguar in South Beach, without a trace of Lloyd or Lena. So, they weren't traveling by car, at least not *that* car. The police were searching the airports, train station and bus depot. I couldn't imagine Lloyd or Lena traveling by bus, but who knows what they might do to throw us off the scent.

I looked over at Jaycee. She'd been unusually quiet since we picked her up on the roadside. She said that she's fine, but I don't know. It must have been quite a hard landing in that trench.

"Honey, are you okay?" I asked her again.

She squinted her eyes and shook her head, as if clearing the cobwebs. "Mom. There's another ship. They're on another ship."

"What ship, Jaycee?"

She was staring into space. I knew that look. She was seeing something in her mind's eye and trying to make sense of it. How frustrating it must be for her! To search for the answer, for a vision to solve the puzzle going round and round in her mind.

"I *fucking* don't believe it!" Anderson said as he jammed his cell phone back into the pocket of his tan linen sport coat.

"I know...I know!" said Sloane. "We were so close."

"Has anybody heard from Ivy?" Crystal asked.

"Not since she called about finding Jaycee," Anderson said.

"Thank God she's okay. If anything, ever happened to her...Ivy would...well, I don't know," said Sloane.

Anderson felt his phone vibrate. "Ah! Well! So Garrett finally decides to check in." Anderson said as he hit the answer button. "What's going on Garrett?"

"We think that they're headed for Montenegro. Can you check it out? See if anyone fitting their descriptions boarded. Names are not important. They probably have fake IDs." said John.
"That's a long shot Garrett. It's a huge ship, and those two are probably going under the radar. They'll have to check every lounge chair on the Lido Deck."
"You got any better ideas, Anderson?"
He didn't want Garret to know he was at a dead end. "Wilson...check with Royal Caribbean. See if they can track down anyone fitting the Snow's description on the ship sailing to Montenegro."
"I have another idea! Come on Crystal." said Sloane.
"Where are we going?"
Sloane grabbed her by the elbow and propelled her across the parking lot to the Range Rover.
"We're going to the Royal Caribbean offices."
Her hunch paid off. The cruise line had video surveillance of all passengers boarding their ships. Grand Slam! The monitor picked up Lloyd Snowboarding the ship right behind daughter Lena, dripping in Bianca Villa's diamonds. A cellular second later, and Jaycee's vision was verified!

My phone rang. It was Sloane. "What's up? Where are you?"

We met up with Anderson at the accident scene. Apparently, Lena ran Alvero down. He's in pretty bad shape, but he's alive. Now, we're at the Royal Caribbean offices. I had a hunch, and it paid off. They're on their way to Montenegro!

I looked at John. "They're headed for Montenegro on the Royal Caribbean."

"Ivy...I have an idea," he said.

"What?"

"Hang on. He pulled out his phone and made an overseas call.

CHAPTER FIFTY-SEVEN

The wine steward popped open a bottle of Veuve Clicquot and poured two flutes. Lena lifted hers to her lips and giggled at the sensation of tiny bubbles tickling the tip of her nose. A soft breeze tousled her wavy hair as she breathed the salty ocean air. “You know, Daddy, it isn’t really a bad idea, reviving the *Snowstorm*.

“It’s bloody brilliant! A toast is in order. To the *Snowstorm!* There’s about to be a blizzard in Europe!”

Lena laughed as they clinked glasses. “So, what’s the first order of business when we reach Cetinje?”

“We hole up at the Gradska Hotel and get the lay of the land. We must be discrete. We don't want any notoriety with the police or the *Pink Panthers.* They won’t embrace the idea of competition.”

“That’s putting it mildly,” said Lena.

“We bide our time, and plan carefully, as we always do. Then we’ll make a stealth strike. They’ll never know what hit them.”

"What do you think they'll do when they realize that we've out maneuvered them? After all, they've had the *jewelry procurement* business tied up in the eastern block for decades. Nobody dares move in on their turf."

Lloyd gazed out at the sun dappled sea. "It will be too late. By then we'll be gone. I really liked your idea of the Maldives."

"Always ready to segue back to plan A Daddy."

A gentle rap on the cabin door announced that their dinner was about to be served.

Lena always knew that the *Snow Storm* had to come to an end eventually. Lacey was becoming more and more suspicious of Lloyd's activities. At first, she accused him of having an affair because of his frequent and unexplained absences. But he was able to convince her of his fidelity, seeing that there were no other women in the picture. Only his daughter, Lena.

Lacey *knew* that something was going on however, and her suspicions were not quelled. She began poking around in places where she was not welcome. Unfortunately for Lacey, the time had come for tea.

It was a windfall of good fortune when Ivy was accused of the murder. Lena could hardly hold back her hysterical laughter. But she was never one to tempt fate. She knew that it was time to strike out on her own. The sky was the limit...and nowhere was the sky bigger than Texas USA!

Lena's lovely reminiscence was interrupted by Lloyd's return. He gently placed a silky pink pashmina over Lena's shoulders.

"Thank you, Daddy," she said demurely.

He took his seat across the table from her and picked up the tiny sterling spoon to stir his espresso. Lena's stare stayed fixed on him as he lifted the delicate china cup to his lips. He devoured the contents in one swift swallow. He leaned back in his chair and smiled at his daughter. Lena remained very still, not uttering a word. They sat in silence for what seemed an eternity.

Lloyd spoke at last. "It's been quite a wild ride, hasn't it darling?"

Lena turned, gazing into the blackness where the sea awaited. "Yes Daddy."

It was at that moment that she knew that *he* knew. He's known all along. He knew of her part in her own mother's demise, and of Lacy's. It was the reason that he'd tried so desperately to see that Ivy was held responsible for Lacy's death, to protect her. That, and the insurance money, of course. She wondered if he knew about Bianca Villa? Of course, he did. How else would she be in possession of Bianca's necklace...the jewels...all of it?

Lloyd breathed a heavy sigh. "You know Lena, the awful truth is that if you hadn't done what you did, I might have been forced to act myself. But it would have been unnatural for me. My mind, although somewhat devious at times, is nevertheless sound. Yours my dear, being of Benedict blood, is not. But you're not to blame, Lena. Madness is inherent in the Benedict line. Unfortunately, it proliferated when they lost their fortune. I often saw signs of it in your mother."

"You abandoned me. You left me out there all on my own. Then, when you needed me Daddy...well you know what you found!" Lena whispered.

Lloyd rose from the table and went to stand at the ship's railing. It was a black starless night.

So black that he couldn't tell where the night sky ended, and the fathomless sea began. He turned and looked at his daughter for the last time. A grin...then a grimace as he doubled over and fell into the depths below.

No sooner had Lena disembarked the ship, when a distinctive London dialect stopped her dead in her tracks. She recognized the voice. Inspector Fiona Wescott of Scotland Yard.

"Stop. You're under arrest" Inspector Wescott said.

Lena froze. Shivers ran up her spine. Her eyes grew wide with fear…then anger.

"Turn around slowly. Hands where I can see them," Fiona said.

Lena Benedict Snow Alvero turned to face her fate.

CHAPTER FIFTY-EIGHT

The horses were loaded on their transport trailer and were already on their way back to Pennsylvania. Crystal and Robert hosted a lovely farewell dinner for us all (thanks to Palm Beach Catering). We were finally able to savor the seabass that we forfeited the night Julia held us at gunpoint, and Lena and Enrico made their escape.

"I'm going to miss you guys," Crystal said.

I hugged her tightly. "Promise you'll head back up north for Memorial Day. It'll be a hundred degrees here by then, and you'll be ready for some crisp mountain air."

"I'm packing already," said Robert.

I had such mixed feelings about leaving. Of course, I missed Jayson terribly, and I had to get my nose back to the grindstone at work, but I had an uneasy feeling. A feeling that was, however, oddly familiar. It came back to haunt me at various times in my life when the winds of change were blowing through my heart. The feeling of unfinished business. My father's untimely death in the racing accident robbed me of his love. I longed for the special moments we would have shared as I was growing up. Then, my mother's horrible murder at the hands of my stepsister. I had a hunch that Lloyd must have known, or at least suspected that Lena did it. He would be all too willing to sacrifice me for her. After all, Lena was his birth daughter, not I. But Vincente did save me...at the exorbitant cost of our love and our future, striking that filthy bargain with Bianca.

I looked over at Jaycee as she settled in next to Trina, both girls squirming to adjust their seatbelts. Sloane sprung for first class tickets home, so that we could avail ourselves of a comfortable flight to decompress.

I turned to look at John. He was staring out the window deep in thought. I don't know what I would have done without him. He protected me from ex-husband Bart's insidious attempts to destroy me. And now the sacrifices that he's made to come to my rescue again. Flying all the way to London to try and stop my mother's cold case from being reopened. Helping me solve Bianca's murder to vindicate Vincente. His valiant effort to rescue Jaycee. John is a hero in every sense of the word.

I needed to get some sleep on the plane. I'd had too many restless nights trying to get

Vincente Villa out of my mind. Seeing him again after all these years. Learning of the sacrifices he'd made to save me from a murder conviction. Entering a loveless marriage and banishing all contact with me for what he thought would be the rest of our lives. But it wasn't for the rest of our lives. Now we were both free. I was deliberately leaving Palm Beach without seeing Vincente again. He'd left several messages for me at The Breakers, and his phone messages and texts were left unanswered. I knew that if I saw him again, things would never be the same...winds of change.

I reached into my bag for my sleep mask. I saw an unfamiliar envelope nestled among my things. Unfamiliar until I turned it over to see the Villa crest stamped into the wax seal. I looked over at John, who had succumbed to a peaceful sleep. Did I dare to open this envelope? I had to. I was overcome with curiosity. I reached inside and drew out a one-way ticket to Buenos Aires.

THE END

Special thanks to Rebecca Winters, Sally Burgman, Patty Turjan and Robert C. Chance 5th for their help and inspiration.

Made in the USA
Middletown, DE
12 September 2024

60811548R00283